The Appraisal

The Appraisal

Brielle Montgomery

www.urbanbooks.net

Urban Books, LLC
300 Farmingdale Road, NY-Route 109
Farmingdale, NY 11735

ISBN 13: 978-1-64556-228-3
ISBN 10: 1-64556-228-X

First Trade Paperback Printing July 2021
Printed in the United States of America

10 9 8 7 6 5 4 3 2 1

Distributed by Kensington Publishing Corp.
Submit Orders to:
Customer Service
400 Hahn Road
Westminster, MD 21157-4627
Phone: 1-800-733-3000
Fax: 1-800-659-2436

The difference between school and life? In school, you're taught a lesson and then given a test. In life, you're given a test that teaches you a lesson.

~ Tom Bodett

CHAPTER ONE

Some men were just too damn easy, it was almost pathetic.

Jayla licked her lips as she watched him approach her. She had to admit, though, he was much better looking than his fiancée had described. She watched his thick lips curl in an approving smile as his fingers stroked the smooth cut of his goatee. Hershey's chocolate skin, muscles rippling through the black T-shirt, and a wide, confident walk, like his dick was too damn big for his jeans. She would be the judge of that soon enough.

"Excuse me," he said when he reached her side. "I don't mean to bother you, but you are damn sure the finest woman in this bar tonight."

She returned his smile with a seductive one of her own. He probably wouldn't feel that way if he knew his fiancée, Tracy, was shadowed in the DJ booth. Jayla could almost feel her calculating eyes watching their every move.

Jayla crossed her legs, allowing the slit of the fire-red dress to inch up. As if on cue, his eyes dipped to the exposed area of her caramel thigh, and she felt her pussy heat up in response. She ran her manicured fingers through the black tresses of her wig. "Thank you," she said. "And you are?"

"Marcus."

Bold one to use his real name, Jayla thought as she took a sip from her drink.

"And you are?" he prompted when she intentionally made no move to speak again.

Jayla winked. "Very interested in you, Marcus," she said.

"Is that so?"

"You're damn right," she said, standing. Her titties were nearly spilling out of the low V-shaped neckline of her dress, and she boldly pressed them against his solid chest. The gesture made her nipples harden between them. She leaned up until her cheek grazed his, her lips a whisper from his ear.

"I would absolutely love to dance with you," she said and slowly licked her lips, making sure the tip of her tongue touched his earlobe in the process. Not bothering to wait for his response, she slid past him and made her way to the dance floor.

The slow reggae mix had a collection of slick bodies grinding and swaying in the multicolored glow of the strobe lights. Jayla maneuvered through the crowd. The mixture of musk, perfume, and alcohol was so thick it was nearly edible. She felt Marcus's arm circle her waist and pull her body to his. She pressed her back against him, leaned her head on his shoulder, and began rocking her hypnotic hips to the beat.

She let her body take over, gyrating her ass against him until the prominent bulge in his pants tightened. When he placed his hands on her waist, she put her hands on top of his and gripped his fingers. Slowly, she guided them up to cup her titties and heard his muffled moan against her hair.

He used his thumbs to massage her nipples until it seemed they might pierce the satin material. He began to thrust his hips forward against her ass, his dick straining against the thick material of his pants. Jayla wiggled against him and was pleased when she saw that his eyes had drifted closed. A look of sheer pleasure had taken over his face, and his mouth was hanging slightly open. He was good and ready. And judging by the heated moisture that had dampened the crotch of her thong, so was she.

Tracy had made the instructions clear in the contract—take him as far as he would allow. Hopefully, he knew how to put it down, so she could at least get some satisfaction.

"I hope I'm not being too forward," she whispered, a combination of liquor and practice giving her voice a sexual rasp. "But I've got a case of Coronas in my fridge that I would hate to see go to waste. Why don't you follow me home so I can . . . give it to you, Marcus?"

"I would hate to waste good beer," he said.

Jayla took his hand and headed toward the door.

This part was always difficult for the women to watch. She'd even had one client storm up to her on her way out with a man, and the combination of sobs, curses, and a strong Spanish accent had rendered the woman completely incomprehensible. If this one interfered, Jayla would politely back off, as agreed. Her clients were always made aware up front that even if they stopped the evaluation before it was completed, the payment was the same.

As soon as they stepped outside, she opened her mouth to speak and gasped when he dragged her toward him. She didn't have time to process her reaction before his other hand grabbed the back of her neck and then he crushed his lips against hers.

She tasted the lingering Corona on his tongue, felt the urgency in the kiss as his hand lowered to squeeze her ass. He seemed to be trying to mesh their bodies together, his package taut against her leg. She flicked her tongue on the roof of his mouth before taking a step back.

"Soon," she said. She then turned on her heel and headed to her SUV. He was at her side in two strides, and Jayla gasped when he grabbed her arm again and whirled her around to face him once more.

"Can't wait," he said, his voice thick. He took her hand and placed it on his dick. "You feel this shit? I need your ass now."

Jayla bit her lip, pretending to consider the proposition. Luckily, she had the tape recorder already rolling in the truck.

She had to admit, Tracy's request for a tape recording was strange, but she would oblige. Some clients just needed hard evidence. As if it would make a difference.

"I'm parked over here." She tipped her head toward the darkened SUV, the crisp black paint and the tinted windows glistening in the moonlight.

Jayla hadn't even completely closed the door to the back seat when Marcus attacked her body. She bit back a curse when she heard the rip of satin, then winced when she felt the sudden bite of air on her exposed skin. The hair on his face scratched her breasts as he devoured them. He polished her nipples, flicking his tongue, licking, and sucking until they were hard and nearly dripping wet.

"Yes, please fuck me, Marcus." Her words came out in an anxious breath. She scooted to lie back on the chilled leather, then spread her knees to welcome him. Her panties were already stained with her pre-juices as she rubbed them against her pussy lips. She nudged the flimsy material to the side and stroked her swelling clit, giggling to herself when she saw his eyes dancing in anticipation.

"Oh yeah, baby, I'm gone fuck the shit outa you." His breath came out jagged and rough as he fumbled with his pants.

Jayla dipped her fingers inside her sugar walls and allowed her nectar to spill onto them. As he watched, she lifted her fingers to her mouth and sucked them clean. "Baby, don't you want to sample it first?" she teased.

He nodded and dove in, his tongue thrashing over her clit. His slurping noises echoed in the car as he put his lips to her hole and attempted to fuck her with his tongue.

Jayla frowned, swallowing her disappointment. His tongue was the size of his hand, but he damn sure didn't know how to work it. It was much too wild and messy for her. But oh well. It wasn't like he was her man. So, she moaned and ground against his mouth, like he was eating her to kingdom come.

"Yes, yes," she whispered, exaggerating, as she allowed her flavor to coat his taste buds. "Eat that shit, Marcus. Eat your pussy, baby."

When she faked her orgasm, he sat up and pulled his dick from his boxers. Jayla took the condom from him and, with the fingers of an expert, ripped open the package. The sound of the crinkling latex had her smiling as the material stretched over his erection. No, size was not an issue at all. After swinging her leg over his lap to straddle his waist, she lowered herself slowly to savor each generous inch and watched the rapid succession of emotions play on his face.

She started slow, clenching and releasing her pussy muscles in a massaging technique and moaning, as if his size was unbearable. She leaned over so her body rested on his and felt his desperate clutch to keep her in position.

A thick heat had permeated the inside of the car, causing the windows to fog up. She tasted the faint hint of sweat as she licked his neck. When his eyes rolled back, she quickened her pace and bounced her ass even harder. She felt the throbbing of his dick as he braced himself for the anticipated orgasm.

"Oh shit!" he all but yelled as he came, lifting his body from the seat with the force of his release.

He sighed as Jayla slowed to a stop, laughing to herself. Was that all? she thought. Damn! That was a quick ten thousand dollars.

She didn't even bother lingering. Just lifted off him and moved to settle on the seat beside him. She blew out a breath, feeling the first beads of sweat dot her forehead under the synthetic hair of the wig. Now to get him out of the SUV without all that extra shit.

"Damn, girl," he said, eyeing the filled condom. "You got some good stuff."

Jayla smiled as she smoothed her dress back into place. He had ripped it on the side, and the hole in the fabric did little to cover her plump breasts. She sighed, already knowing she and Tara would have to get back out to the mall so she could get another. It was one of her favorites.

"You were great, Marcus," she said, sneaking a glance at the digital clock on her dashboard. "I definitely needed that."

The ego stroke had him grinning like he'd just won the lottery. "Anytime. You keep giving me that ass like you just did, I'm all yours."

Jayla watched him slide the condom off and fold it back into the wrapper. "You got a girlfriend, Marcus?" she asked.

Silence.

He lifted his shoulder in a half shrug, as if pretending to be totally engrossed in the act of pulling up his pants. He mumbled something to the effect of "Not really," and this had Jayla rolling her eyes. Of course not. He had a fiancée, which was even worse. The wedding was in two weeks, but of course, she wasn't supposed to know that. *A dog, through and through.*

"I got someone I'm talking to," he went on. "But she don't mean nothing. She definitely ain't as fine as you." He leaned in and used his index finger to trace her lips. "Besides, I would rather get to know you better."

Jayla nodded and reached toward the front seat, grabbed the pen and scratch paper she had placed in the cup holder. She scribbled a fake number on the paper before kissing it and handing it to him.

"Call me," she whispered.

He planted another kiss on her lips before opening the door. "Most definitely," he said. "I think I'm in love." He laughed at his own joke before climbing out of the SUV and shutting the door.

Jayla released a disgusted breath. The trifling bastard didn't even know her name. Pa-fucking-thetic. Tracy would be lucky to get rid of him. *If* she got rid of him.

Jayla climbed into the driver's seat. She reached under the steering wheel and stopped the recorder. She knew it was a case of *if* because the woman seemed desperate, naive, and downright dumb enough to stay with the man even when she knew the truth. Jayla figured the evidence she had collected wouldn't matter one bit.

The sudden banging on her passenger window had Jayla screaming. She squinted through the tinted glass and let out an aggravated sigh when she recognized Tracy's tight-lipped frown, brooding hazel eyes, and inches of weave hiked into a hasty ponytail. *What the hell?*

Before Jayla could lock the doors, Tracy slid into the front seat, and Jayla looked toward the back when she heard another door open. Tracy's sister, Lauren, jumped in, looking pissed, and frowned at the wet stains on the leather seats.

"What the fuck are you two doing here?" Panic had Jayla shouting the question as she snatched her wig off, letting her mane of auburn hair spring free.

Tracy sniffed the air and frowned at the distinct odor. "So, I guess you fucked him, huh?"

"Hell yeah, they fucked!" Lauren's voice was laced with a bitter angriness. "Can't you tell? Shit, it smells like nothing but ass in this car. I told you that nigga wasn't shit, Tracy."

Unsatisfied, Tracy stared at Jayla, her eyes tight with hurt and restrained anger of her own. "Did you fuck him?"

"What the hell do you think?" Jayla snapped, rolling her eyes. "Isn't that what you paid me to do? Fuck him? Or have you forgotten our little contract?"

"Tracy, let's beat this nasty bitch," Lauren yelled.

"Beat me? For what?" Jayla looked from Lauren, who was bouncing on the edge of her seat in anticipation, to Tracy, who just sat eyeing her in silence. "I just saved you from making a big-ass mistake by showing you what kind of lying sack of shit you were about to marry. I just proved your nigga ain't shit, so what the fuck you questioning me for? Y'all need to be thanking me."

Silence.

Jayla smirked as Tracy sat hunched in the seat like a whipped puppy. She was almost as pathetic as her man. "I don't know why you're pissed," Jayla went on. "He can't fuck or eat pussy, so y'all lucky I'm not charging extra for wasting my damn time."

Tracy's slap carried enough force to throw Jayla backward. She winced, partially from the stinging of her cheek and partially from the impact of her arm as it slammed against the door. Fuming, Jayla lunged toward Tracy, prepared to fight Lauren off and punch them both through the damn window. She stopped short when Tracy burst into hysterical sobs.

"I'm sorry." Tracy buried her face in her hands. "I just can't believe he did this to me. I loved that bastard."

Jayla pursed her lips, still seething from the slap. It was time for these crazy bitches to leave. She snatched the recorder from under the steering wheel and dropped it on the seat beside Tracy. "Consider this my final report," she said. "Give me my damn money and get the fuck outa my car."

Tracy's face was tear stricken as she gazed at the tape recorder. She sighed. "Lauren, give her the money and let's go."

Lauren smacked her lips and pulled an envelope from her Coach purse. "Take it, then, you trashy bitch," she said as she snatched the crisp bills from the envelope and threw them in Jayla's face. Money rained down to pool in Jayla's lap and litter the floor. "And we better not see your ass on the street, or we gone fuck you up. Believe that, you skanky bitch." Lauren got out of the car and slammed the door behind her.

Tracy glared at Jayla as she grabbed the recorder. "I hope it was worth it for you." She had lowered her voice and sounded almost sinister. Then she stared a moment or two longer.

Jayla narrowed her eyes. Fear was beginning to inch its way up her spine. "Get away from me," she whispered through clenched teeth.

Without another word, Tracy climbed from the SUV and shut the door.

Jayla waited until both sisters had crossed the parking lot before she let out a staggered breath of relief. She looked in the rearview mirror and saw her heavy eye makeup had begun to smear and her cheek had colored to a light red from the hit. Jayla rolled her eyes. She could almost bank on the fact that even after all the theatrics, Tracy would still probably say, "I do," and become Mrs. Marcus Harris.

Oh well. She had done her job and gotten paid for it. Everything afterward had nothing to do with her. The money was getting so good, she considered hiring herself an accountant to help her hide it. Money was good, life was good, and Jayla loved how shit was always in her favor.

CHAPTER TWO

"You're such a bitch!" Despite the drunken stupor and anger that had the slurred voice raised, Jayla easily recognized Yolanda, another satisfied but unsatisfied client.

Jayla grimaced as her feet pounded the treadmill, harmonizing with the breath coming from her parted lips and roaring in her ears. She'd gone without headphones this time, and now, with only two minutes left on her run, she didn't bother to break stride as the words on her voicemail pierced the air.

"How do you live with yourself?" Yolanda barked, continuing her rant. "Fucking other women's boyfriends? A glorified prostitute, that's what you are. I hope you rot in hell. Better yet, I hope you catch AIDS or some other shit that kills you, you fucking slut!" A pause followed by muffled sobs. "How could he do this to me? I loved that man. I hate you for this! It's your fucking fault, throwing yourself on my man like a—"

Jayla tuned the voice out, a burst of renewed energy willing her legs to sprint faster. The sweat pooled in the small of her back, the base of her neck, and peppered her forehead like jewels glistening on her caramel skin. The message was not unlike any she'd had before. Just the nature of the business.

Time and experience had dulled the impact of the vicious remarks. How quickly they forgot that *they* had come to her. How quickly they forgot the numerous secret meetings to go over the infinite details, the constant reassurances of "Yes, I want you to do it. I need to know." But ignorance was truly bliss, because when the truth was out, they pointed the finger, not at the man, but at her.

The timer signaled the end of her hour, and with a satisfied sigh, she slowed the machine down to a leisurely walk. Shaking her head, she snatched her water bottle from its cup holder. She had to admit, though, part of her heart went out to Tracy. And Yolanda. And hell, all the women, actually. A small part. The other part of her crossed into the adjoining office to erase the evil message.

One thing was for sure. Converting to email only for business communication was complete genius. During the first year of business, she'd thought the personal contact via phone was a great mechanism to build trust and establish relationships with her clients. Then, however, the threats, profanity, and frequent hang-ups had become aggravating and had begun to make her uncomfortable. Jayla just wished she had thought of the email idea sooner, because now some of the women who had her number still liked to call and remind her what a low-down bitch she was. And since changing the number would be detrimental to business, Jayla had to just tolerate their backlash.

The second cell phone she carried for work rang now, and Jayla blew out an exasperated breath. "Exhibit A," she mumbled. She glanced at the caller ID. It read *Kayla Brown's Carl*. She had to put the clients' names in first, so she could keep their men in order. Sometimes, there were just too damn many investigations going on at once. She really needed a team of people to watch her back, screen her phone calls, and sift through emails, but her line of business required secrecy. Now, a security team would be beneficial, but Jayla did not see the absolute necessity of that . . . not yet.

Jayla took a breath and swiped the phone's touch screen to answer the call. "Hi, Carl," she gushed. "I was hoping you'd call me back. I haven't been able to stop thinking about you since we met last week."

She heard his strained chuckle between gasps of breath. Probably from the three hundred-plus pounds he carried around. She thanked her lucky stars his wife didn't need her to full out fuck him for her to be satisfied with his infidelity. Though why he had the nerve to be out trying to get some pussy when he had a wife willing to lay up with his fat ass was beyond Jayla.

"Me too," he said. "I just can't get that soft, round booty of yours outa my mind."

Jayla cringed but forced a flirtatious giggle. "Really?"

"Oh yeah," he went on. "I've been thinking about you all day and night. How you doing?"

Jayla stretched out on the floor, not wanting her sweat-stained body to soil her sofa. "I'm good," she said. "Just finished working out a little while ago. Now I'm just taking a bath."

"A bath?"

"Yes," she cooed, sugarcoating the lie. "I wish you were here."

"Oh yeah? And what would you do?"

Jayla closed her eyes, struggling to get in the mood. She pictured her cut buddy Chris, his iron body, and his delicious dick stroking all up and through her honey tunnel. "Mmm," she moaned as her pussy began to throb. She raked her fingernails up her stomach to massage her nipples, envisioning her fingers were Chris's lips. "I would lick over every inch of your body. From your neck down your stomach . . ." His delighted groans prompted her to continue. "I would then put my face between your thighs and suck that juicy dick of yours. Running the tip between my lips, rolling my tongue up and down while

I massaged your balls. I would suck and suck until you came all in my mouth, and I would swallow it up and lick my lips at the delicious flavor."

She smiled as Carl's moans roared in her ear so mightily, she could've sworn he was there in the room. All the way turned on, thinking about a real man, she ran her fingers down to her pussy. "Your turn," she whispered, nearly breathless. She felt herself straddling an orgasm. "What would you do to me?"

"I would take each one of your titties in my mouth, roll my tongue over the nipples like you probably like it. Watch you squeeze your eyes shut as you struggle to keep from creaming."

Jayla's bit her lip as she continued to pleasure herself to his words. Damn, he was pretty good at this. For the moment, she had completely forgotten what Carl looked like.

"Then," he went on, "I would lift you up and sit you on my face so you could ride my mouth, and I would flick my tongue over your clit, using my thumb to finger you at the same time."

Jayla moaned again as she demonstrated his exact words: first, rubbing her finger on her clit before inserting two fingers. She began to grind against her fingers, wishing they were a dick, a tongue, anything. Her breath grew heavy, and she listened to his gentle urges. She quickened her pace.

"Cum for me, babe," he whispered, and as if on cue, her muscles clenched, and she felt a release so strong, it startled a scream from her parted lips.

She let out a shaky breath and looked down at her yoga pants, now wet with her thick juices. Well, that was unexpected but very much appreciated.

"Damn, girl."

Jayla pouted as Carl's laborious breathing brought her back to reality, slicing her post-orgasmic high like a knife.

"You sound so good when you cum," he said. "Almost as good as you look."

"Thank you for that, sweetie." Jayla staggered to her feet. "Let me call you back later. You got me all messy, and I need to clean up."

"You gone call me back? I want to meet up with you so I can make those things happen."

"I'm gone call you back," she lied and hung up.

Fat chance, she thought and giggled at her little joke as she put his number on block. His case was closed.

Her desk phone rang just then, and Jayla decided to ignore it. She needed a shower, anyway.

When she came back downstairs, casually dressed in a tank top and some capris, she crossed straight into her office. She noticed the red light blinking, signaling she had messages, but first things first: she needed to type up her report and call Carl's wife. She dropped into the high-back executive chair and opened a blank template on her computer. She pulled Carl's file from her cabinet and fumbled through the paperwork until she found the phone number. She dialed.

"Ms. Brown," she greeted when Carl's wife picked up. Putting the call on speaker, she said, "Just letting you know the evaluation is complete, so we need to set up a time to go over everything together."

"No problem." Ms. Brown didn't sound upset or worried at all. In fact, she sounded very nonchalant about the entire situation. "Did he give in?"

"We should discuss this face-to-face," Jayla insisted. "Let's set up a time to meet, and I'll give you all the details."

Ms. Brown grunted. "That means yes. With his fat, weak ass."

Jayla chuckled to herself. It always amazed her what drastically different reactions she received from her clients.

They arranged a time to meet to finalize the paperwork and exchange the remaining balance. Jayla hung up and finished typing her report while the details were fresh on her mind.

Done with that, she sat back and pressed the PLAY button on her phone.

Yolanda's psychotic ass had called another fourteen times. More cussing, more crying, more threats. Jayla massaged the beginnings of a headache at her temples as she deleted each of the fourteen messages one by one. Then she played the last message she'd received.

"Um, hi. I'm . . ." The timid woman paused, as if she was unsure if she should divulge her real name. "Heather. Heather Frederick. I got your number from my friend Melanie and . . ." Another pause. Then a frustrated sigh. "Look, I'm sorry. I don't even know why I'm doing this. I'm . . . I heard you were good, and my boyfriend . . . he's . . . I'm sorry. I'm not really sure how this all goes. Can you just please give me a call?"

Jayla jotted down the number on a notepad. She glanced at the clock as she fingered the slip of paper. Yeah, she had time. Jayla punched in the phone number she had scribbled on the notepad, then cradled the phone between her ear and her shoulder.

"Heather Frederick?" she greeted once the woman answered.

"Yes?"

"Denise." Middle name, and middle name only, for business purposes. "I received your message about an evaluation."

"A what?"

Jayla glanced at the notes scribbled on the pad in front of her. "Your friend Melanie gave you my number," she said, clarifying. "For the evaluation." She waited while the woman seemed to be collecting her thoughts.

"Oh yes. About my . . ."

"When would you like to meet?" Jayla said. No business details over the phone. Only in person.

"I'm sorry. Meet? Can we talk now?"

"Well, there are a lot of details to go over, so it's best if we can get together for a face-to-face discussion."

A pause. "Okay. Can we meet today?"

Jayla glanced at the open desk calendar next to her keypad. She had expected to have a nice relaxing afternoon, a small indulgence for the previous week's demanding schedule.

She had opened her mouth to suggest an alternate time when Heather added, "I know it's such short notice, but I am actually leaving town tomorrow, and I'll be gone for a week."

Jayla sighed. Pleasure would have to wait. This was business.

"That's no problem," she conceded. "Are you familiar with Shogun? The Japanese steakhouse near Atlantic Station?"

"Yes, ma'am."

"Perfect. How's one thirty?"

"Um, okay," Heather stammered.

"Great. Please bring a pen, paper, and a photo ID, and I will see you in a few hours." Jayla hung up and jotted down the appointment in her calendar. Her shoulders had tensed, for some reason, and she rolled them on a yawn.

The rigorous morning workout was catching up, and the spontaneous orgasm had her body craving a nap. Too bad.

The doorbell ringing had Jayla's brow furrowing at the unexpected interruption. She dabbed her face with a towel as she stepped into the hallway and pulled the French doors to her office closed behind her, and then she headed to the front door. All suspicion evaporated when she saw the familiar face through the peephole. She pulled the door open and watched her best friend breeze past her.

"I would hug you." Tara pivoted on the six-inch heels of her Jimmy Choo strap sandals. "But I ain't trying to wrinkle my new outfit."

"Yes, ma'am." Jayla eyed Tara's distressed skinny leg jeans and sheer crop top. "Where you headed dressed like that?"

Tara grinned and did a model twirl. "Girl, a cookout with Kevin," she answered, following Jayla into the kitchen.

"Cookout? In those heels?"

Tara's grin widened as she playfully lifted her foot onto a barstool to show off the designer shoes. "Oh, these things?" She feigned innocence. "If I have to sit there, bored shitless, at another one of my husband's corporate events, the least I can do is look good while I'm there."

"Yeah, and your damn feet are gon' be crying," Jayla said with a laugh. She reached into the refrigerator for the bottle of wine.

"And you know what pisses me off?" Tara was still rambling on. "Why we have to be the token black couple when we go somewhere. This shit it getting on my nerves." Tara talked on about her diminishing tolerance in having to smile and feign interest in Kevin's uppity coworkers. As she poured wine into two wineglasses and then placed the glasses on the kitchen island, Jayla caught a few more snatches of the conversation before Tara switched topics.

"So . . ." Tara tossed Jayla a grin as they both took a seat on barstools at the island. "Tell me about this guy."

Jayla frowned. "What guy?"

"Bitch, don't play me," Tara replied, pushing. "You remember the other day, when I wanted to stop by. You said you were going out . . ." She paused.

Jayla turned up her nose, vaguely remembering flashes of the disappointing Wednesday night assignment. He had insisted on some movie she didn't remember, and the sex had been terrible. A forgettable evening. But the girlfriend's check had cleared, so she'd forgotten the guy even quicker.

"Oh," Jayla shook her head, dismissing the topic. "Nothing worth talking about."

"That's all?" Disappointment had Tara's lip poking out. "Damn, Jayla. I'm married, so I have to live vicariously through you. But you don't even have stories worth trying to relive."

Jayla smirked. Tara had been her best friend since college, but she didn't even know the sordid details of Jayla's employment. And it was better that way. As far as she was concerned, Tara and everyone else was better off thinking she was a marketing consultant who had a good amount of sex.

"Girl, I'm sorry." Jayla laughed at Tara's dejected expression. "The men nowadays are sorry. You and a select few scooped up the last few good ones we had left."

"So I guess no getting married and settling down for you no time soon?"

"Not hardly."

"Well, I can introduce you to some of Kevin's friends from work."

Jayla rolled her eyes. "Now, you just went on and on about how uppity they are. Damn. Thanks, Tara."

"Most of them are," she agreed, laughing. "But one guy, Derrick, he's pretty fine. He's, like, the only other black guy there, so he and Kevin have hit it off good. I think he just got promoted in from the Chicago region."

"No thanks."

"You'll like him," Tara said. "Let me give him your number."

"Tara, do you even know if this guy is married? Got kids?"

"That's for you to find out. At least consider it."

"I'll consider it."

It was an obvious lie and had Tara smacking her teeth. "I'm starting to think your ass is gay, girl," she teased.

Jayla chuckled. "I'll consider that too." She blew her friend a playful kiss, and they shared a laugh.

Heather was running late.

Jayla stood outside the restaurant, dressed in a professional gray pencil skirt suit, Chanel pumps, and a splash of purple from the silk blouse peeking out from under her blazer. After much effort, she had managed to tame her long hair in a neat bun at the nape of her neck. And the glasses weren't even prescription, but Jayla liked the added touch. She also liked the briefcase she carried. All in all, a very calculated image to overshadow the nature of her business. Meticulous.

Jayla angled her wrist to eye her watch once more. She looked up just in time to see the young white woman ducking low as she scurried across the brick walkway, tossing anxious looks over her shoulder. Her tight fingers gripped a Gucci purse to her chest like a life vest. Jayla swallowed a grin. The poor thing looked petrified, her already pale skin not helping the fearful image. She looked as if she was attempting to blend in. And failing miserably. From the crisp jeans and satin blouse to each strand of blond hair secured in the ponytail resting on her shoulder.

"Heather," Jayla called when the woman breezed past.

Heather looked back, and it was clear the professional black woman was not at all what she had expected. After a moment, she turned around and walked over to Jayla.

Jayla dismissed the awkward pause and reached out to shake the woman's hand. "I'm Denise."

"Oh, yes," Heather said, then hesitated. Her eyes darted around before she accepted the hand. "I'm sorry. I . . ."

'It's okay," Jayla assured her with a smile. "I completely understand. Why don't we go have some lunch and talk?" She turned to lead the way to the Italian restaurant across the street.

"Wait," Heather said, glancing at the restaurant. "I thought we were going to

Shogun."

The little white lies were necessary on occasion. Especially with new assignments. Hell, Jayla didn't know this chick from a can of paint, and some women had ulterior motives. She'd had her share of run-ins with them too. But instead of revealing that, Jayla simply said, "It's a little too noisy there."

The two women entered the dimly lit Italian restaurant, and the hostess led them to a private booth in the back and gave them menus.

They stared at the menus for a few minutes.

"Relax, Heather," Jayla said, her voice hushed, as the waitress walked over to take their order. "You're drawing unnecessary attention." She turned her attention to the waitress. "I'll have a glass of water," she told her. "And the house salad with balsamic vinaigrette dressing."

"And for you, ma'am?"

Heather shook her head. "Nothing, thank you." Her voice was almost a whisper.

The waitress left, and Jayla sighed as she pulled a pen, a notebook, and a tape recorder from her briefcase. The woman was already one step from a nervous breakdown, and Jayla hadn't even slept with her man yet.

"Why don't you tell me a little about yourself, Heather?" she prompted, clicking on the recorder.

"Um, I'm Heather Frederick. I'm twenty-six. I've been with my boyfriend for six years. We have one daughter together . . ." She trailed off, fidgeting with the strap of her purse.

As Jayla jotted down the information in her notebook, the waitress brought two glasses of ice water to their table. "And how did you find me again?" she asked once the waitress had left the table.

"Melanie. Melanie Stock. You did an . . . evaluation, I guess, on her . . . her girlfriend."

Jayla smiled to herself. Yes, she definitely remembered Melanie Stock and her girlfriend, Angie. It wasn't her first time doing an evaluation on a gay couple. There was something about lesbians that made her job more intriguing. Melanie was definitely a character. She had *wanted* to set up her girlfriend. Wanted to do something spiteful. She had happily divulged information, requested frequent updates, and had generously paid extra for Jayla to sex Angie not once, but three times.

Jayla rubbed her thighs together at the thought of Angie's thick tongue working its magic. Yes, that had been a very eventful and fulfilling month. Sexually and financially.

"Tell me about your boyfriend," she continued as Heather took a sip from her ice water. "What's his name? What does he do? Hobbies?"

"Um . . ." Heather leaned in a bit closer. "His name is Reggie Smith. He's a plumber. We recently moved in together, and he's been . . . I don't know. It seems like he's pulling away from me. He's working all the time, doesn't answer his phone, and he never wants to make love to me anymore. It's probably me, isn't it?"

Instead of acknowledging her question, Jayla sat her pen on her notebook and removed her glasses. "Let me tell you a little about what I do." She started delivering the lines to her routine script. "I am a Heartbreaker. What that means is I evaluate your subject and I draw up a credible estimate of value in an evaluation report. Much like an appraisal, if you will. There are several factors that can influence the results of my assessment. Would you like me to continue?"

At Heather's tentative nod, Jayla pulled a small stack of papers from her briefcase. "How the process works is like this. We have three required meetings before I even begin. First, there is the briefing, where I just provide information about the process. Then we have a consultation, where we discuss, in great detail, the complexity of this evaluation. I have to do a preapproval questionnaire with you, in which you answer very specific questions regarding you and your partner." Jayla did not play around when it came to taking on new clients. She knew all money was not good money.

Heather nodded.

"I place a value in three separate categories," Jayla explained, rattling on. "Mental, emotional, and sexual. In each of these areas, I have subcategories that I review, and the extent of my evaluation will depend on your comfort level. Then we have a conference, where I have you sign a consent contract that is completed based on our agreement from the consultation. At that time, you are required to provide sixty percent of the total cost of service. The other forty percent is due upon completion, and upon receipt, I will provide you a report and all subsequent evidence collected during the process."

"And how much can this cost?"

Jayla smiled at the question. "It really depends on what you would like me to do. It can range anywhere from three thousand dollars to as high as fifty thousand. Or more."

"Fifty thousand dollars?" Heather echoed, her eyes ballooning.

I know it's a large range and a large sum of money." Jayla's voice was gentle. "But this is a large investment of time, patience, and effort."

"Right. I get it." Heather's eyes fell on her twiddling thumbs. "So, how much time does it take?"

"I can typically have a thorough analysis completed in two to three months. Rarely have I needed more time."

Pause. Jayla saw the confusion, the uncertainty in Heather's downcast eyes. "So, after that, if they haven't done anything, is it safe to say they passed?"

Now it was Jayla's turn to frown. "I don't think I understand the question," she said.

"Like, you can report they are faithful."

"Um . . ." Jayla thought back a minute and had to stifle a smirk. Now, that was funny. "I've yet to have that happen," she admitted. "But I guess we'll cross that bridge if and when we get to it." She sat back in the booth, Heather's deflated face wanting to tug on her heart. The truth hurt, she knew. But it was a matter of choice. Either she wanted to know or she didn't. Simple as that. "So now it just comes down to you, Heather," Jayla said. "How important is it to know what your boyfriend is worth?"

Not bothering to wait for the answer, Jayla began repacking her briefcase. That was enough for one meeting. Poor Heather probably needed some time to marinate on the idea. But Jayla figured she would come around eventually. Curiosity was a son of a bitch.

Heather scooted out of the booth, looked at Jayla, mumbled something Jayla didn't understand, and ran past the hostess station. Unbelievable.

Just then Jayla's phone began vibrating. She glanced down at it, saw an unknown number, and ignored the call, not knowing if she would regret it.

CHAPTER THREE

Shit.

Jayla tripped and damn near fell face-first on the cement doorstep. She stumbled a little before she caught her balance and glanced back to see what the hell she had tripped over.

A package.

Curious, she observed the neatly taped flaps and the carefully tied red ribbon and bow adorning the simple brown packaging. A slip of notebook paper was attached to the ribbon, and there was no evidence of a postal service delivery. Not even a stamp. Whoever delivered the package had personally placed it on her doorstep.

Jayla glanced around the quiet neighborhood, half expecting to see someone watching. The sun and a faint breeze created a picturesque vision of the ideal family community. Sighing, Jayla stooped to pick up the package and then carried it back inside. She would just have to be late.

Jayla nudged the door closed behind her and carried the package into the kitchen. Instinct compelled her to press her ear against it. Nothing. She shook it to see if she could guess the contents. Not a sound. Jayla plucked the slip of paper from the package and turned it over to reveal a note. The sadistic message had her heart spiking to her throat as a gasp ripped from her parted lips.

*You fuck over others and you're liable to get
fucked up.*

The threatening words were scribbled in deep-red
lipstick that, even though it had been slightly smeared,
stained the crisp white paper with evident precision.

Jayla wanted to be angry. A psychotic client was
sending her threatening messages. She wanted to be
amused. An immature woman wanted to play the damn
blame game, as if she hadn't asked or paid for the insight.
But all she felt was fear of the faceless, voiceless person
who had been bold enough to write a threatening note,
and who had been vigilant enough to hand deliver it right
to her front porch, like the Sunday paper.

After crumpling the note in her fist, Jayla threw it in
the trash can. She then eyed the seemingly innocent
package a moment longer. She shuddered to think what
was inside, but curiosity gnawed at her like a desperate
itch. She snatched the ribbon and bow off and used her
nail to puncture holes in the tape sealing it together.
Then she ripped off the brown packaging and found a
plain box. Slowly, she opened it.

The glint of the knife was the first thing she saw, as the
edge of the jagged blade was protruding from a jumble
of cotton and plush velveteen. One end of the velveteen
looked like a slashed face, and she realized that the heap
of fabrics used to be a teddy bear. But someone had taken
care of that real good.

Jayla shut her eyes but couldn't erase the teddy bear's
image. Innocence had been replaced with something
evil. She opened her eyes. There was nothing else in the
box, but the slashed bear and the knife were unsettling
enough. She teared her eyes from the remnants of stuffed
animal, then shoved it back in the box and flipped the
flaps to close it once again. Someone was fucking with

her, but who? Jayla remembered Yolanda's hateful message and sighed. But, shit, was it Yolanda? Was it Tracy? Was it Kayla? she wondered. Hell, she had fucked so many spouses, fiancés, and boyfriends, it could be a number of people. It wasn't like she had the most likable of professions, but still, she'd taken care to maintain a sense of anonymity. How the hell did the person get her address?

Jayla carried the box outside and dumped it in the large trash can. Her hands were trembling. Quickly, she climbed in her truck, started it, and sped out of the neighborhood. Fear had really set in now. Jayla felt it snake its way up her spine as her grip tightened on the steering wheel. Calming down didn't seem possible at the moment.

She knew she was late. But after what had just happened, she should have canceled her damn plans altogether. As she sped down the highway, her mind flipped through the faces of her many clients. Too many to count. It could've been anybody.

The driveway at her sister's house was already stuffed with cars, and they also lined both sides of the street. Jayla parked and sat in the car for a moment longer. It was easier to be angry at the situation than afraid, so Jayla quickly latched on to the former emotion as she stepped out from behind the wheel and headed up the crowded driveway. When she found whoever it was, the bitch was as good as dead.

Her sister Jackie leaned against the doorjamb, the distinct aroma of barbecue wafting from behind her. "Damn. Do you know how to get anywhere on time?" she said, a combination of annoyance and mild anger coloring her voice. A frown had settled on her pouty lips, which were identical to Jayla's. "I even called you this morning," she noted, rambling on. "For once, just *once*, I'd like to see you be somewhere when you say you are going to be there."

Jayla rolled her eyes but remained quiet as she stepped past her sister into the house.

A slew of cousins cluttered the living room and dining room. And by taking a quick glance at the sliding-glass door, she determined that even more had spilled onto the patio and into the backyard. Her sister definitely knew how to get the family out, that was for sure.

Jayla lifted her hand to greet several of her cousins huddled around the sixty-inch flat screen. Apparently, a football game had them on their feet, beers in one hand. Some sort of bet had prompted them to pull dollar bills from their pockets and toss them into a bowl on the coffee table. Jayla didn't realize her muscles were clenched until she felt them ache, and she struggled to relax. It did feel good to be around family and friends.

She spotted her other sister, Jocelyn, waddling from the kitchen with a full plate of food in each hand. She headed over. "One for you, and one for the baby, huh?" Jayla teased when she reached Jocelyn's side.

"Girl, shut up. You make it sound like I'm a fat, greedy pig or something."

"Greedy, yes," Jayla said on a wink. "But we're not going to blame that on the baby." She followed her sister to the dining-room table and helped her sit down. "So how you feeling, ma'am?" she asked as she took the seat next to Jocelyn.

Jocelyn sighed and rubbed her protruding belly. The frilly lounge dress accentuated her plump titties and full, pregnant figure. "Pretty good. Tired as hell. Swollen. Back and feet killing me."

"How's my nephew?" Jayla leaned forward to rub her sister's stomach, and a grin spread across her face when she felt a slight kick against her palm.

"He's good. Of course, he wants to wait until all times of the night to practice his karate, so I'm not getting any sleep."

Jayla smiled, masking the slight twinge of guilt she felt. She had been pregnant before. Twice, to be exact. But raising children was about as foreign to her as working a "real" job. She didn't want that for herself, so adoption and then an abortion had been her only options.

"But enough about me," Jocelyn said, pulling Jayla from her train of thought. "You know, Tara's here with her boo . . ." She trailed off, and her lips curved upward, as if she knew the punch line to some secret joke.

Jayla frowned. "Okay," she said. "They're always here. What's so funny about that?"

Jocelyn remained silent as she shoved a forkful of baked beans in her mouth.

"What, Joce? What is it?"

"I'll let you find her," she said. "Wouldn't want to ruin your surprise."

Jayla grimaced. No telling what her "surprise" could be. "Let me go get something to eat," she said instead and then rose and crossed into the gourmet kitchen.

Jackie's daughter, Jasmine, was in the refrigerator, fumbling through Tupperware and foil-wrapped plates. Jayla immediately noticed how much her ass was filling out her jeans, a drastic change since she'd gone off to college.

"Damn, what they feeding you at State, girl?" Jayla joked and poked a finger at her niece's plump ass. "How your body look better than mine and you ain't but nineteen?"

Jasmine snickered and tossed her twists behind her shoulder. "I gained a little weight," she admitted. "But in all the right places." She tossed her aunt a wink, and Jayla couldn't help but laugh at how grown up she was.

"Auntie, I'm glad you're here." Jasmine took a peek at the living room to make sure no one was within earshot. "I need some advice."

"What's up?"

Jasmine let out a frustrated sigh. "You remember my girl, Keela? How about I saw her boyfriend at the movies with some other chick? That shit pissed me off. So me trying to be a good friend, what do I do? I tell her, and this chick gets mad at me, saying I'm lying. I guess that's what the fuck I get for not minding my own damn business, right?"

"Girl, no." Jayla leaned on the laminate counter. "Keela should appreciate a friend like you trying to give her a heads-up on her shitty-ass boyfriend. You didn't do anything wrong."

"But now I feel like I should've kept my mouth shut. She won't even answer my calls."

Jayla rolled her eyes. "So? Fuck her," she said. "You did the right thing."

Jasmine's lips turned down in a frown. She was obviously unsatisfied with the nonchalant answer.

Jayla eyed her niece more closely and noticed the smooth bronze complexion, the hazel eyes, the dramatic arch of her narrow eyebrows, and those genetic pouty lips. Her niece was absolutely gorgeous. Plus, she had ass for days and titties that looked to be catching up.

Jayla's mind went to work, and she couldn't help but grin at the brilliant thought. "Do you have a job for the summer?" she asked.

"Nah."

"I think I have a job for you."

Jasmine grinned. "Really? Doing what?"

"Bitch, does it matter?" Jayla laughed. "You'll be making money. A lot of money, I might add. I'll talk to you about the details later. Just keep this between us, though."

"I'm down. Thanks, Auntie."

Jayla nodded, excited about the prospect of her niece working with her. With Jasmine helping with the evaluations, Jayla could pull in twice as many clients. And it appeared Jasmine already had the right attitude, given her situation with her friend. It was perfect. "Oh, one more thing," she added as Jasmine headed to the door. "Are you a virgin?"

Jasmine's eyebrows drew together at the random question. "Auntie, really?"

"I just want to know."

"Yeah."

Jayla lips folded into a doubtful smirk. "Bitch, don't lie to me, because you think I'm going to tell your mom."

Jasmine laughed. "I'm for real."

Jayla's mouth fell open at the sincere expression on her niece's face. "Girl, you lying? No anal? No oral? Nothing?"

Jasmine shook her head. "Why?" she joked. "Is that a problem or something?"

"Girl, get on. We'll talk about it later." Jayla frowned as she watched Jasmine head back into the living room. She hadn't expected that. But that damn sure wouldn't stop no show. There was a first time for everything.

Aunt Bev marched into the kitchen and slapped Jayla's shoulder, with a frown and a smack of her teeth. "Child, you need to eat."

Jayla sighed. Sheer love for the woman had her biting back a smart comment. "I do eat, Aunt Bev," she said.

"Skin hanging all off you like you done had gastric bypass," Aunt Bev continued as she began to prepare her plate. "What man gone marry you without some meat on your bones?" As she spoke, her own round frame and abundant rolls clearly stretched the little souvenir T-shirt she wore.

"I'm healthy," Jayla said and watched as Aunt Bev rolled her eyes.

"You young girls. Can't nobody tell you nothing. Just skin and bones."

The not-so-subtle jealousy lacing her words was too obvious. Even though her long-standing battle with diabetes had packed the weight on her, those extra pounds were, nonetheless, *extra*. It was enough to prompt people to voice their comments on the drastic change in her weight. But Aunt Bev had raised Jayla and her sisters after their real mother had passed, so Jayla had too much respect for her to refuse to take her advice.

Jayla reached for a plate. "Well, I'm going to fix a plate now to make you happy," she said with a smile. "Where is Uncle Ron?"

Aunt Bev lifted a Styrofoam cup to her plump lips and slurped. "Who knows?" She shrugged and gestured toward the patio. "Who cares? That bastard made me so mad this morning, it's ridiculous. I probably need to go ahead and divorce his fat ass."

Jayla rolled her eyes. Those two had been married for forever, plus some years. No one even bothered to take their little arguments seriously anymore.

"Yeah, I need to go ahead and get me a young, fine thing that can keep up with me." Aunt Bev smirked as she patted her thigh. "Someone your age. Someone like . . ." She trailed off as her eyes, lit from apparent appreciation, traveled to the doorway. "My, my! Now, who is that?" she said.

Jayla glanced over but did not recognize the stranger. One thing was for sure. The bald head, the thick lips, and the deep chocolate skin certainly did make for an attractive package. As he approached them, he flashed a smile, and Jayla seemed magnetized by those deep-set dimples winking in each cheek. She drew in a breath.

His cologne smelt deliciously masculine; the distinct fragrance was like a refreshing blend of rich cinnamon and citrus. He dressed like a man who took great pride in his appearance. The khakis and polo shirt hung like they were tailor made and only hinted at what, Jayla assumed, was a defined physique underneath.

"Good afternoon, ladies," he greeted. His voice was erotically smooth and had a sexy undertone. Hell, everything about him seemed to drip sex.

"Well, you are most certainly not a relative." Aunt Bev offered her hand. "I'm Beverly, but just call me Bev, sweetie."

"Pleasure to meet you. I'm Derrick Lewis. I'm a friend of Jayla's."

Jayla lifted an eyebrow. "A friend of mine?" she said.

"Well, my niece has certainly been hush-hush about you, because she hasn't said anything about any *friends*."

While Aunt Bev was talking, Jayla realized that Derrick was not shy about sizing her up: he casually ran his eyes over her lips, returned to her eyes, and then gave her a full-body once-over and a murmur of approval. She shifted. Damn, that turned her on. She could almost hear her kitty purr at the candid attention.

"Well, I definitely hope to see more of you," Aunt Bev said, with a knowing grin. "We'll have to get our girl Jayla here to stop hogging you and bring you around more often."

"We sure do." Derrick kept his eyes trained on Jayla as he spoke.

Jayla didn't bother responding when Aunt Bev patted her arm before she edged out of the kitchen.

"Friend of mine," Jayla said once they were alone.

"New friend, I hope," he replied, clarifying matters, and then his lips stretched back in another one of those sexy grins. "I came with my coworker Kevin and his wife, Tara."

Jayla nodded. *Of course. The final piece of the puzzle.*

"She couldn't stop talking about you the whole way over," he went on. "Said once I met you, I wouldn't be disappointed. And I must say, Miss Jayla Morgan, I am very far from disappointed."

Charming. She had to give him that. Her smile broke loose before she had time to hide it. "So I guess you're supposed to be my surprise," she said.

His grin widened. "Damn, I hope so."

Jayla's sigh was regretful. Boyfriends were a big no-no. It just wouldn't work. Yes, she hated it, and yes, she sometimes missed the companionship, but her pay-off was worth the sacrifice. "Listen, Derrick . . ." Her voice was gentle, already filled with compassion, in an effort to, hopefully, soften the sting. "It was a pleasure meeting you, but I'm not really interested."

Derrick didn't waiver. "Why don't you give me a chance first?" he said. "You don't want to get to know me, Jayla?"

Jayla ignored the boyish charm, those damn dimples, and shrugged at the flirtatious questions. "I'm sorry," she said. "But, again, it was nice to meet you, Derrick." Without waiting for a response, she carried her plate over to the open sliding-glass door and stepped outside. It was better this way. But too bad. Too damn bad. The man definitely had her body thirsting.

The heat from the sun warmed her legs, and she was glad she'd opted for capris today, despite the overcast clouds outside her window earlier. A thick screen of smoke and barbecue aroma drifting across the backyard. Someone had put on some old-school jams, and while the pool looked enticing, instead, people had spilled across the deck and onto the grass, bobbing to the music.

Jayla saw Jackie's husband, Quentin, motioning for her to come over, and she obliged, stepping across the manicured lawn toward the blazing grill.

"Hey, Jaye." He put an arm around her shoulders and pulled her in for a friendly hug. "I know you weren't gone come out here and not speak to me."

"Never that, Que," she said, fanning the smoke away from her face. "You throwing down out here. Got it smelling good. You never cooked like this for me when we were together." Jayla had no filter. Nothing new.

Que glanced around to make sure no one had heard the sneaky comment. He cleared his throat. "We were never together," he replied.

"Oh, you're right. We just fucked a couple times."

"Jayla." His head whipped around, and he stared her in the face. He was pissed, just that quickly. "Not here. Not now. Quit making those damn smart-ass comments."

Unfazed, Jayla stepped forward. A quick image of her riding Quentin like he was a runaway stallion flashed through her mind and had her grinning. "Oh really?" she taunted, her eyes twinkling. "If I recall correctly, I thought you liked my smart-ass mouth." Boldly, she puckered her lips to blow him a kiss, and then she strutted past him just as Jackie headed in their direction.

Jayla waved and greeted some more family members before heading over to Tara, who was bent over and pulling a drink from the cooler.

"Very sneaky," she said, and she had Tara frowning in confusion.

"What—"

"Derrick," Jayla interrupted with a smirk. "I guess you're going to tell me he just so happened to stop by when you and Kevin were on your way out, and you thought it would be nice to bring him along."

Tara shrugged and casually popped the top on the soda in her hand. "Not really," she said. "I told him he should come because I knew you would be here. I already told you I wanted y'all to meet." She nudged Jayla's arm. "He's fine, though, ain't he?"

Jayla tried to hide her amusement. She glanced over to the sliding-glass door as Derrick stepped out onto the patio. She had to admit, the man was fine. She watched him grin at her and lift his beer bottle in another flirtatious greeting.

"Yeah, he's fine," Jayla admitted, unable to contain the hint of wistfulness in the statement.

"Well, then, what's the problem?" Tara said. "You better jump on that while he's available. You know, he hasn't been in Atlanta long, and some chick gone try to scoop him up quick."

Jayla snatched her eyes away from that hypnotic smile. Of course, this wasn't the first time she'd had to turn a blind eye to a potential boyfriend. She'd had her share of relationships, and some had appeared to be great investments. Call it a test. Just to see if maybe, maybe she could have a little sliver of happiness. But her job called for deception, cheating. So she'd walked away from those relationships. So, as ironic as it was, it was only fair to herself and to potential suitors that she didn't entertain false hopes anymore. No time to search for Mr. Right at this stage. And she was content with that.

"I appreciate you trying," Jayla said. "But he'll have to just admire me from a distance. I'm not interested in a relationship."

Tara didn't appear to buy it, but instead of arguing, she merely lifted her can to her lips and took a quiet sip.

It seemed like Jayla spent the rest of the party trying to sneak peeks at Derrick as he mingled among her family. Thanks to Aunt Bev, a rumor had spread that the sexy guest was with Jayla, and everyone insisted on an in-depth interrogation, with jaded questions about marriage and kids. Every so often, her eyes would lock with his across the room, and each time embarrassment had her tearing her gaze away from that penetrating stare. *Intrigued.* Maybe that was it. She was intrigued by his mysterious confidence.

As the party wound down, she took refuge in the bathroom. When she finally came out, she was surprised, pleasantly so, to see him posted in the hallway, waiting.

"Are we following each other now?" she said.

"Not at all. I'm waiting for the bathroom." He didn't budge, and Jayla wanted to laugh.

"There are two more bathrooms in this house."

He nodded. "Yes, I know," he said.

The fact that he stood there, leaning against the wall, his eyes taking her in as leisurely as if he were savoring a glass of water was intoxicating. Jayla shifted under his gaze, struggling to keep her breathing steady.

"Is there something else you wanted?" she said.

Something flickered in his eyes. What, she couldn't tell. But it was definitely something. And the excitement that radiated through her body was enough to leave her dazed. And aching.

"I'm just waiting for you." His movements were slow. The hallway wasn't narrow, but he eased by her, his face just inches from hers, as if space was at a premium.

Disappointment had Jayla frowning when Derrick merely passed by her, disappeared into the bathroom, and closed the door. She didn't know what she had been expecting, but she sure as hell didn't get it. She shrugged and made her way to the living room.

"Where is your friend?" Aunt Bev asked when Jayla took a seat opposite her in the recliner and right next to Uncle Ron. He draped his arm around her shoulder.

Jayla shook her head. "Aunt Bev, I don't know that man," she said for what had to be the hundredth time. "He came with Kevin."

"Well, child, you better get to know him." Aunt Bev clucked her teeth. "It's not like you got a man. And that one sure has an eyeful of some Jayla."

Jayla's lips curved upward at the thought, even as she let out another regretful sigh. Too damn bad. Jayla was not about to feel bad for some thirsty-ass dude. She didn't want to hurt his feelings, but her passive-aggressive behavior had done just that.

Aunt Bev locked eyes with Jayla and whispered, "I'm telling you, Jayla, keep your eyes open. He just may be *the* one."

CHAPTER FOUR

Jayla locked her legs around his sweaty waist, forcing him to penetrate her deeper and harder. His labored breath roared in her ears as his condom-covered tip stroked her walls, which were already slick from the two orgasms she had barely gotten over. She gripped his tightened arms, her own ragged breaths in sync with the banging of the leather headboard against the wall.

"Oh yes! Shit, babe! Get it," she gasped as he gripped her waist. And with one final thrust, she felt the condom tighten with the explosion of his nut, and his heavy body collapsed on hers from complete exhaustion.

Before she could nudge his shoulder, Chris was already rolling over, unconsciously pulling with him the sheets tangled around his waist.

She let out a satisfied breath and rose up on her elbows. Yes, this one was definitely a great fuck buddy. And after all the dry assignments she'd had in the past week, she'd needed a genuine and uninhibited orgasm.

They lay quiet for a moment, breathing in ragged unison before slowly calming down. The ceiling fan sang overhead, causing a slight breeze to prick her slick skin. Confident she could stand on her weakened knees, Jayla tossed the sheets back and prepared to leave.

"Why do you always rush off?"

Jayla paused not from the question but from the unexpected hand on her arm. She tossed a weary look over her shoulder. "You already know why."

Chris rolled his eyes, his lips turned up in a cross between a smirk and a frown. "I know," he said. "I'm just saying, can you just chill out for a second? I mean, damn. You always quick to throw your clothes on and bounce afterward. Like we about to cuddle or some shit."

Jayla sighed. He was right. Despite their mutual understanding, part of her feared he wanted something more. So distance was best. Until she got horny. And much to her surprise and, she had to admit, gratitude, he had been satisfied with their arrangement for the past two years.

Chris had been an assignment once upon a time, a boyfriend who'd been adamant about remaining faithful. But her persistence had paid off when she'd followed him to a restaurant with his girlfriend and hemmed him in, in the men's bathroom, with nothing on but red stilettos and a slim trench coat. He'd long stroked her pussy over the sink in a matter of minutes.

One saying in particular was self-evident and was the ultimate reason for her business's success. *You can hook any man. You just need the right bait.*

Jayla couldn't explain why she'd called him afterward, and she had not been surprised when he divulged his recent breakup. Now, years later, a mix of comfort, familiarity, and bomb-ass sex had them still going at it when either one had a craving.

She sighed and lay back in the bed and was grateful when he made no move to touch her. That mushy shit was for the birds. Instead, he shifted to give her more of the sheets, and she covered her breasts and tucked the edges of the fabric under her arms.

"I met this chick," he said absently. Pause. He was obviously waiting for her reaction.

Jayla thought about the blanket statement and was slightly relieved when it didn't prompt any adverse emotions in her. "Tell me about her."

"Well, she's definitely not Megan."

Jayla winced at the reference to his ex-girlfriend. She still had some reserve, but she couldn't help the guilt that emerged at times. Especially after she'd seen the outcome with Chris. Never before had she stuck around to see the direct effects of the evaluations. Never before had she cared to.

"But she seems cool," he continued. "A little younger, and she fine, got a nice ass . . ."

Jayla laughed before she realized it. "Okay. Nice ass. But anything substantial?"

"Oh, her ass is very substantial," he said with a wink. "But seriously, she seem like she got a good head on her shoulders. Only thing is, she got a kid, though."

Relaxed, Jayla looked over to study him. He was staring at the ceiling, his face wrinkled in concentration. "So what?" she said.

He shrugged. "Yeah. I guess you're right," he murmured, not bothering to delve deeper.

"And . . . you're telling me this because?" she prompted gently.

Chris finally turned to face her, his eyes intense. "Because we'll probably have to kill this," he said.

Jayla nodded. "You sure about that?"

"I mean . . ." Chris sighed and repositioned himself in the bed. "You cool and all, and I like what we got, but I know you're not trying to get serious. I know I fucked up a good thing with Megan, so I think it's time I grow the fuck up. Settle down. Get married and shit."

"Get married and shit?" she echoed.

"Yeah. Get serious about life. I'm pushing thirty-five, girl. My birthday is next month, and I'm looking around like, damn, life is just flying by."

Jayla sighed. "This ain't no dress rehearsal," she murmured.

"Exactly." He paused, and she could tell he was attempting to tread lightly. "You mad?"

Jayla shook her head no and smiled to reaffirm her answer. "Not at all. That's good. Just . . . just stay faithful to her. A good piece of ass ain't worth losing the one you love for."

Now it was his turn to laugh. "Says the 'good piece of ass' I lost the one I loved for."

"Touché."

"Well, I'm not in the habit of making the same mistakes over again. What about you?"

Jayla frowned at the question. "What *about* me?"

"You like just fucking around? Are you cool with that?"

"What makes you think I'm just fucking around?"

The reverse tactic had Chris rolling his eyes.

Jayla shrugged. "I'm content," she told him. "Not looking for anything more."

He opened his mouth to say something else, but his phone rang. He reached toward the nightstand and grabbed the phone.

"What is it?" Jayla asked, watching him frown at the screen.

"It's Megan," he said. "Damn, I haven't talked to her in a while. Wonder what she wants?"

Jayla pursed her lips and watched him stare at the ringing phone in his hand. "Answer it," she suggested, tossing the sheet from her body. "It could be important." She quickly stood up. snatched her clothes from the floor, and left the bedroom.

Apparently, Chris waited until she had left the house, because she didn't hear him answer the phone until she'd stepped outside. The phone call out of the blue seemed strange, but Jayla quickly dismissed the thought as she climbed into her SUV. She needed to mind her own business. And Chris wasn't her business unless she craved his dick.

She had intended to go straight home, but Chris had her body on empty. Jayla maneuvered her SUV into the parking lot of the first deli she spotted.

The smell of fresh dough greeted her as she stepped into the corner eatery. Since the lunch rush was over, Jayla made her way to the glass case, ordered, and took a seat at a high-top table near the window once she had her food.

Something was wrong, and the fact that Jayla couldn't interpret her own emotions disturbed her. Even more so because she couldn't figure out why. *Was it loneliness?* Maybe the conversation with Chris had gotten to her more than she had realized. Maybe part of her would miss his companionship. Either way, the turkey sandwich wasn't doing much to ease the hollow feeling inside her. Instead of dwelling on it, Jayla tuned in to the jazz music wafting softly through the speakers and to the leisure bustle of downtown traffic outside.

The sky was overcast, but the threat of rain didn't prompt Jayla to eat any faster. She couldn't help but smile as she remembered Chris's rough hands as he'd pawed at her skin. The man definitely knew his way around her body. The giggle slipped from her lips without her realizing it.

"Is it that funny?"

The husky voice startled her, and Jayla glanced up. There he stood, with that damn smile and those bedroom eyes.

"Inside joke," she said. "What are you doing here?"

Derrick held up his to-go bag. "Late lunch. I work right up the street."

Jayla nodded. She kept her eyes on his but was still able to see the alluring drape of the tailored suit.

Not waiting for an invitation, Derrick took the seat across from her. "I was going to eat at my desk, but I would much rather look at you while I eat."

Jayla's breath caught at the suggestive comment. Damn, he was good. Her face remained calm. "Are you flirting with me, Derrick?" she asked boldly, holding back a smile.

He didn't seem taken aback by the direct statement. Just smiled. And, damn, was that smile sexy. "Actually, I am," he said. "You seem like the kind of woman who likes it direct."

This time, she did smile. He was clearly teasing her. And she liked it. She even felt her kitty watering in response to the sexual innuendos. "I am," she said. "And you seem like the kind of man who is not into playing games."

"I am." He paused, his chocolate eyes piercing hers. "So now that we can agree on that, we should get together to learn more about each other."

Jayla held his gaze for a moment longer, the denial prepped on her tongue. He seemed like he could match her, physically and mentally. And she was mesmerized. She pictured his body on top of hers, his lips caressing her thighs. . . .

Jayla wanted to laugh out loud at the vulgar thoughts. Here she was, still warm from Chris's good dick, and she felt her body vibrating at the delicious image of Derrick stroking her from the inside out.

She was usually in good control of her body, could almost get her own juices flowing as easily as if she'd flipped on a switch. Another key to her success. Now, the fact that Derrick's smile alone had her moist . . . Needless to say, the sensation felt damn good.

Jayla kept her eyes fixed on the man across from her. Of course he looked good, no question. But he also seemed very intelligent. Too intelligent to settle for just a fuck buddy. He probably had standards. He wanted a full-fledged relationship, she would bet. Shit, he would probably be one of the ones who could remain faithful for a long time before he cheated. Unfortunately, it wouldn't work.

"You're charming," she said. "And I do appreciate the offer. But I told you before, I'm not interested."

An element of surprise flickered on his face before he masked it with another smile. "I did say you were direct."

"You did," she agreed and rose to her feet. He remained silent as she busied herself with collecting her half-eaten sandwich. The sexual tension was high, and that she could handle. But it was something else that hung between them that was beginning to make her feel awkward.

"Hopefully, you'll change your mind," he said as she turned to go.

Jayla tossed an apologetic smile over her shoulder. "No, hopefully, you'll change yours. You enjoy the rest of your day, Derrick Lewis."

Back in her car, Jayla let out a staggered sigh. He was already making this complicated, and he wasn't even her man. Jayla's phone rang, and she answered it, thankful for the distraction.

"Hey, Jasmine," she greeted. "What's up?"

"I've been thinking about your proposition. I'm not sure I can do it."

Jayla rolled her eyes. She had talked to Jasmine until she was blue in the face after the cookout, trying to convince her niece she wasn't joking, dripping words of encouragement in her ear about the money and the thrill of the business. Jasmine's agreement had been reluctant, but it was an agreement nonetheless. She would come around once she stopped being so damn shy and opened up to her sexuality.

"Did you do what I told you?" Jayla said, struggling to restrain her frustration.

"Yeah. I called Keela, told her that I was wrong and that we should meet up to talk about it."

"Good. And did you call her boyfriend?" She started the SUV and pulled out of the deli parking lot.

Jasmine groaned. "Yeah, I called Tony, too, and said I wanted to meet up with him. But that's what I'm saying. I don't want to be the one to set him up. I can't do it. If Keela comes to the restaurant and sees me and Tony hugged up, that bitch is going to trip."

"So the fuck what, Jasmine?" Jayla was nearly yelling into the phone as she shot through an intersection. "That nigga is a two-timing snake, and she deserves to see him for what he really is."

"But can't I just try to set it up so she catches him with another girl?"

"Fine, Jasmine." Jayla gave a sigh that was laced with pure agitation. She hadn't been this difficult for her own mentor when she first started out. "Do whatever the hell you want. I'm just trying to prepare you before I start giving you some assignments. If you want to be that scared bitch, then be that scared bitch. But I tell you this. You're going to be that scared, broke virgin bitch that's too damn scared to speak up when you see foul shit going on."

Jasmine remained quiet, and Jayla lowered her voice. Maybe she was being a little harsh. "Look, I just don't want to see nobody take advantage of you. You're my niece, and I love you with all my heart. I'm just trying to prep you for some real shit out here. After college, you on your own, sweetie."

"You're right." Jasmine's voice was nearly a whisper.

Jayla wheeled onto the expressway and pushed the gas pedal. The speedometer climbed to eighty-five. "I'll tell you what," she said. "Why don't you go with me on one of my assignments? See how I do it. Would that make you more comfortable?" At Jasmine's hesitation, Jayla pressed. "Listen, I'm not trying to send you out somewhere, and you don't know what the hell you're doing. That's how you get hurt. If you're not ready, I'll back off. But this first assignment I was going to throw your way is an easy one for fifteen thousand dollars. But I want you to be one hundred percent prepared."

"Okay. That's fine."

Jayla smiled. "Good. I'll give you a—"

Her sentence was cut short when someone slammed into her car from behind. The impact threw her forward in her seat, and she dropped the phone to grab the steering wheel with both hands. *What the fuck?* Jayla looked in her rearview mirror just in time to see a black Toyota Sequoia speeding toward her like a bullet. Panicked, she sped up and attempted to get over, but she was not fast enough, and the truck collided with her trunk once more.

Metal scraped against metal, and the sound of shattering glass pierced the air. "*Shit!*" she screamed as the impact knocked her against her steering wheel with enough force that she hit her forehead. She felt her skin split open and the first drops of blood dribble down her face. Jayla swerved again, struggling to keep her truck in her lane.

Another glance in her mirror and she saw the driver of the truck ease off her tail before gunning the engine once more. Jayla held her breath and braced for the collision. She clenched herself and was surprised when the truck made a sharp swerve into the adjoining lane to ride alongside her.

Jayla watched the truck shoot by and frowned when she couldn't make out the driver through the tinted glass. Her breath got caught in her throat as she watched the truck swerve to cut in front of her. The brake lights' sudden glare in front of her ripped another scream from her throat. She snatched the wheel to the right, and the side of her truck scraped the back of the psychotic driver's truck and narrowly missed a car coming up in the adjacent lane.

Horns blared, muffling Jayla's terrified scream, as she spun out, then rolled onto the bank of the expressway.

Jayla sat still, her body shaking, as if she were having a mini seizure. She took desperate gulps of air. Someone had tried to kill her. She shuddered at the thought and squeezed her eyes shut, struggling to erase the traumatic episode from her memory. The fear was a death grip, nearly suffocating her. She inhaled sharply through her nose and blew out a quivering breath, willing her heart to steady itself.

Blood trickled into her eye, causing a faint red haze to cloud her vision. Calling the police was out of the question for Jayla, as she knew her line of work would be questioned, and she couldn't chance it. She had done enough research to know that prostitution charges would stick, but even worse, she didn't want to chance her family and friends finding out the truth about her. So just as quickly as the thought of 911 entered her mind, she dispelled it.

It was then that she glanced behind her at the road. Of course, the traffic sped along, as if a *Fast & Furious* movie shoot hadn't just taken place.

When Jayla was sure she could drive, she eased back onto the road and made her way to the hospital, barely able to see and crying like a baby. Jayla could not help but wonder when her vengeful client or clients would give up and move the fuck on.

CHAPTER FIVE

The outfit was nearly see-through, a dangerously sheer black piece entirely too tight, too short, and too low cut. Jayla grinned as she angled herself so that she could look at the view from the back in the full-length mirror. The matching thong was clearly visible underneath, the material disappearing in the crevice of her juicy ass. Jayla puckered her lips in a frown, and after deciding against the panties, she slid them off. She smiled. *Much better.*

She had fixed her hair to cover the stitches, and with a little makeup, they were barely noticeable. Jayla cringed when she remembered the previous week's near-death experience.

Hell, yeah, she'd been shaken up. But after the hospital had drawn blood, stitched her up, and given her some feel-good drugs, Jayla had been back in the streets. It had taken some time for the anxiety to wear off when she got behind the wheel. Especially since every time she'd looked at her ride, she'd seen the dents and cracked glass. But after a few more days, and after picking up her truck from the body shop, she'd put the incident out of her mind as much as she could. But she was damn sure more vigilant now.

Jayla checked her clock before glancing around the room. Since this was just for her clients, the studio apartment was small, but it sufficed. The furniture was minimal, and with the exception of the bed, all else was purely for decoration, to make the place look more lived in. Hell, the forty-two-inch flat screen she'd had mounted on the wall didn't even have cable attached to it. Just a Blu-ray player was connected, for movies if her clients needed a little coaxing first. Jayla especially loved that she had opted for a studio, because there was clear view into the "bedroom," and so she could go in and change clothes in front of whoever was in the living area.

In the kitchen, Jayla pulled out the half-empty bottle of sangria. She had to admit, part of her was surprised when that Heather chick had called back after their initial meeting. But during their subsequent meetings, the woman had seemed to have grown a backbone, because she sure as hell hadn't seemed as timid as she had at the restaurant. Either way, she had signed the paperwork, had paid her deposit, and had been more than generous with details of her and her plumber boyfriend. The ink hadn't even been completely dry on the contract before Jayla shoved a dishrag down her sink, got it tangled in the garbage disposal, and called the plumber to set up an appointment. Hopefully, this would be another easy one. Especially with her outfit.

The phone vibrated on the stainless-steel countertop, and glancing down at the caller ID, Jayla grinned and clicked on the speaker.

"Hi, *papi*," she said, flipping through her mental Rolodex. *Eric Lawrence, Puerto Rican and black mixed, wavy black hair, live-in girlfriend, Kimberly.*

"Hola, *mamacita*," he greeted, his Spanish accent coating each syllable. "How are you?"

"Much better now."

"That's what I like to hear. I'm at work, on a break now, but I was wondering if I could come by later."

"How about I just come over to your place?" Jayla suggested.

"That would be great, but my sister is staying with me, and I don't want her all in my business."

Jayla rolled her eyes at the lie. "No problem," she said. "Come by around eight." She rattled off the address to her studio apartment and hung up. Quickly, she punched in Jasmine's phone number. She sucked her teeth when the girl's voicemail came on.

"Jasmine, it's me," she said. "Be at my house at six thirty sharp tonight. Don't be late." Her niece was beginning to pluck her nerves.

She punched the OFF button on her phone just as the doorbell rang. Jayla hiked up her sheer lingerie a bit more, so it rode high on her succulent thighs. Licking her lips, she strolled to the front door.

"Yes, I'm coming," she called, then swung open the door.

Jayla smiled to herself when the man caught sight of her and his jaw visibly dropped a few inches. She leaned against the door, placing a hand on her hip and sizing him up at the same time.

He was buff for a white guy. His tanned complexion and blond hair suggested he had been riding waves on the West Coast rather than working knee-deep in clogged pipes. And the image did look appetizing. Plus, by the look of the instant bulge beneath his jeans, he was packing too. She waited while he cleared his throat and shifted his eyes to his tool belt.

"You must be the plumber," she said when he made no move to introduce himself. "I'm so sorry, but I just woke up. I think I forgot you were coming this morning."

He cleared his throat, keeping his eyes downcast. "It's no problem, ma'am. Do you need me to come back?"

Jayla pretended to contemplate the idea. "No, no, I think now will be fine, if that's fine with you. No need for you to waste a trip." She stepped out of the way, barely, and she couldn't help but chuckle as Reggie made a huge effort to ease into the small foyer without grazing her exposed body. She caught the faint smell of cigarettes and coffee and wanted to groan out loud. She could already taste the burned tobacco. *Great.* She prayed no kissing would be involved.

Jayla closed the door, and the sound of the lock sliding into place echoed in the empty room. She turned with a smile and caught him eyeing a picture on the wall.

"That's nice." He gestured absently, and she knew he was trying to diminish the tension in the room. By the look of his eyes fishing greedily for something to focus on, anything but her, she almost felt sorry for him. Almost.

"Thanks," she said, not knowing or caring which picture he was referring to. She stepped around him and led the way into the adjoining kitchen. "I don't know what exactly is going on." She feigned innocence as she waved a hand in the direction of the sink. "It just stopped working. And it's making some kind of whirring sound."

Reggie seemed grateful to get to work. He unclipped his tool belt and sat it on the floor. Then he flipped the switch for the disposal. Sure enough, a grinding and stuttering sound came out first; then there was silence. He turned the disposal off, and after giving the switch a few more flicks, he opened the cabinet and disappeared underneath the sink.

"It's probably just something caught in there," he said, guessing. Jayla hopped up on the kitchen counter. She made sure to keep her knees apart, giving Mr. Reggie a full-fledged peep show, thinking he would stop acting so damn weak and indulge himself.

"Can I get you something to drink? Coke, wine, coffee?"

"No, ma'am."

She frowned. He was good at pretending to be focused. *Fine.* She could wait until he was done.

Jayla remained on the counter, getting herself off by watching his muscles ripple underneath the tight shirt, watching the bend and stretch of his jeans as he leaned in and worked to remove the pipes. She imagined herself wrapping her slender legs around his waist while he gave it to her good and rough right there on the countertop. She'd had a few white guys before, and she'd been disappointed by their short compensation. Maybe Mr. Reggie would be a little different.

He leaned back on his heels and pulling the shredded dishrag into view. "Here's your problem," he said. His eyes ballooned when he glanced over at Jayla.

She smiled, pleased at his reaction. She had taken great care with shaving her pussy and was enjoying the feeling as it grew hot under his shocked stare. Still, she pretended to be oblivious.

"Thank you so much. I'm so glad you were able to fix it."

He cleared his throat and tore his eyes away. "I'll put everything back together and be out of your way shortly." His movements were brisk as he disappeared underneath the sink once more.

"Oh, you're not in my way," she said.

He didn't respond, just continued reaching for pieces of the pipe he had scattered on the tile kitchen floor. As soon as he was finished, he stood, and Jayla hopped down. She walked toward him, and he immediately took a step back.

"Miss," he gasped when Jayla pressed her body up against his and her groping hand snaked up his leg to grab his bulge. He didn't move. Just stood silent as she continued to finger the zipper and leaned in to lick his neck.

Abruptly, Reggie snatched away from her grasp and headed for the living room. "Miss, this is not that kind of maintenance call," he said with surprising strength.

Jayla smiled again. *Fine. Straight to level ten.* She had no problems keeping up. In one swift motion, she reached behind her to the fastener hooked tight at her back. After unclasping the corset, she let the entire piece fall to her feet. She placed her hands on her hips and arched her back to give him a full view of her body in all its naked glory.

"I understand," she said. "But that doesn't make me any less horny."

Reggie turned, and his eyes sucked in her body like a savage. Her size D cups were plump and perky, the nipples beckoning him. His face shaded to a rich crimson hue as he backed up to the door. His clumsy fingers fumbled with the lock and the doorknob, all while his eyes took in every inch of her. As if realizing his mistake, he shut them and turned around.

"I'll send you an invoice," he said before snatching open the door and sprinting out to his truck. In his haste, he hadn't bothered to close the door behind him. Slight aggravation had Jayla sighing as she moseyed over to shut it herself.

She moved to the window and peered through the blinds to see if he was really leaving. Sure enough, he was damn near on two wheels as he backed out of her driveway, swerved, and barely missed the mailbox. As he sped away, Jayla eyed the black Mini Cooper parked across the street.

It didn't seem too out of place, except for the fact that it was facing the wrong way. And perhaps it was parked at the property line between two residences, so she couldn't tell which house the vehicle belonged to. The tinted windows blocked any evidence of someone actually in the vehicle, and she dismissed her rising suspicion with a roll of her eyes. The car accident had her on edge. It wasn't like she lived over here. Hell, people were moving in and out all the time, and she probably wouldn't recognize a neighbor if he or she knocked on her door. She eyed the car a moment longer before letting the blinds fall back in place. *First night fail. No problem.* She'd be better equipped next time she met Mr. Reggie.

She didn't notice the car speed off when she turned from the window.

"Won't he have a problem if I'm just sitting right here, watching?" Jasmine asked. "Or be suspicious or something?"

"Girl, he'll probably be too damn drunk to even care," Jayla admitted with a shrug, finishing up the last little bit of her makeup. She stood back, smacked her lips together to even out the burgundy lipstick, and smiled at the results. "Would you feel better if I made you watch from the closet?" She turned around, completely naked, to face her niece.

Jasmine shifted uncomfortably on the couch. "No, not really." She wasn't really sure what she was getting herself into, and Jayla wasn't too concerned about turning her niece on to this lifestyle.

"Okay then." Jayla nodded, resting her hands on her narrow hips. "I'm trying to teach you like I was taught. Let's not make this difficult. Just watch and learn. And, hell, if you want to participate, I'm sure he won't mind one bit. Let's go have a drink while we wait."

Jayla sauntered into the kitchen and opened the fridge.

Jasmine took a seat at the bar and tried not to stare at her aunt's perfectly sculpted body as she went about pouring them each a glass of wine. "How do you do it, Auntie?" she asked finally, once Jayla had slid a drink in front of her.

"Do what?"

"I mean, how do you get them every time?" Jasmine said, clarifying. "I guess I'm still shocked that men cheat with you left and right. Like they have no morals. Has it always been this easy?"

Jayla sipped her wine and shrugged. "Not always," she said. "Back in the beginning, I used to have to . . . speed things up a little."

"What do you mean?" Jasmine frowned.

"Well, I can deliver in two to three months, and usually, I can do it with no problem. But sometimes, you get those real stubborn ones. Sure, I know they'll cave eventually. I mean, look at me." Jayla did a twirl to show off her plump titties and equally voluptuous ass. "But," she went on, "it takes some longer than others to give in. Meanwhile, a bitch has clients rolling in, bills to pay, and I ain't got time for niggas to be pussyfooting around, trying to convince themselves they don't want me. So I would slip them a roofie or something. 'Let's go ahead and get this shit over with, so I can get paid and move on to the next one,' I'd tell myself."

Jasmine's eyes ballooned at the admission. "You would drug them?"

"Shit, I still do sometimes," Jayla said. "But now that I've got this thing down pat, I know what works, what doesn't work, and I rarely need to. Which reminds me. I'll give you some before you leave tonight. Just think of it as your trump card. Especially because you're new at this."

Jasmine didn't respond. She took a huge swig of her wine and struggled to put on a brave face.

The doorbell rang just as Jayla was polishing off her own drink, and she quickly sat her glass in the sink. She clasped her hands together and tossed Jasmine an encouraging smile. "Ready?"

Jasmine merely nodded.

Jayla went to the front door and peered through the peephole before swinging the door open.

Eric was on her body in an instant, groping every piece of her delicate skin, his tongue shoved down her throat. He backed Jayla into the living room and kicked the door closed behind him.

Jayla laughed as she wiggled from his desperate grasp. "Eric, baby, wait," she said as he took the opportunity to snatch off his jacket. "Do you mind if someone watches us?"

Eric didn't even bother acknowledging the woman perched on the barstool as he pulled his shirt over his head and fumbled with his belt buckle. "I don't care," he huffed.

Jayla tossed Jasmine an "I told you so" glance as she looked on in wonderment. Jayla wasted no time lowering Eric to the floor and straddling his face. Then she situated herself in the sixty-nine position. Eric's tongue lapped hungrily on the underside of her dripping kitty as she stroked his dick before slipping every inch through her parted lips. Fueled by the audience, Jayla stroked and sucked at the same time, flicking her tongue over his tip. Jasmine's wide-eyed stare turned her on even more as Eric continued to slurp her pussy, nuzzling his lips against hers as she wiggled on his mouth. She moaned when he slapped her ass, and the light sting sent her into overdrive. She grabbed his hips and guided him in an upward thrust so the tip touched the back of her throat.

Eric took his mouth off her pussy long enough to groan and mumble something in broken Spanish.

Jayla felt his dick tighten, as if he was about to explode, and she quickly pulled away. After turning her body so they were face-to-face, she hovered over his dick for a moment, allowing her moisture to drip on him, before she took him in. Her pussy slid down the length of his shaft like a figure skater, leaving behind a trail of her creamy juices against his honey skin.

She was easily ready to take Eric into the next century, but he was quick, snatching her over until she was on her back and he was positioned between her slender legs.

"I can't let you win that easily," he said in a breath and began drilling Jayla's pussy, nearly leaving her breathless from the rough force. She wrapped her legs around his waist and angled her head toward Jasmine.

Sure enough, Jasmine had hiked up her skirt and was generously fingering her own kitty. Her eyes were glued to Eric's ass as he continued his deep, hard plunges. As awkward as the situation was for Jasmine, she was beginning to enjoy it all.

Satisfied, Jayla moaned out loud, heightening the stimulation. When she erupted, she felt the gush of her cream spill against her thighs and saturate Eric's lap. As if on cue, she heard Jasmine let out a startled cry of her own, and this was followed by shrieking and gasping, as if she couldn't breathe.

Jayla smiled at the accomplishment. Not only had Eric finally caved after three laborious months, but also Jasmine was good and ready to get that cherry busted wide open.

CHAPTER SIX

"I'm sorry I didn't tell you, but I knew you probably wouldn't come if you knew," Tara told Jayla as they stood outside the restaurant.

The curse word seeped through Jayla's lips before she had time to catch herself. She should've known something was up. "Damn, Tara, really? A double date?" She turned to leave, but Tara caught her arm.

"Jaye, please. I just thought you needed a little nudge."

Jayla opened her mouth to respond once more, but she immediately pursed her lips when she saw Derrick strolling up.

She smelled his enticing cologne before he was within arm's reach. His polo button-up and his slacks hung casually enough from his frame to draw a few noticeable glances from the women leaving the restaurant. She gave credit where credit was due: this man was fine, and he knew he was fine. But it wasn't arrogance that he projected, but subtle confidence. This was obvious by the hint of a smile flirting at the corners of his lips when his eyes met hers.

Jayla opened her mouth to greet him but gasped when she felt his hands slide around her waist and pull her body to his. She felt the bunch of muscles through the thin cotton material of her dress, and the movement caressed her nipples until they hardened like pearls. She hadn't realized she was shuddering in his arms until she heard his low moan of approval at the involuntary reaction. Stepping out of the intimate grasp, Jayla cleared her throat and ran a shaky hand through her hair.

"Um, hi," she mumbled and cursed herself for the idiotic response.

Tara's muffled giggle had her wanting to kick herself. What was this man doing to her?

"Good to see you again." Derrick touched her shoulder, and Jayla felt her breath catch when his fingers grazed her skin. She needed to gain control of herself. She hated this vulnerable feeling.

"So . . ." She cleared her throat again. "I guess you figured you would get me to go out with you by any means necessary, huh?"

Derrick's smile fell into a frown as he glanced at Tara.

"Yeah, I kind of didn't tell Jaye you were coming," Tara said. "But we are all here now, so let's have some drinks and make it a good evening." She tossed Jayla another apologetic, but encouraging smile before making her way inside the restaurant to join her husband, Kevin.

Jayla let out a sigh and turned back to Derrick. She was definitely craving a drink after seeing how these dominos were falling. "Sorry," she said on a smile. "I thought you were in on the setup."

Derrick let his hand slide down the length of her arm before lacing his fingers with hers. "Unfortunately, no, this had nothing to do with me." His eyes swept over her body. He clearly approved of her choice of attire. "But I must say, I've never been so damn grateful for a setup before."

Jayla chuckled and slipped her fingers from his. "Don't even get the wrong idea." She relaxed when she felt the natural inclination to flirt a little. "This dress is just eye candy. No touching."

Derrick nodded and let his gaze linger on her body a moment longer before meeting her eyes. "I'm a very respectable gentleman. Won't do anything you don't ask me to do. Fair enough?"

Relief or disappointment? Jayla wasn't sure which had her frowning at the seemingly simple question. "Fair enough," she answered.

An hour in and Jayla had to admit that perhaps the double date idea wasn't so bad, after all. Tara was so damn commanding, she could carry a conversation by herself. And the way she toggled between reminiscing with Jayla and probing Derrick, she seemed to be handling the routine date questions for them. At first.

"So what do you do?" Derrick finally asked after Tara and Kevin had made their way to the dance floor.

Jayla sighed. It was only a matter of time. She toyed with the small piece of salmon lingering on her plate. Sure, she was a bit hazy from the few drinks and was currently babysitting another, but she wasn't that damn drunk to recognize that question.

"I'm in marketing." The way she delivered the practiced statement was so convincing, as if it were the truth. "A marketing consultant, actually."

"Nice. So you work for a company I would know?"

"No. I work for myself."

"So you do the business and own the business?"

Jayla grinned and gave him a wink as she twirled the straw in what remained of her frozen daiquiri. "Oh yeah. I do the business and own it. JM Enterprise." She went on before he could ask for more details. "So what do you do with Kevin?"

"I'm in the financing department," he said. "You know Kevin is in IT, so we really don't see each other much."

Jayla glanced at Kevin and Tara. They were grinding much too provocatively to the slow song floating through the speakers. "So let me ask you this, Derrick. What did Tara say about me?"

He grinned. "She said you were a workaholic that needed a steady man in your life."

"Well, she is wrong." Jayla caught the glint in his eye as he knocked back the last swallow of his Hennessy.

"Is she, now? So you're not a workaholic?"

"Ha ha. You know what I mean." And normally, she probably would've been pissed at Tara for putting that shit out there, but she was too busy enjoying herself. "I don't want a steady man in my life."

"She didn't say *want*."

Jayla narrowed her eyes, refusing to be charmed. "Since you're so sure about my needs, what about yours?"

Just as she had intended, the casual innuendo caused a flash of desire to color his eyes. When his tongue rolled over his bottom lip, Jayla released a stuttered breath. Even as her heartbeat picked up, she kept her eyes trained on his in a silent dare.

Derrick stood and held out his hand. "I need a dance," he said. "For now."

Maybe it was the liquor. No, it was definitely the liquor. But Jayla couldn't find any kind of excuse to refuse the invitation. So she yielded, allowed herself to be steered to the glistening oak parquet dance floor. She didn't object when he guided her arms to circle his neck and his hands lowered to grasp her waist. The sultry melody prompted the gentle sway of her hips, and she eased her body against his. It felt so natural. So right. And so damn good. Yes, *definitely* the liquor.

She felt the need to wake up. Jayla lifted her lids, squinted against the beginnings of daylight seeping through the blinds. The dull throb of a headache had her rolling over in the satin sheets on a groan.

Damn, she shouldn't have had all those shots. She could've kicked herself for trying to "turn up" like some virgin college freshman. She barely remembered the events that had taken place. Fuzzy images of knocking back Patrón and tequila, sipping a few margaritas, and dancing flitted through her mind. She'd had a great time. That she did remember. Derrick had enjoyed making her laugh, and she'd been completely relaxed in his presence. Even after Kevin and Tara had called it quits, she'd insisted on staying longer, listening to him joke about work, crazy college roommates, and an ex-fiancée who had gotten cold feet and had disappeared without so much as a backward glance.

Jayla pulled the comforter over her head and shut her eyes against the gleaming rays spilling through the flimsy material. Five minutes. Just five minutes and she'd be able to muster enough energy to get up, bathe, and hopefully find something edible in the fridge. She prayed for coffee in the cabinets, even though she couldn't remember her last trip to the grocery store. She sure as hell needed painkillers.

Jayla heard a slight rustle and a cough laced with the edges of slumber. She rose to a sitting position and had to pause, as the quick motion had initiated a brief wave of dizziness.

The room was foggy, but gradually, she focused on a black dresser, a mounted flat-screen TV, and a picture of an older woman she'd never seen before sitting in a frame perched in front of a mirror. She leaned on her elbows, and the aching in her head had her moaning as she continued to take in her surroundings.

His place, she concluded as she gazed at the masculine furniture, the black and red comforter set, and the weight bench and barbells on the bedroom floor. She caught her reflection in the mirror, saw the sheets pooled at her waist, to reveal her black lace bra and panty set, noticed that her hair was tied back from her face with a rubber band. Damn. What had she done? And where was he?

She heard another cough and realized it was coming from *below*. She moaned as she crawled to the edge of the bed to peer over the footboard. There he was, lying on the floor. He'd discarded his shirt and changed into some basketball shorts. Jayla allowed her eyes to sweep over the muscles that rippled on his arms, chest, and stomach, torn between surprise and satisfaction. He lay on his back, a sheet the only barrier between his body and the tan carpet. He hadn't bothered with a pillow but was using his hands as a support.

"Figured you'd sleep longer," Derrick said, his eyes still closed.

Jayla opened her mouth and closed it again wearily. "Did we . . . ?" she began and saw his lips curve at the insinuation.

"What do you remember?" he taunted.

"Not sex."

Derrick propped himself up on his elbows, his eyes glinting with obvious amusement. "Must not have been as good for you as it was for me."

Jayla studied him and had to roll her eyes at the joke. "You're not funny," she said. Sighing, she lifted her hand to her head as the pain intensified. Even as she sat there in her panties and bra between the sheets of his king sleigh bed, with only a few snatches of memory, she knew he'd been as respectable a gentleman as he said he would be.

"We didn't do anything," he assured her. "I promise. I just brought you home . . ."

"Undressed me?"

Derrick nodded. "Yes. Undressed you. Admired your gorgeous body, since you insisted you were just eye candy. But I did not touch you inappropriately." He lifted his hand and used his index finger to cross his heart.

Jayla smiled. *Yes, a charmer.* And she was definitely attracted. "Thank you."

"But," Derrick went on, "I can't promise I will be so respectable next time."

"Next time?"

"You want some coffee? And breakfast?" His grin spread, and Jayla saw the hint of cockiness.

"Real smooth," she said with a laugh.

He rose to his feet, and Jayla tried not to notice how the shorts rode low on his hips. "Why don't you clean up?" he suggested. "There are some towels in the bathroom." When he tossed her a casual wink, Jayla was surprised to feel a blush warm her cheeks. Where the hell was the sudden coyness coming from? Amused, she couldn't help the unconscious grin that touched her lips.

When he shut the door behind him, Jayla pulled herself from the bed and stretched. She eyed the picture on his dresser once more and noted the glaring similarities between Derrick and the older woman. His mother, she guessed, and felt the tiny sting of pain. Her own mother had passed while she was in college, and though they weren't close, the painful void from her absence was like a poorly bandaged wound. Jayla ran a finger down the faux leather frame and sighed.

The gorgeous bouquet of lilies she had taken to her mother's grave a while ago was probably a pile of wilted petals. Jackie had been closer to their mother, so she went more often, but that was still no excuse for Jayla's infrequent visits. A shame. The guilt that deterred her from going as often as she wanted was the same guilt that compelled her to make the trip to the countryside cemetery once a month. The guilt resulted from the fact that her mother had conveyed to Jayla that she was somehow inadequate, and that had strained their relationship.

Jayla ignored the rising distress she felt, willed her mind to extinguish the familiar sentiment as quickly as it had come. She tore her eyes away from the photograph and swept her gaze over the other items that littered his dresser. Nosiness tempted her to open his drawers, but she quickly dismissed the idea. Maybe it was her evaluation mindset. Jayla caught her frown reflected in the oversize mirror. It wasn't like he was her assignment. So what the hell was she looking for? And, more importantly, why the hell did she care? She turned and crossed into the connecting bathroom.

The water pelted her skin like a soothing massage, but it did little to help her headache. Jayla sighed. Her mind was overflowing with thoughts of Derrick. The problem wasn't her acknowledging these feelings. She was a big girl, and, hell, she wasn't ashamed. Yes, she liked the man. A lot. But she was torn. She wasn't supposed to like him. Couldn't afford to. Didn't want to. That was the damn problem.

Jayla stepped from the tub, then used a towel to dry her body before wrapping it around her. She wiped the fogged-up mirror and shuddered at her pitiful reflection. The heat from the shower had flushed her light skin to a warm scarlet hue. Her hair had frizzed, and her eyes reflected every bit of the hangover she felt. Derrick was just going to have to settle for her worst today. Given the circumstances, the scales were tilting away from the embarrassment side to the "too tired to give a damn" side.

Jayla changed into the clothes he had left out on the bed, and then made her way down to the kitchen.

The scent of fresh ground coffee beans caught her; then she heard the sizzle of grease and the low murmurs of an old-school radio station. Jayla paused in the kitchen doorway and watched as Derrick busied himself with scrambling eggs on the stove.

"Hey you," he greeted.

When he turned, she accepted the mug of coffee he offered. The steam wafted up to warm her cheeks, and she inhaled the aroma with a relaxed smile.

"Here." Derrick handed her two pills.

Without speaking, she knocked them back, grateful for the relief.

"Feel better?" he said.

Jayla's appreciative smile spread. "I do. Thank you." She watched him plate some eggs and bacon. "You didn't have to do all this," she said before taking another sip of the coffee.

"I wanted to. I didn't have any grits or oatmeal." Derrick began setting out the food buffet-style on the bar area. "So we'll just have to settle this time."

"This looks great," Jayla commented as she climbed onto the nearest barstool. "You don't look like the cooking type."

Derrick smiled as he dished out healthy portions on her plate first, then on his own. "A man has to be able to feed himself, right?" He placed her plate in front of her, then slid on the stool next to her and set down his own plate. "And his companion," he added.

They ate in silence, their knees bumping companionably against each other under the counter.

"Thank you," Jayla finally murmured as she savored the delicious breakfast. She wasn't aware Derrick had been watching her until she felt his finger nudge her hair behind her shoulder.

"Why are you making this so difficult for us, Jayla?" he murmured.

She paused, felt his gentle lips touch her shoulder. She sighed. *If only.* "Listen, Derrick." She turned to face him, surprised by the close proximity. She didn't see the gesture, only felt the hand circle the back of her neck, the fingers tangle in her hair and then drag her toward him. She could stop this. He seemed to be moving slow enough to see if she would. She had time to catch the lust in his eyes for a split second before his mouth crushed hers.

She hadn't expected or prepared for the tenderness. That was what scared her. Rough, wild, quick, she could handle. But this man was taking his time, coaxing her mouth wider so he could gently suck her tongue. He seemed to be igniting something she hadn't felt in years. *Interesting*. Her pussy was aching, but it wasn't just a sexual desire clawing at her. It was more.

She sucked in a desperate breath, soaked in the sheer pleasure as he tore his mouth from hers and began sucking her neck. She hadn't felt his hands crawl underneath the T-shirt, but they were caressing her titties now, his thumbs massaging her nipples until they ripened against his fingers. Jayla's eyes flew open. It was a weak attempt, she knew, but she forced herself to pull away.

Derrick didn't push. "How long are we going to play this game, Jaye?"

She wanted to smile when she heard his voice, thickened with desire. At least she wasn't the only one. "Derrick. This isn't a good idea."

"Why?"

She fumbled for an excuse. "I'm not looking for a relationship right now."

She kept her eyes trained on his when he stood and gave her another one of his leisurely full-body once-overs, as if he were committing each curve to memory.

"You haven't given me a chance," he said finally.

"I'm not interested in sex." She almost had to swallow a chuckle at the ironic statement. When he leaned closer, she leaned back, and she was surprised when he grinned in response to her unconscious motion.

"Derrick." She hadn't intended to sound like she was pleading. But the way he stared at her, as if he could devour her right there, was becoming more than she could handle. And she could handle a lot. If it was just sex, maybe that would be more tolerable. Sure, she could pleasure him left, right, and sideways, but that was all she was good for. This man had made his intentions crystal clear. He wanted all of her. And she was fucking up. She had allowed herself to like this man.

"I want to see you again, Jayla," he said.

She remained silent. She couldn't do it to him. Couldn't do it to herself. If she wanted to keep her sanity, she needed to stay as far away from Derrick as humanly possible.

Jayla left the restaurant a few short minutes behind her client. She'd handed over another evaluation, and now she needed to get to the bank to deposit the money before they closed.

She hurried down the sidewalk, at the same time pulling out her cell phone. She dialed a number, and Jasmine answered as quickly as if she had been expecting her call.

"I have an assignment for you," Jayla said as she stopped at the ATM. "You think you can handle it?"

"I think so." Her voice sounded slightly hesitant, but still more confident than before.

Jayla smiled. "Good. His name is Benny. I just got the initial deposit from his wife yesterday, so this is a completely new task." She began depositing her money, tossing an absent glance over her shoulder. "Tonight he'll be at that hookah lounge in Midtown. You know the one I'm talking about?"

"In the shopping plaza?"

Jayla finished her transaction and turned around to scan the streets. Pedestrians hurried by, cars eased through the busy downtown district, but she just couldn't shake the feeling that she was being watched. Her heart rate quickened as she glanced around for some sort of sign that something was off. She saw none.

"Auntie?"

Jayla snapped back to the conversation. "Yeah, sorry. What did you say?"

"I asked if you meant the one in that shopping plaza?"

"Yeah, that's the one." Jayla shook off the eerie feeling and hurried back down to the parking lot where she'd left her car. "His wife says he usually gets there around seven, and he tends to stay a few hours. Now, I don't know how this guy is. The wife is not sure if he's a cheater, so he may reject you. Either way, don't push. Just feel him out first and then see how you want to make your next move. If you don't think he'll bite tonight, just let me know and we'll set him up again."

"All right . . ."

Jayla climbed into her car, quickly shut the door and locked it. She sighed. "Hey, you can do this," she assured her niece.

"Okay." Jasmine blew out a breath. "Auntie, how much is this one?"

Jayla did a quick calculation. At first, she figured Jasmine could have the whole fee, but shit, she still had to do the legwork on the assignments, considering her niece was a newbie. To be honest, she really didn't expect Jasmine to be successful on her first night.

"You'll get ten thousand dollars," she said after deducting a generous 60 percent cut. It wasn't personal. It was business. And the wife had paid well over the amount Jayla had planned on charging, so she didn't mind sharing. "Call or text me and let me know what goes down."

***

At one in the morning, Jayla was surprised to hear the alert to an incoming text. She rolled over in the bed and grabbed her phone from the nightstand to read the message. It was from Jasmine.

You didn't tell me the man was fifty-eight.

Jayla rolled her eyes and quickly punched in her reply.

What damn difference does it make? Dick is dick. Did you get it done or not?

She waited, drumming her fingers impatiently on her leg. She surely hoped Jasmine hadn't punked out or done some weak-ass shit that could potentially ruin the whole assignment. Moments later, her phone vibrated again, and Jayla could only grin at the message.

It's done.

CHAPTER SEVEN

Jayla zeroed in on his black Range Rover as soon as she wheeled her truck into the crowded parking lot of Spades. She had never been to the place, but in a quick update, Heather had informed her that Reggie frequented the popular hangout every Thursday night. So here she was, showing every piece of curve in the tight skinny jeans, meticulous razor-slashed holes adorning each thigh area, and a cream crop top that dipped suggestively off her shoulders. She had decided on wedge heels for comfort, and her hair was swooped into a casual ponytail. As far as she was concerned, she was dressed to hunt, and if she played her cards right, she'd be straddling this plumber before sunrise.

The sports bar was in an uproar. Apparently, some football game had brought out every man in Atlanta. They either nursed shots and Coronas around the crowded bar or sat munching on hot wings at the high-top pub tables. Every seat was in view of an angled flat screen, all showing the same game currently in progress. An occasional touchdown or penalty call unleashed unanimous cheers and high fives, and even a few exchanges of money, as the gamblers made good use of the anticipation. The scent of lit Black & Milds, cologne, and liquor hung in the air like a stale blanket, and someone had turned down the music enough to hear the football game.

She may have been the only female in the place, but Jayla was satisfied with that. She didn't need the jealous

stares from women as their men gave her all the attention. She ignored the whistles, the groans of appreciation,
even the bold one who grabbed at her hand as she made
her way to the bar. She was used to it. She basked in it.
She knew she looked good, and everyone who came into
her inner circle knew it too. But she was fishing for one,
and only one. She'd play the tease to everyone else.

"What can I get you, sexy?" The female bartender, who
had a tattoo sleeve laced up each arm, sat a napkin on
the marble bar. She winked, the piercing in her eyebrow
glistening with the gesture, and despite her huge breasts
and curvaceous body, she had her eye on the candy just
like everyone else in the room and could hide her huge
grin.

Jayla's grin was polite. "Surprise me," she said.

The woman nodded and began mixing vodka, rum,
and a combination of fruit juices. She tossed a few cubes
of ice in the mixture, poured it into a glass, and sat the
glass on the napkin. "I call this a Cherry Popper." The
bartender licked her lips after that statement. "It's on me,
babe."

Jayla lifted the glass and grinned over the rim. A free
drink was always worth a little flirting.

The woman scribbled her number on a bar napkin and
slid it to her. "I get off in an hour," she said.

Jayla accepted the napkin, smiled once more, and
slipped away from the bar. Not really her type, but that
was completely irrelevant. She began to scan the crowd
for Reggie.

A group of men posted around a pool table off to one
side were obviously torn between their game and the
TV. Once she made her way over, she smiled when she
recognized Reggie among the men at the pool table. He
leaned casually on a pool stick, his eyes on the flat-screen
TV mounted on the wall. Two other guys stood around,

as well, and another was leaning over the table, already in position to take a shot.

One of Reggie's friends saw her first and let out a low whistle, apparently approving of the newcomer. "Damn, girl," he said. "You know you a fine one."

Jayla smiled as her eyes met Reggie's. The fearful look on his face was priceless. "Thank you," she said and also acknowledged the comment with a wink. "I'm Slim," she added.

"*Shit*," one of the other guys exclaimed. He didn't bother hiding the head-to-toe scan of her body. "I'm Bruce, by the way." He gestured to the other three men. "That's Mike, Reggie, and DW."

"I don't mean to impose," she said, still watching Reggie. "Unfortunately, my date stood me up. So . . ." She glanced around, pretending to look for someone.

"Aye, man," said the one named DW as he nudged Reggie. "You know her?"

"Not really," Jayla said before Reggie could respond. "He did some things for me, though."

"Plumbing," Reggie explained when the others turned his way. "Work. It was work."

"That's what I meant." Jayla took a sip from her glass and watched his uneasiness.

So was this all she needed to do to make this man break? Show out in front of his friends? Too easy. She glanced down at the pool table, feigning interest. "Oh wow. I haven't played pool in forever. You guys mind if I join?"

"I don't think you can afford us, sweetheart," Mike said with a grin, exposing a gold cap on one tooth. "We don't play for free around here."

Jayla nodded. Taking care to exaggerate her movements, she ran her hand along her breasts for a moment before sticking her fingers into her bra. She pulled a stack of twenty-dollar bills into view. The attention had her adrenaline on an all-time high.

She looked to Reggie again for confirmation. "Only if it's okay with you, though, Reggie." She could tell he was getting flustered from the heightened tension, but his absent shrug had her reaching for a cue stick. She let Bruce rack the balls while she chalked her cue tip.

"Ladies first, Slim," he said.

She leaned over, felt every set of eyes on the jeans hugging her ass. *Fine*. He wanted to act tough. She knew how to break him. She smirked as she took her shot.

One hour and three drinks later, Jayla scooped up the bills the men had piled on the pool table. A combination of premium liquor and a nice winning streak had a triumphant smile planted on her lips. Even Reggie had loosened up a bit. So much so that he had started talking smack like the rest of his friends in a weak attempt to throw off her game. But it was a public display of his relaxation, nonetheless. She was juiced.

"I underestimated you." Bruce touched her waist lightly. "You fine, but you damn sure can play."

"Thank you." She glanced at Reggie again. "It's getting a little late, so I'll head out. You mind walking me to my car?"

Reggie nodded, laid his pool stick down, and followed her outside.

It felt late. Much later than it was. The July air was crisp and gently tickled her skin, coaxing a slight shudder from the temperature. She slowed, allowing Reggie to fall into step beside her.

"Sorry about your date," he mumbled, and she could tell it was his attempt to break the awkward silence.

She shrugged. "Hey, you know what? It's his loss," she said. "And I had a great time with you and your friends."

"I bet you did." He laughed. "Hey, how is your garbage disposal?"

"Good. You do excellent work. I'm definitely going to give you some referrals." She stopped at her car and turned to lean on the hood as Reggie stuck his thumbs in his front pockets.

"I appreciate it," he said.

Jayla bit her lip and swallowed her slight impatience. She was going to have to speed up this thing if she wanted to get it over with. White boys liked that damsel in distress shit.

She shifted and stumbled, and her intentional clumsiness prompted Reggie to grab her arm to catch her fall. Exaggerating even more, she allowed him to pull her upright, but then she stumbled again, and this time she leaned on his chest when he grabbed her. "I'm sorry." She faked a chuckle. "I think those drinks are finally getting to me."

Worry creased his forehead as his eyes studied hers. "You probably shouldn't drive," he said. Jayla leaned in closer, pushing her protruding titties against him. She glanced at his full lips, then back up at his eyes.

"You want to take me home?" she whispered. She felt his body stiffen. Before he could pull away, she leaned in and pressed her lips against his.

He remained stiff as she gently prodded his mouth open with her tongue and then drew his lower lip into her mouth to suck. The beer taste was strong, but she ignored it as she wrapped her arms around his neck. When he still made no move to return the kiss, she slid her hand down his chest and into the waist of his jeans. Her hand snaked past the elastic in his briefs, and her fingers got a possessive grip of his dick. That was the switch.

Reggie came alive, hardening in her hand and beginning to suck her wild tongue. He nudged her back against her hood and, in one movement, gripped her plump ass and lifted her legs so she would wrap them around his waist. He reached in the top of her shirt and pulled out one of her titties. The sudden exposure to the brisk air startled a gasp from her lips. Then, with an urgent moan, he tore his lips from hers and leaned down to devour her supple flesh. His movements were hasty, as if he needed to feast. Thank goodness nobody was in the parking lot, but Jayla wouldn't care when all was said and done.

Jayla purred. "Damn, you're big," she whispered.

He groaned, and she felt his fingers flick the button of her jeans open. Then they snatched down her zipper. Her lips curled when his hand brushed her naked pussy. No need for panties tonight. It was ready for him. She felt his fingers dancing around her clit before dipping inside her, allowing her juices to spill. She moaned and bucked against his hand, urging him to go deeper. He obliged, shoving in his second and middle finger to stroke her walls as well. Her head fell back as he continued to finger her, his rhythmic pace increasing as she gyrated her hips against his hand. Harder. Faster. She felt his thumb caress her clit with the motion, and she braced herself.

Then, as quickly as he had started, Reggie snatched his hand away. The abrupt withdrawal had her stumbling to catch her balance.

"I . . ." A combination of fear and embarrassment tinted his face. "Damn! I'm sorry. I . . ."

"What's wrong? I want you, Reggie. You are so damn sexy, and I want you. Don't you want me?"

"I have a girlfriend," he said. "Shit. I have a girlfriend. This is wrong."

Jayla hadn't expected the confession, and she bit her lip in consideration. *Next move, next move. What to do? What to do?*

Just then his cell phone went off, slicing the sexual tension like a knife. He fumbled for the device before pulling it from his pocket. After wiping Jayla's juices off his hand, he answered, "Yeah?" He glanced back at the bar.

Jayla smacked her lips. Damn hating-ass friends. Probably jealous she had all but thrown it at him all night and not them.

"I'm coming," he said and hung up. He looked at Jayla again and mumbled a short "Get home safe" before turning and trekking back across the parking lot.

She sighed. The regret had been more than prominent in his voice. *Fine.* Next time she saw Reggie, she would pull the apology card, make herself seem weak, vulnerable. That shit would probably turn him on even more than the direct approach.

Jayla had just slid behind the wheel when her own phone rang. She already knew it was Heather before she picked up. "Hello?"

"How did it go?"

"It will be in my final report," she said, exasperation bringing on a slight headache. "If you want to discuss details prior to that, remember it must be done in person." She sighed.

"I know. I'm sorry." It was Heather's turn to sigh. "I don't know. I just. . . You're right. Guess I just got a little anxious when he didn't come home and didn't call."

"I'm not done yet," Jayla said.

Pause.

"Okay, um . . ." It was too obvious she had something else to say.

"What is it?" Jayla prompted, slightly irritated. "Do you want me to stop?"

Another pause.

"No," Heather answered finally. "No, I'm fine."

Jayla hung up and laid her head back on the headrest. *Any man can be hooked. You just need the right bait.* Jayla closed her eyes at the thought. She had proven the concept true thus far. It was only a matter of time. But one thing was for sure. She was horny as hell, thanks to Reggie.

Not bothering to assess her actions, Jayla punched in a familiar number and waited while her phone rang in her ear.

"Fuck me," she said once Chris answered. She heard him sigh.

"I can't—"

"Come on, Chris." She didn't care that she was almost whining from desperate frustration. "I need you. It'll be quick." She took note of his brief hesitation.

"It's over," he said finally, his voice firm. "I told you. We're done. I'm seeing someone."

"That didn't stop you before." Jayla hadn't meant to snap, but the rejection was eating at her. A little more than usual. She was surprised to hear the click. Damn, he was really serious. Never before had he hung up on her.

Jayla squeezed her thighs tight, moaning as her clit throbbed for attention. She used her fingers to rub between her legs. She was warm, and the coarse jeans material was rough against the supple flesh of her pussy. *Fuck Reggie and Chris.* She'd handle herself right in the middle of the parking lot.

Jayla fumbled with the zipper of her jeans before she stopped short, remembering the busty bartender. Her eager fingers reached in her pocket for the bar napkin. Sure enough, the woman's phone number was legible. Jayla held the napkin between her thumb and forefinger as she considered the proposition. The woman seemed down for a no-strings-attached cut buddy for the night, and since Chris had cut her off, it wasn't like Jayla had someone to satisfy her at the moment.

Jayla dialed the number. *What the hell.* She had nothing else to do.

The woman picked up on the second ring. The noise in the background was deafening, a monotonous hum of activity that had Jayla pulling the receiver away from her ear.

"This is Joi," the woman yelled over the noise.

Jayla smirked at her own behavior. *Joi*. It occurred to her she was ready to fuck this woman sideways, and she hadn't even known her name. Or cared what it was, for that matter. "It's me," she said. "Cherry Popper. You off yet? I need that sexy-ass tongue of yours on my pussy." Jayla could almost hear the woman grinning at the bold statement.

"Come around back, so I can let you in."

By the time Jayla had walked around to the back of the building, Joi was already standing outside, leaning against the door to prop it open. Jayla saw her licking her lips as she motioned her over. Anticipation had Jayla on the edges of an orgasm, and she quickened her pace, trotting over to meet the woman at the door.

Joi led her to small storage closet, and they stepped inside. The smell of cleaning supplies and dust permeated the tiny space. It was stuffy as hell in there, too, but Jayla didn't care.

She was already snatching her jeans down as Joi shut and locked the door. With the exception of a sliver of light peeking through the crack of the door, they were enveloped in darkness, which only fueled the rising sexual tension.

Jayla grinned as a sneaky idea crossed her mind. She dialed Chris's number and placed the phone on the floor. Since he had insisted he didn't want her anymore and had had the nerve to hang up her on, let him get an earful of what exactly he had rejected. She waited until she heard him answer the phone before she went in.

"I need you to fuck me, Joi," she cooed, then gave a seductive moan.

"You damn right I am. You said something about wanting this tongue on your pussy."

"Oh, please, give it to me."

Jayla heard the desire coating Joi's voice as she pressed her body against hers. Joi's nipples protruded through the thin material of her top, and Jayla found this inviting and deliciously tempting. Jayla pulled one of the woman's titties out from the low-cut neckline and leaned over to take the nipple between her lips. The faint smell of Joi's soft flesh was distinct as Jayla flicked her tongue around the hardened pearl. *Cocoa butter*, she decided. She heard Joi moan, and so she grip the back of her head as she indulged, alternating between generous sucks and feathery licks. She felt Joi's fingers inch down her stomach to brush her pussy lips, and she moaned. Joi's fingers were cold, but the contrasting sensation sent a tingle through Jayla's thighs. Joi gripped Jayla's clit between her index and middle finger, then moved her fingers back and forth to massage it until it swelled against her touch. Jayla felt her knees get weak, and she ground against Joi's hand, urging her to keep going.

"I want you to ride my face," Joi said, and obediently, Jayla lowered herself to a squatting position. She felt Joi position herself between her legs, her heavy breathing loud and jagged. Jayla lowered her pussy onto Joi's lips and groaned as Joi gently spread her open and began using her tongue to massage the inside of Jayla's walls. The stimulating sensation was enough to drive her damn near crazy as she bounced on top of Joi's stiffened tongue, simultaneously using her thumb to stroke her clit with each upward movement. The only sound that could be heard was Joi's appreciative moans and the lapping noise as she slurped Jayla's abundant juices.

When Jayla felt the muscles tense in her legs, she lowered herself to her knees and leaned forward on her hands for support. Then she gyrated her hips in sync as Joi moved to sucking on her clit like a pacifier. She squeezed her eyes shut, and the tension mounted as Joi worked miracles with her tongue, swirling it around the hood before taking the inflated clit between her lips once more. Damn, she was good. Jayla felt Joi's hands on her plump ass, nudging it faster as she licked her sugar clean and then some. When Jayla released, she bit back a scream, and the warm cum ran down her thighs to pool like a moist beard on Joi's chin. She shivered and collapsed, her body jerking with the orgasm.

"Uh." Joi's muffled groan had Jayla lifting her hips from the woman's wet face. "Damn, you taste good, girl."

Jayla smirked as she stood. Damn right, she knew. She needed her kitty in tip-top shape for whatever scheduled or spontaneous affair occurred. Which reminded her . . .

She scooped her phone up off the floor and saw that Chris had hung up. For some reason, that tickled her.

She found her pants scattered on the floor, and she leaned against a wall to put them on. Her pussy still tingled with the aftereffects of the orgasm, and she sighed in relaxation.

"Do I get to see you again, Cherry?" Joi asked.

Jayla rolled her eyes, grateful the darkness concealed the slightly irritated gesture. "I know where you work, Joi," she said instead. She didn't object when she felt Joi feeling for her face and when Joi pulled her lips against hers. Jayla tasted her own fresh juices on the bartender's tongue as she allowed the woman one final kiss.

A combination of the oral sex and the hastily arranged boxes in the storage closet had Jayla stumbling to the exit. She didn't bother looking back after she opened the door. She didn't even bother thanking Joi. It was a great release and was damn sure what she needed.

As soon as she made it back to her car, she quickly dialed Chris's number but was not surprised when his phone went straight to voicemail.

"Hey, lover," she gushed in the phone. "Just wanted to call back and see if you enjoyed the show. I figured you needed an idea of what you were missing. You know you'll be back sniffing at this pussy, Chris. In case you need a reminder, just remember how that woman was sucking on all this juicy pussy." She made a kissing noise before groaning. "Yeah, I know you liked the sound of that, boo. Call me when you're ready to play in it some more." She hung up and fell back in her seat, laughing.

That was what his ass got. Now, with all of that out of the way, she could refocus on the task at hand.

CHAPTER EIGHT

The phone's incessant ring snatched Jayla from some good sleep. She sat up, grumpy as hell and instantly pissed off at whoever was calling this early. She grabbed her phone off the nightstand and answered the call.

"What?" she barked.

"Girl, don't come at me like that," Jackie tossed back.

"Whatever, Jack. I'm sleepy."

"Well, that's not my problem."

Jayla groaned and fell back into her pillows. She didn't have time for this shit this morning. "What is it?" she asked.

"I was wondering, have you seen Jasmine?"

"What are you talking about?"

"She hasn't come home in a few days. I'm starting to get worried. I figured she was hanging out at Keela's, but I called over there, and she hasn't seen her, either."

Jayla shut her eyes against the sun spilling in through her blinds. She vaguely remembered sending Jasmine on another assignment, but of course, Jackie didn't need to know all that.

"I talked to her yesterday," she said. "She was fine."

"Fine? But what the hell is she out doing?"

"Jackie, she is grown. Leave that girl alone."

"I don't give a damn if she is grown. She's living in my house, and I don't appreciate her coming home at all times of the night. Hell, when she even bothers to come."

Jayla sighed.

"You could be a little more concerned, Jayla." Anger had quickly elevated Jackie's voice.

"Calm the fuck down, Jackie. Damn. I said she is grown. Stop treating her like a fucking kid."

"Jayla, you can be a real bitch sometimes." *Click.*

Jayla smacked her lips and tossed the phone on her bed. She yawned, and reconsidering Jackie's words, she picked up the phone again and dialed Jasmine's number. It rang twice before the call went to voicemail.

"Jazz, it's me. Call me when you get this. Your mother is worried about you."

She hung up, and just as quickly, the phone buzzed in her hand. Not bothering to look at the caller ID, Jayla quickly answered. "Jasmine?"

"Nope, it's me," Jocelyn answered. "Something wrong with Jasmine?"

Jayla sighed. "No, I just left her a message, and I thought she was calling me back."

"Everything all right?"

"Yeah." Jayla quickly changed the topic. "What's up, sis?"

"I need a favor. Come baby shopping with me."

Jayla prepped her lips to decline—she already had a no on the tip of her tongue—but instead she stifled a groan. This was her baby sister. And it wasn't like Jocelyn had an active baby daddy to do that type of stuff with.

"Come on," Jocelyn urged, already sensing a rejection. "It's Saturday. We can make a whole day out of it."

Jayla sighed. She hadn't spent time with her in a while. "Fine," she said.

"Cool. I'll pick you up in an hour. Thanks, girl."

Jayla hung up and checked to see if she had a missed call or text from Jasmine. Nothing. She tried her again and frowned when she got her voicemail. It wasn't like her not to answer or return phone calls. Jayla punched in a quick text.

Jazz. Call me as soon as u get this.

Not completely satisfied but having exhausted all options, Jayla headed to the bathroom to start getting herself ready. It would feel good to relax a little today. It felt like she was constantly juggling men, evaluations, meetings, and money. She was successful, yet the work was strenuous. Sometimes there were just too many desperate women needing answers at one time. And she only had three holes to go around.

Jayla stepped out of the shower, beads of water trickling down her body and soaking the plush rug under her feet. Her mind immediately went to Derrick. She wondered what he was doing, then immediately cursed herself for the thought. She had tried her best not to think about him, but she couldn't help questioning why he hadn't tried to call since their last encounter a week ago. Part of her felt relieved, but she had to acknowledge the tug of disappointment as well. Tara hadn't even said two words about him since the surprise double date, and it was taking everything in Jayla's power not to bring him up.

An hour later, the doorbell rang, and Jayla swung the door open and allowed Jocelyn to waddle through. Jayla cringed when she looked down at her sister's flip-flops and saw that her feet had swelled to the size of melons.

"Your feet look like they hurt, Joce."

Jocelyn forced a grin. "I'll be all right. Here." She handed Jayla an unsealed envelope. "This was on your door."

Jayla eyed the simple letter *J* someone had scribbled across the front of the envelope. She hesitated, then turned the stark white envelope over. Nothing on the other side. No indication of its source. "Did you look inside it?" she asked.

"Of course not. What is it? Who sent it?"

Jayla wanted to explain that it was from some psycho-path whose man she'd fucked and sucked sideways for money. She thought of the stabbed teddy bear package and shuddered. She hadn't received anything since, and she'd had no more vicious road encounters, so she had convinced herself the madness was over. She led the way to the kitchen.

"What is it?" Jocelyn asked again as she followed.

Jayla absently tossed the envelope on the counter. "Nothing important." She smiled to hide her discomfort.

"Uh-huh." Jocelyn grinned. "Since when do you have a boyfriend?"

"I don't."

"Then who is it from? A secret admirer?"

Jayla turned to the refrigerator. "Something like that," she said, reaching inside for the gallon of apple juice. "Here. Drink something. And how about after the baby store, we go get a pedicure? My treat."

"I'm thinking about Bryce if it's a boy." Jocelyn hadn't stopped talking since they had arrived at the mall. Or eat-ing, for that matter. Even now, as they rode the escalator, she was knocking back Whoppers by the handful. "Or maybe Brycen. What you think?"

Jayla nodded as they stepped off the escalator. "I like Bryce. I'm surprised you don't want to keep the *J* thing going like Jackie."

"Girl, I've always hated that idea," Jocelyn said.

Speaking of which, Jayla snuck a glance at her phone again. No word from Jasmine. What the hell was that girl doing? she thought.

Jocelyn led the way into the baby store. Soft pastels and hushed lullaby music created an inviting and re-laxing atmosphere. Cribs, dressers, and changing tables had been neatly arranged to simulate mini nurseries in varying styles. Racks of baby clothes lined the back wall, and strollers, car seats, and high chairs were on display. The place had it all.

"I saw this the other day and thought it was so cute." Jocelyn pointed to a mahogany-brown converter crib, already decorated with a blue plaid comforter set. "And it converts into a bed, too, so seems like it'll be a good investment."

Jayla nodded absently. Her mind wanted to wander to the what-ifs of her own unplanned pregnancies, but instead, she fingered the price tag dangling from a rail on the crib.

"Excuse me." The voice from behind had both ladies glancing up, and Jayla sucked in a breath. Tracy.

She immediately flashed back to the car incident after her evaluation on Marcus. Tracy and her sister had damn near been at her throat. Now her hair was shorter, and the hint of a pregnancy belly protruded underneath an I SWEAR I'M A VIRGIN maternity shirt. But still, it was definitely her. *Damn. What are the odds?*

"I just wanted to see where you got that dress from," Tracy was telling Joce. "They are so hard to find."

Jayla pretended to be heavily engrossed in the changing table, but she clearly caught the wedding rings blinking from the woman's finger. She started to inch away from the pair as they lapsed into an erratic exchange of pregnancy stories. Neither seemed to notice as she headed toward the back of the store. The sight of the man headed her way with an armful of onesies had her stopping short. She made her way back to the ladies.

Marcus made eye contact and nearly collided with a nearby rack as he froze. *Shit.* Jayla remembered the black wig she wore with him, but apparently, her face was crystal. She tried to stifle the rising panic as she pivoted on her heels once more and maneuvered toward the exit. Joce stopped her.

Tracy's eyes met hers. The series of emotions that played on her face was like watching a movie. Her eyebrows crinkled in confusion, her eyes rose in shocked recognition, and then her tiny lips pursed in restrained anger. And it was that anger, that quiet glint of some seething hatred, that had Jayla narrowing her eyes. Tracy had finally recognized who she was. *The death threats.* Jayla didn't know how this bitch had found out where she lived to send them, but her own anger outweighed her curiosity to the point where she wanted to slap the shit out of her right there. Even more so when Tracy gave her a slick smile and turned to Marcus.

"Can you meet me outside, Marcus?" she asked.

Marcus seemed grateful for the dismissal, and he hurried to the front of the store.

Jocelyn glanced at each woman, obviously sensing the suffocating awkwardness and increasing tension. "Do you two know each other? This is strange."

Tracy's smile widened. "Absolutely," she answered, her voice dripping with sarcasm. "We're good friends."

Jayla lifted an eyebrow. "Can you give us a moment, Joce?" She waited until Jocelyn had disappeared to the back of the store before she lowered her voice and growled, "You're such a grimy bitch, Tracy."

Tracy chuckled. "Excuse me?"

"You heard me. I know you're the one sending me those damn packages. And was it you who tried to run me off the road a few weeks ago? I ought to report your ass to the cops."

"Bitch, please." Tracy's eyes carried a knowing glint. "Do you really think I believe you would go to the cops and risk me exposing all this little bullshit you got going on?"

"So it *was* you."

When Tracy rolled her eyes, Jayla stepped forward, her glare menacing. It was taking every ounce of her willpower to keep her from wiping the floor with this chick. "If you come near me again, I swear I'll kill you."

"I don't care about none of that bullshit you barking about, bitch. I do know that you're not about to stand here in my face and threaten me. I take it you're mad that I'm with Marcus. Mad your sour pussy couldn't keep him away from me, right?" She wiggled her fingers to let her wedding rings catch the light. At the same time, she rubbed her protruding belly with a smug smile.

Jayla's eyes ballooned in shock. "Bitch, are you serious? You're the idiot who is still with him and is now about to have a baby by him, and you know he's fucking around. And you gave me eighteen thousand dollars to prove what you already knew. But at least you have a souvenir. Still enjoying the tape recording I put together for you?"

Tracy's eyes blazed at the comment.

"Yep," Jayla said, gloating, happy to have gotten under her skin. "He feasted on this delicious pussy like he was on death row. And went back home to kiss you. Tell me, how do I taste?" She could almost feel the wave of heat from Tracy's simmering anger. Jayla blew her a final kiss before breezing by. "Checkmate, bitch," she murmured.

Jocelyn had checked out, and Jayla found her waiting outside the store, a questioning expression already fixed on her face.

Jayla let out a breath, not bothering to look at her sister.

Jocelyn dove in as soon as Jayla was beside her. "So what the hell was that about?"

"Just some work mess."

"Work?" Jocelyn looked back over her shoulder at Tracy, who was watching them walk away. "That seemed a little more personal. *Good friends.*"

Jayla turned up her lips in disgust. "Please, that bitch is not my friend. She was just being a smart-ass. Don't worry about it."

Jocelyn's next statement was cut short by her phone ringing. She pulled it from her purse and smacked her lips once she saw who the caller was. "Alex." She spit her baby's daddy name like it left a bitter taste in her mouth.

Jayla laughed at her sister's reaction. "What does he want?"

"One sec. Let me see." She answered the call and put the phone to her ear.

Jayla moved in the opposite direction, allowing her sister a little privacy. Those two had been on again, off again for nearly eight years. Perhaps this was an "on" week for them.

When Jayla heard the familiar ringtone muffled inside her purse, she inched toward a bench near the mall's indoor fountain to take the call. She didn't bother glancing at the phone before she swiped the touch screen with her thumb and placed the device to her ear.

"Hello?"

"Jayla?" The masculine voice was so seductive. Renewed excitement had her lips curving.

"How did you get my number?" she said and heard Derrick chuckle.

"Come on, now. You know better."

She wanted to ask what had taken him so long to call but thought better of it. "How have you been?"

"Can't stop thinking about you," he said, as if he had been waiting on the question. "When can I see you again?"

"Derrick, we talked about this—"

"No, I think I asked, and you shut me down a couple times," he interrupted. "But you never gave me an explanation."

"I don't owe you one."

"True."

He paused, and Jayla glanced over to see Jocelyn chatting away on her own call.

"So tell me something," Derrick went on. "Do you want me to leave you alone? Honestly?"

Jayla remained silent. Of course she didn't. But still . . . "I just think that's best," she said. It was a weak answer, but she tried to put some conviction in her tone. "I don't want to get into a relationship."

"Who said I was looking for a relationship?"

Jayla remained silent. *Good point.*

"Listen, I like you," he said. "I'm direct. I don't like bullshit. Can't we just start off by being friends and let whatever happens happen? That's not to say it won't, but that's not to say it will, either."

"We'll talk about it another time," she said. "We'll see. Fair enough?"

"Fair enough," he agreed. "Have a good one, beautiful."

Jayla waited for the call to disconnect. She didn't realize she was grinning like an idiot.

Jocelyn waddled over and slid beside Jayla on the bench. "He can be such an asshole," she murmured about her baby's daddy.

"What did he want?"

"He just wanted to know where I was and when I was coming back home. I told him he should've been the one here with me, and he wants to cut me off, saying he's not trying to hear my fussing."

"*Home*?" Jayla had picked up the subtle hint and lifted an eyebrow.

Jocelyn sighed. "Yeah, I let that nigga move back in. *Again.* That was stupid, huh?"

"I don't know why you let him walk all over you," Jayla said, shaking her head. "That shit is getting old."

"He promises to do better," Jocelyn insisted, even as Jayla's disapproving frown deepened. "He really does. He said he's going to get a job, we're going to save up for a wedding, and he'll be a good daddy. All of that. I need to give him a chance to prove himself."

"So where is he now, Joce?" Jayla motioned around the crowded mall and watched Jocelyn's eyes fall to her lap. "Exactly. Like I said, that shit is getting old." She remained quiet when Jocelyn didn't respond. Maybe she was too aggressive. On the other hand, her sister could be weak at times, and she damn sure needed to get with the program.

It wasn't until after she had sent her sister on her way that Jayla remembered the envelope in the kitchen. Of course, it hadn't moved from where she'd thrown it earlier. She saw the letter *J* once more, the simple personalization like a finger pointing at her. *This* is *for you, bitch.*

Jayla turned the envelope over, plucked off the solitary piece of tape keeping the flap closed. After lifting up the flap, she pulled out a card. It was some sort of child's card. Well, it used to be. On the front was a picture of a teddy bear, his arms across his chest. Someone had taken a red marker and crossed out the original message, *Do you know how much I love you*? And they had scribbled the question *Do you know how much I am going to enjoy killing you*? The words seemed to tear a hole in her, so much so that she dropped the card on the floor.

It sprang open, revealing a much larger teddy bear. Someone had taken the liberty to turn the bear's smile into a sinister snarl, complete with sharp teeth. The front of the card said, *Do you know how much I am going to enjoy killing you*? And the answer to that question was on a banner in the larger teddy's hands, outstretched in 3D pop-up fashion: *This much. This much. This much.*

Her phone rang, startling her, and a scream came from her throat. She ripped her eyes from the evil message and eyed her phone. She took a grateful breath when she saw Jasmine's number flashing.

"Jasmine," Jayla gasped when she answered the call. She forced herself to focus on her niece and not the threatening card. "I've been looking for you. Where are you?"

"Out," she snapped.

"What the hell is your problem?"

Jasmine's attitude was all the way on as she blew out an irritated breath. "I've been out here busting my ass, Auntie. I've gone on four assignments, and I don't think I'm getting enough money for the shit I have to put up with."

Jayla rolled her eyes. A little taste of the good life and the bitch had the nerve to get greedy. Money was already changing her. Which was why the ungrateful heifer didn't need to know Jayla was skimming her cut off the top.

"You should have almost fifty thousand dollars in the bank," Jayla shot back. "The fuck you mean, you're not getting enough?"

"I'm saying I got niggas begging for my pussy, and I should be upselling the shit outa these ballers," Jasmine said. "So that's why I've been setting up my own assignments."

"What?" Confusion had Jayla squinting at the phone. Had she heard correctly? "Setting up your own assignments? You don't know what the hell you're doing."

"Please. Come see me at the Sheraton off Main Street and tell me I don't know what I'm doing. Suite twenty-two-oh-four." And with that, Jasmine hung up.

Jayla stared at the phone for a moment. How quickly Jasmine had turned into her was enough to make her skin crawl. And what the hell was Jasmine trying to show her? She didn't bother dwelling on it any longer. Whatever it was, she was headed to that Sheraton to knock her niece's ass off her pedestal.

Stepping off the elevator on the second floor, Jayla glanced both ways down the empty hall. She eyed the sign with the room numbers and then walked briskly toward suite 2204. Jasmine had gotten out of hand. Got her first taste of dick, and she thought she had gold between her legs.

Jayla stopped in front of the door and lifted her hand to knock. That was when she noticed the door was cracked open. As if on cue, muffled moans drifted out of the suite. Jayla nudged the door open and stepped inside.

She noticed Jasmine first, straddling a man's lap. Her back was to the door, and Jayla's mouth dropped open as she watched the scene unfold.

Jasmine was working that dick like a pro, rotating and gyrating until her ass clapped and jiggled with the intense motions. "Oh, fuck yes," she was moaning, and she lifted her face to the sky, as if in prayer. Her eyes were squeezed shut as she leaned forward for the man to grab her bouncing titties. His thumbs fingered the rings glinting on her erect nipples as he lifted his hips to stab his dick deeper. Each thrust had a wet, sloshing sound echoing in the room.

Jasmine must have sensed Jayla was watching, because it was then that she tossed a smirk over her shoulder and gave her a bold stare. The movement had her shifting to the side, and Jayla's eyes ballooned when she recognized the man's face twisted in utter pleasure.

"Jasmine, what the fuck!" Jayla yelled and lunged across the room to snatch her niece's naked body off the man. At just that moment, he came, and once Jasmine fell from his lap, his cum squirted on his thighs and pooled on the sheets.

Jasmine took her time getting to her feet, then threw her hair behind her shoulder and crossed her arms over her breasts. "What's the problem, Auntie?" she said. "Surprised I'm a long way from a virgin now?"

"No, bitch. I'm surprised you're fucking Alex! Jocelyn's baby daddy!" She gestured wildly toward the man, who was beginning to doze off, his dick now lying limp on his stomach. Jayla's eyes caught the overturned pill bottle on the dresser. "And you gave him roofies?"

Jasmine shrugged. "What's the big damn deal? I can't believe you're taking up for this nigga. We all know he ain't shit, and Aunt Joce is better off without his ass. Shit, it's bad enough she's having his baby."

Jayla put her hands to her head; the utter confusion of the situation had brought on a slight headache. "What the hell has gotten into you?" Jayla eyed her niece, and for the first time, she saw a monster. "What the hell were you thinking?"

Jasmine stepped forward, bumping her titties against Jayla's. "I was thinking I was doing the right thing and saving my aunt from a bullshit relationship."

"Yeah, so now you fuck for free?" Jayla tossed back. "Since you know every damn thing and got it all figured out, who the fuck is paying you for this? Because it damn sure ain't me or Jocelyn."

Jasmine grinned and scooped her clothes up off the floor. "Don't worry. This one's on the house." And with that, she sauntered to the door.

CHAPTER NINE

"I know it's a large range and a large sum of money," Jayla recited, watching her potential client shift in the booth. "But this is a large investment of time, patience, and effort. As far as time goes, I can typically have a thorough analysis in two to three months. So now it just comes down to you. How important is it to know what your husband is worth?"

"It's important." The woman sighed, fingering the glistening wedding band she wore. "But I just don't know if I want to know the truth."

Jayla nodded. "That's completely up to you. But don't feel like you have to make a decision today. You have my contact information. You let me know if you want to proceed."

The woman stood up, toying with the strap of her purse.

Jayla stood and held out her hand. "It was an absolute pleasure, and you have a good day, Ms. Walker," she said. The woman accepted the hand and hurried off.

Jayla sat back down and lingered there for a moment longer. She doubted the woman would pursue the evaluation, but she really wasn't surprised. Some women were comforted by the ignorance.

She felt the first few sprinkles of rain on her arm as she stepped out of the restaurant. Jayla glanced up and frowned at the threatening clouds. Even the smell of the impending storm hung thick. That was fine. She wanted nothing more than to go home and climb back under the covers. Maybe she would pick up a bottle of sangria on the way home, order a pizza, and watch some ridiculous movie on TV. Maybe Tara would want to stop by.

That last thought prompted Jayla to pull her phone from her purse, and she glanced at the voicemail indicator on the screen. She had one voicemail. She lifted the phone to her ear to listen to the message. Her lips curved at the sound of the familiar voice. It had been over a year. Way too long.

Hey, Puma. Yes, I know it's been a minute, but you know I did some traveling when I first retired. Been all over the place, but I'm back now, and I would love to catch up with you. Call me. She rattled off her number, and since the rain was picking up, Jayla ducked under the umbrella of a patio table and punched the digits in her phone.

As it rang, Jayla could almost feel her heart rate pick up speed. *Her mentor.* She didn't know why she still felt the need for Patricia Dixon's approval, but the woman had practically groomed her for success, taken her under her wing. Jayla had always tried to make her proud, and even now, ten years later, she wanted that established rapport to remain intact. She was a mentor to Jasmine and would never leave her side, and Patricia was the same for her, but so much more.

"Puma," Patricia said when she answered the phone. That nickname carried so many memories. And Jayla was just like that big cat, a solitary, adaptable hunter. "It has been entirely too long."

"Yes, it has. You wanted to see the world," Jayla reminded her.

"But I would've never thought we would go so long without speaking. I'm sorry for that. But I'm sure you've had plenty to keep you occupied." The insinuation was clear.

Jayla grinned. "I have to update you on everything when you get some time."

"Well, I am back in town."

"For good?" Jayla asked, hopeful.

"I did buy a house," Patricia said after a minute. "So, I think I'll settle down for a while. Come by and see me."

"Now?"

"Sure. Why not? I can fill you in on my adventures, and you can fill me in on yours. I'm retired from teaching college, but not from teaching my Puma."

Jayla glanced at the darkened sky. The rain was coming down in sheets now, cascading off the umbrella like a waterfall. There was a slight chill to the air. That bed and movie idea was still appealing, but she couldn't think of anything she'd rather do more than visit Patricia.

"What's the address?"

It suited her perfectly.

Jayla eyed the massive house as she maneuvered her truck up the paved circular driveway and braked at the front door. Knowing Patricia, she had definitely expected to find a mini mansion nestled amidst a manicured lawn and a thicket of trees. She knew it was not so much so the pension of a retired college professor that had made Patricia's extravagant purchase possible. It was definitely the stockpile of cash Patricia had put away from her days as a Heartbreaker.

By the time Jayla stepped from her truck, the rain had stopped and the sun was trying to peek through. She angled her head to observe the gorgeous stone house, with its oversize windows, jutting rooftops, and large wraparound porch. Just then, Derrick called, but Jayla let it go to voicemail. This was not the time or the place.

"It's about time." The voice, made husky from years of Virginia Slims and shots of vodka, carried easily from the porch.

Jayla grinned as the figure seemed to glide over to her. Despite the time, those mature wrinkles creasing her gorgeous face, that hair in a pixie cut and dyed black to mask the silver streaks . . . Patricia Dixon had not aged a bit.

"I've missed you so much," Patricia said, enveloping her in a hug. "I feel like I haven't been around for you like I should have."

"You taught me well," Jayla said. "I've been doing great, but I'm so glad you're back."

Patricia hooked her arm through Jayla's and steered her toward the house. They climbed the porch steps and went inside.

The house's interior was as sweeping and majestic as the exterior, with beautiful, expansive ceramic tile floors, elaborate archways, and heavily adorned chandeliers hanging from cathedral ceilings. A light jazz tune came through the built-in speakers, and the subtle smell of honey and jasmine coated the air.

Jayla took a seat in the living room, kicked off her heels, and stretched her legs out on the plush couch. "This place is gorgeous," she said as Patricia made her way to the bar. "Your retirement present?"

Patricia brought two Long Island Iced Teas to the couch and sat opposite Jayla. She handed Jayla a glass. "Something like that," she said and took a sip of her drink. "You know I enjoy the finer things in life." Patricia wiggled her fingers for effect, allowing the expensive diamonds on her rings to glitter in the light. "And I can afford it, so hell, why not? You only live once, right?"

"So true."

"But I want to hear all about you, ma'am," Patricia said with a sneaky grin. "What's new? Who you been into lately?"

Jayla laughed and relaxed, a smile on her face. It felt good to be able to discuss this with the woman who had started it all for her, the woman who knew her, and this business, better than she did.

"Business is still successful," she said with a proud smile. "Got an influx of clients at one point, but I've gotten it under control. Sometimes, it can get a little crazy, a little overwhelming, but you know I'm good, so I can handle it." She paused. "Thanks to you," she added, raising her glass in a mock toast of gratitude. She debated telling her about her niece but quickly decided against it. Not until she got that girl on some kind of leash or something.

"I didn't do anything but open you to a new way of thinking," Patricia said. "You were the one that caught on so quickly. Eager and determined. You were always one of my best and brightest students. I know my girl. Nothing you can't handle." Patricia's compliment was laced with a subtle innuendo, one Jayla was more than familiar with. Patricia let her tongue linger on her bottom lip while she lowered her eyes and let them graze over Jayla's body.

The sexual gesture had Jayla smiling at the thought. She hadn't had Patricia in what seemed like a long time. She loved Patricia, almost in a motherly sort of way, but she thought of the way Patricia could make her pussy sing, and she was reminded that Patricia wasn't anything more than a woman. A woman who had the best body money could buy and who got her money's worth with her enormous appetite for sex.

Jayla remembered that while she was in "training," Patricia had taken a direct, hands-on approach. She had shown her how to give and receive pleasure, had allowed Jayla to watch her on assignments. Patricia had even exposed Jayla to her first threesome, and Jayla remembered she had absolutely loved watching her sex herself with toys. But it hadn't been all about sex. She'd helped Jayla with makeup, given her counseling, shopped with her for disguises. Hell, she'd been there for her since day one. And Jayla would probably always feel indebted to the woman.

"Damn, I missed you, Puma." Patricia's voice had lowered with desire. "Take off your clothes and let me see how much you've grown."

Jayla sat her drink down and did as she was told. She stood, peeled off her clothes, and let them pool at her feet. The slight chill in the air caused goose bumps to form on her arms and thighs. Her nipples hardened under Patricia's scrutiny as she stood there naked, quiet, as Patricia's eyes absorbed each and every curve.

"Turn around," Patricia instructed.

Jayla almost felt weak from the sexual tension that had suddenly overtaken the room. She felt her pussy heat up from the attention as she turned her back to Patricia. She was glad her mentor was still proud of her.

She heard the rustle of clothes as Patricia undressed, and Jayla's breath caught from excitement. It had been too long. She gasped in surprise at the sudden sting when Patricia slapped her ass, then gripped each cheek in the palm of each hand. Jayla shut her eyes and swallowed a moan as Patricia gave her a gentle massage, kneading each cheek like dough. Then she replaced her fingers with her lips and tongue. Instinct had Jayla bending over to brace herself against the wall, allowing more exposure. She had almost forgotten Patricia had always loved her plump ass. Sure enough, she felt Patricia bury her face between her crack and heard her moan at the glorious feeling of the supple flesh swallowing her face. She used her hands to spread Jayla's cheeks apart and devoured her, letting her tongue glide up and down her crack before using it to moisten her hole. Jayla tossed her head back in ecstasy. The woman damn sure hadn't forgotten how she liked it. Cum trickled down her thighs as Patricia continued her feast, using her tongue to massage Jayla's ass while she simultaneously smacked it for emphasis. The clap of flesh pierced the air, heightening the glorious feeling even more.

Jayla murmured something inaudible, a cross between a plea and a moan, and as if reading her mind, Patricia reached between Jayla's spread legs and began stroking her clit with her thumb.

"Come for me, Puma." Patricia whispered the encouragement.

Shit, shit, shit. Jayla let her head fall and let out a weak cry as she came, feeling the gush of her juices spill over Patricia's hand and wrist.

Jayla slid down the wall on a breathless sigh, struggling to calm down from the orgasm. The smell of sex was strong and delicious, a fragrance completely normal to the pair. She didn't move as Patricia took off her pants, revealing long, slender, smooth mahogany legs that led to a clean-shaven pussy, none of which held any evidence of her actual age. She grabbed Jayla's outstretched foot, positioned her toes against her own swollen clit. Jayla smiled, wiggled her toes and rubbed Patricia's pussy lips until her toes were wet. Patricia gripped Jayla's foot to keep it in place as she rotated her hips with the movement. When she felt Patricia's pussy clench with the impending orgasm, Jayla quickened her pace. Knowing how she liked it, Jayla stuck her big toe in to catch the steady stream of cum as it burst free. Patricia clenched her thighs, and her body jerked.

When she sighed and relaxed, Jayla shifted to lie down beside her. She wasn't one to cuddle, but Patricia liked to cuddle with her, and it had been a minute. So she lay in the crook of Patricia's arm and sighed as Patricia gently stroked her shoulder. The plush carpet was soothing on her skin. They lay in silence for a moment, basking in the afterglow of their lovemaking. To anyone else, their relationship could have seemed strange. To Jayla, she couldn't have asked for a better mentor.

"I guess that was your 'welcome home' present," Jayla murmured.

Patricia laughed. "You still got it," she said. "I can see why you are so successful."

"I was taught by the best."

Jayla could almost feel Patricia's satisfied smile at the compliment. Then Patricia moved her lips, like she wanted to say something, but she didn't speak.

Sensing the hesitation, Jayla lifted her head and stared into the woman's gorgeous face. "What is it?" she prompted.

"I just don't want you to get stuck in a never-ending cycle," Patricia said. "Don't feel compelled to ride this golden goose out for twenty or thirty years. That's one advantage of it being so lucrative. So you *can* retire young and sit back." She gestured to the massive living room. "And reap the benefits."

Jayla nodded. "You're right. But I'm enjoying myself. I'm helping women and getting paid."

"Let me ask you this." Patricia shifted slightly and began gently stroking Jayla's hair. "I asked you this once, and I'll ask you again. Where do you see yourself in five years? Still working?"

Jayla pondered the question. The scrutiny had her averting her eyes, and feeling slightly uncomfortable, she sat up. *Ten* years wasn't really long at all. Shit, Patricia had been in the mix for nearly twenty.

"I don't know," she answered. "I know *eventually* I'll stop. I just don't see it right now."

"Jayla. Don't get so sucked in, you can't find your way out. Stay on top of your game, remember?"

Jayla nodded. She thought she was. "There's something else," she added, and Patricia lifted her eyebrows. "I met someone. A guy . . ." She trailed off as Patricia stared. "I don't know what to do about him. He won't go away."

"Of course not. Look at you."

"But still. He's determined. And I'm tired of fighting him off. Plus . . ."

"You like him," Patricia said, finishing her sentence for her. She didn't bother waiting for a response. "Yeah, those are the tough ones. But are you ready to let this man in your life? Seriously?"

Jayla bit her bottom lip in consideration.

"What about trust?" Patricia added. "Do you trust him?"

"I don't know him." She sighed and felt Patricia's knuckles lightly graze her back.

"Maybe this is your sign."

"Sign?"

"Sign that you need to reevaluate your own life and see where you are. You've been working for years. Have you even come up for air?"

"No." Jayla pouted with the admission.

"Exactly. You've set goals for yourself. Have some fun. You don't want to wake up at my age, alone." Her voice cracked with the last statement and had Jayla glancing up in confusion.

"That doesn't sound like the Patricia I know," she said.

Patricia laughed. "Oh, it's still me," she said. "I didn't say, 'Fall in love.' Just enjoy your life. You need to decide, what does Jayla Morgan want?"

Jayla turned to straddle Patricia, and playfully, she began rubbing on her titties. She smiled suggestively.

"Jayla Morgan wants to hear all about what you did on this fabulous trip and then afterward." She leaned down and flicked her tongue on Patricia's neck. "I want to play."

Patricia frowned and ran her nails through her cropped hair. It was obvious she wanted to say something else. But she smiled instead.

Hours later, after the two had fallen into a hazy buzz, laughed over Patricia's travel pictures, and had had fuck fest round two, Jayla eased out of the driveway. Impulse had her pulling out her cell phone as she steered the truck with one hand.

She didn't expect Derrick to answer when she returned the call. It was after eleven, but she was feeling good and horny again. Damn, Patricia could have a bitch thirsting, but for some reason, she wanted to speak to him.

"Hey, you," she greeted when he answered on the third ring.

"I must have been on your mind," Derrick said. "Because you were definitely on mine."

Jayla grinned. "Actually, you were. I was just talking about you to a friend."

"Is that so? And what were you saying?"

Jayla grinned as she remembered the sexual play. "Just . . . stuff," she teased. "But I did want to hear your voice. What are you doing?"

"Watching some sports highlights. You sound like you're driving."

"I am. On my way home."

"Well, be careful out there."

His concern had her glowing. Jayla hesitated with the next statement. *Fuck it*, she decided and blurted it out. "Let me come over." She could tell she had finally caught him off guard with that bold statement.

"Why?"

"Because I want to see you," she said. "If sex just so happens to come into play, I damn sure won't stop it." Jayla was feeling bold after the powerful sex sessions with Patricia.

Derrick chuckled. "Your offer is tempting, but I don't want you to get the wrong idea."

"And what is the wrong idea?"

"I want us to maybe build toward something," he said, his voice carrying a gentle patience. "And I don't want you to think that's all I'm wanting from you."

The respectable gesture turned her on even more. Damn, the man seemed perfect. And challenging. She thrived on a challenge.

"Well, what if I just come over and we watch a movie?" she said.

"I want you, Jayla. Bad," Derrick admitted.

Jayla had to tighten her thighs to keep from creaming right there on her leather seat.

"But," he went on, "I want you in the right way. Not like some cheap piece of ass."

Jayla pouted. Funny. That was exactly what she was feeling like at the moment. "Okay," she mumbled, not bothering to hide the disappointment in her voice.

"How about we start with a date?" Derrick suggested, his voice seeming to drip with the sexy appeal of the idea. "We don't have to worry about Tara or Kevin. Just you and me. We can do it the right way and let whatever happens happen." He was silent for a moment. "And then," he added, "when the time is right, I can lay you down and make love to that gorgeous body. Sex you in all the right places." He moaned for effect, and Jayla's eyes widened at the delicious thought. "Fair enough?"

Hell yeah.

"Fair enough." She hung up and tossed the phone on the passenger seat. She hadn't lied. It was a fair deal. But she didn't play fair.

Jayla didn't realize where she was headed until she pulled into the parking lot of Spades. Her mind already fixed on Joi, she headed into the club and went straight for the bar.

Joi was leaning against the bar, as if she'd been waiting for her. Her eyes lit up when she spotted Jayla. Without a word, Joi led her to their freak storage closet once more, where she proceeded to prop Jayla's leg on a box, bury her face between her thighs, and lavishly drink her orgasms. Even after Jayla's weakened knees had her slithering to the floor, Joi feasted by the mouthful, leaving Jayla's pussy saturated and swollen.

When she was done, Joi removed her own clothes and placed her pussy against Jayla's, their legs in a scissors position. Their kitties purred against each other, clit caressing clit.

It didn't take long for Jayla to come once Joi began slapping their pussies together, and she shook with the force of the release as their juices mixed and ran down their thighs and their ass cheeks.

Immediately, Jayla rose on shaky legs and, without uttering a word, staggered to the door.

"Cherry, wait," Joi called, but Jayla stepped out and shut the door behind her and hurried back to the parking lot.

Her phone started ringing as soon as she had made it safely back to her truck. She glanced at the caller ID and rolled her eyes. The bitch had some nerve.

"What is it?" she snapped when she took the call.

"Damn! What's supposed to be your problem?" Jasmine said. "I know you not still tripping about Alex."

"It doesn't even matter, Jasmine. What do you want?"

"I need some more assignments," Jasmine answered, as if it was obvious. "You haven't been throwing nothing my way."

Jayla scoffed. "Hell nah! Not after how you've been acting. Not to mention you've been setting up your own assignments, remember? So you should be good."

"Auntie, stop tripping. Do you have some assignments for me or nah? I'm trying to get this money."

"No," Jayla lied, not caring if Jasmine believed her. She'd be damned if she continued feeding this monster. "Fresh out."

"So now you want to bullshit me? Really? It's like that?"

"I don't have anything right now, Jasmine," Jayla repeated. A long pause.

"Fine. Be a bitch, then," Jasmine mumbled before hanging up.

Jayla's phone rang again, and without looking at the screen, she answered the call. "What the fuck do you want now?"

No response. Just silence. Jayla looked the screen and noticed the call happened to have come from an unknown number. By the time she arrived home, the same scenario had occurred several more times. Even when Jayla answered and cussed out the mystery person to hell and back, the caller remained silent.

CHAPTER TEN

Jayla blew out a hard breath as she slowed the tread-mill and stepped down from the running belt. She felt the sweat trailing down the small of her back and a burning sensation, which signaled that she may have slightly overexerted her already toned muscles. She took a swig of water and pulled the damp sports bra over her head as she started up the steps. She had agreed to meet Derrick in a few hours, and she needed to get her body right.

Her phone rang as she stepped from the shower. She took the call.

"Hey, Jaye."

Jayla immediately frowned at the discomfort in her sister's voice. "What's the matter? Are you in pain?"

Jocelyn sighed. "Just a little. This baby is sitting on every organ in my body, but I'll be fine. Not too much longer, the doctor said." She paused.

Jayla sat on the bed, waiting for her to continue. Her sister definitely sounded like she wanted to say more but didn't know how. "So . . . is everything all right, Joce?" she asked finally.

"Not really," she admitted. "Girl, I'm so damn pissed. Someone emailed me some pictures of Alex sexing another woman."

Jayla sucked in a breath. She damn sure hadn't ex-pected Jasmine to do that. "Um," she said, fumbling for a response. "Damn. I'm sorry, Joce. Did you see who the girl was?"

"No. But that's for her own damn good. I would probably fuck her ass up."

"You need to be fucking Alex's ass up."

Jocelyn sniffed. It was obvious she had been crying.

"Did you put him out?" Jayla asked tentatively.

"You damn right I put him out," Jocelyn snapped. "I
was so disgusted, Jaye. I really thought we were working
toward something serious. I hate to say, you were right."

Jayla struggled to erase the image in her mind of
Jasmine grinding on Alex in the hotel. That damn smirk,
though. The sneaky bitch had known exactly what she
was doing.

"But that's not why I called," Jocelyn went on. "I have a
question, but I'm not sure how you're going to react."

"What's the matter?"

"I was wondering if I could move in with you until I
have the baby," Jocelyn said and rushed on before Jayla
could answer. "I know how you feel about your space, but
I really need someone to help me. Getting around this
apartment is becoming more and more difficult. Hell,
even going to the kitchen to get some water is a damn
Boston Marathon. And now with Alex's stupid ass outa
the picture . . . ," she said, trailing off.

Jayla took a breath. She loved her sister. Absolutely
loved her sister. But damn, she wasn't looking forward
to having her around 24/7. Jayla glanced through her
open bedroom door and caught a glimpse of the other
bedroom across the hall.

Her storage room, for the most part. There was a full-
size bed in there, but that was the only piece of furniture
among a pile of boxes, pictures she hadn't hung, and
other junk she'd just shoved in there to get out of sight.
She'd have to clean, for sure.

And then there was work. How the hell was she supposed to work with Jocelyn waddling around? Not

that she thought her sister would go snooping, but she would have to watch what she said, keep her files out of sight, and pretty much walk on eggshells for another couple of months. Not to mention waiting on her hand and foot. Jocelyn was right. It was becoming more and more difficult for her to get around painlessly, and Jayla would have to make herself available. She sighed, already regretting the decision, even as the words left her lips.

"Of course you can." She couldn't very well jeopardize her sister's or, better yet, her nephew's health and safety. She would just have to make it work.

By the time they got off the phone, Jayla had promised to move her in that weekend. Plus, she had decided it was best to move her office into the spare bedroom upstairs and her sister into the space downstairs that was now her office. That way, the office was out of the way, and Jocelyn would have no reason to worry about climbing to the second level. The room downstairs had gorgeous French doors for privacy and more than enough room for bedroom furniture. Jayla glanced in the second bedroom again, did a quick scan of the full sleigh bed. She would see if she could find some matching dressers. Two months sure as hell wouldn't go by quick.

Her phone rang in her hand, and already expecting more instructions from her sister or bullshit from the anonymous caller, she clicked it on and placed it to her ear. "Yes?"

"Bitch." The harsh whisper stung her ear and had fear snaking up the back of her neck. "Your time is almost up, you fucking slut bitch. I can't wait to watch you die." *Click.*

Jayla dropped the phone, as if the person was about to come through the receiver and choke her right then and there. She didn't realize her hands were shaking until she covered her mouth and felt her fingers tremble on her lips. The caller had spoken to her this time, and it had scared the shit out of her.

Immediately, Jayla's mind flipped through a multitude of clients as quickly as if she were paging through a glossy catalog. Her mind became cluttered with the mixture of women, some angry, some grateful, but all harboring some disgust toward her for being "the one." She could almost taste the fear as she struggled to focus on an image. *Who?* Then, as if in response, she saw Tracy's face as plain as if the woman was standing in front of her. She'd been upset, of course, but she'd been past horror stricken when Jayla played the tape in front of her and her sister. Maybe that had pushed her over the edge. But when Jayla had seen her at the mall, Tracy hadn't actually confirmed or denied making the threats. She couldn't think of anyone else. It had to be Tracy and her raging hormones.

Desperate for an answer, Jayla clutched the thought of Tracy as the evildoer like a lifeline and struggled to swallow the bitter taste of fear. *Crazed bitch*, she thought as she stumbled toward the bathroom. She leaned over the sink, turned on the water, and cupped her hands under the glistening faucet to catch some. She barely felt the sting of the cold water as she splashed it on her face. All she could think about was Tracy and Marcus. He hadn't even been worth it, and she'd just been doing her job. Doing what Tracy had asked. Jayla willed herself to be angry, but the fear gripped her mightily. She splashed water on her face over and over again, until it was in her throat, nose, and eyes. She jolted back, gasping for air. Who could she turn to?

Deciding to ignore the phone for a little while, Jayla busied herself with getting dressed.

When she emerged from the house a few moments later, Jayla couldn't help scanning the neighborhood. All was quiet. A little sun peeked from behind a few clouds, and a gentle breeze rustled the trees. Jayla shuddered. Part of her expected some masked intruder to jump out of the shrubbery, and the thought had her nearly running to her truck.

Her movements jerky and sloppy, she fumbled with her keys when she reached the truck.

Somewhere in the distance, a car's tires screeched, and her breathing hitched. She put her hand to her chest and felt her rapid heartbeat like a steady pounding against her palm. *Breathe*, she instructed herself. She inhaled and exhaled, concentrating on slowing her heart rate.

The voicemail indicator light on her phone flashed on at that moment, and not sure what to expect, Jayla put the phone to her ear to listen to the message.

Hi. This message is for Jayla Morgan. The professional tone caught her completely off guard. *I'm calling from Regency Medical. We saw you last week, after your car accident, and we have received the results of your lab work. Please give us a call at . . .*

Jayla hung up the phone, and though she was curious about why the hospital was calling, she had to admit she was feeling slightly better now, thanks to the fact that the voicemail wasn't another psychotic message.

"What's wrong?" Derrick asked as soon as he opened her car door.

Jayla feigned a smile. "What do you mean?"

"I mean, you look like something is bothering you."

"I'm fine," she lied and looked away, took her time collecting her purse and cell phone. She hated that it was so obvious. She wondered if he could tell that she had checked her rearview mirror numerous times on the drive over. That she had glanced at the pedestrians at every intersection, searching and waiting, for what, she didn't know. And that was the disturbing part.

Jayla flipped down her mirror and pretended to primp a bit while she studied herself, Derrick looking on. She had put on a little makeup, and yes, she looked gorgeous. But her face showed a loss of color, and beneath the shadow and mascara, the fear in her hazel eyes was evident. *Get a grip, girl*, she scolded herself and turned to step out the car.

"Well, don't you look sexy," she commented. She watched Derrick's eyes narrow at her exaggerated attempt to deter his scrutiny. She was relieved when he merely smiled to lighten the mood, and she felt her muscles relax little by little. Jayla didn't object when he grabbed her hand and led the way to his black Nissan Altima. They both climbed in, and he started the engine.

"So where are we going?" she asked as he maneuvered the vehicle out of the complex. "I wasn't going to ask, but you have got me curious."

"Can't you just sit back and ride?"

"Not really. For all I know, you could kidnap my ass."

Derrick laughed. "I assure you, you would go willingly. Or maybe you don't like surprises," he replied.

"Negative. I do like surprises."

"Well, you must not like me."

Jayla smirked at the loaded question. "What's your point?" she asked.

"My point is if you enjoy surprises, and you enjoy me, then you should be able to relax and know you're going to have a good time."

A charmer. She had pinned that label on him the first time she met him. Damn, he was good. "Do you always get what you want, Mr. Lewis?"

Her amused grin froze when he took her hand and lifted it to his face. The kiss was gentle, a reassuring brush of lips on her knuckles, but enough to have her heart stutter.

"I'm not going to say I usually get what I want," he answered. "But I will say, if there's anything I want, I go for it."

Derrick drove leisurely. The windows were down to let the comfortable breeze drift through; the radio was soft enough for conversation, but loud enough to have Jayla nodding along to the music. When he placed his hand on hers on the armrest, she didn't budge at the casual gesture.

After a short drive, Derrick eased the car up a brick driveway and under the arch of a stone building. A spa amor sign hung suspended between two columns, and large windows allowed a glimpse of the elegantly decorated reception lobby.

Before she had even gathered herself, a valet was opening her door and extending his hand to help her out. "Welcome to Spa Amor," he greeted as she stepped out of the car. Then he rounded the hood to the driver's side. Jayla was surprised to feel the simmering of excitement. Her body had grown hot with anticipation.

Inside, candles, plush cream couches and ottomans, lap throws, and glass shelves adorned the lobby. Someone had lit the fireplace, and a mellow flame licked at a stack of crackling firewood, filling the room with the smell of hickory.

Derrick headed to the reception desk, while Jayla wandered to a set of French double doors toward the back of the room. She peered through and admired a pool, hot tub, and rock-formation waterfall, all surrounded by an assortment of palm trees, hammocks, and patio furniture.

"Gorgeous, huh?" Derrick touched the small of her back as he joined her at the doors.

"It really is," she agreed, then turned to share a generous smile. "Thank you for this."

"No problem. First things first, a couple's massage.
Then you can do your girly thing."

She laughed. "What's my girly thing?"

"You know, your nails, face."

"Oh yeah," she said, flirting. "And what's wrong with
my face?"

"Too damn sexy," he responded and had her laughing
again.

They were shown down a spiral staircase, from there a
young attendant led them to their respective areas.

The women's changing room had the same high-end
finishes as the rest of the mini resort, from the deep
chocolate lockers lining each wall to the patterned tile
floor in rich shades of rust and sage.

When she removed her socks and shoes, Jayla could
only smile as the underfloor heating radiated gentle
warmth to each foot. As instructed, she changed into
the monogrammed spa robe, savoring the distinct smell
of honeysuckle that infused the locker room and drifted
suggestively into the attached bathroom. *Damn.* The
depth of this serenity had her body nearly throbbing in
appreciation. Yes, she would allow this place to spoil her
for the day. She deserved it.

The attendant led them into a European-style room,
dimly lit and decorated with a range of earth tones.
The room had two massage tables. "If you two will get
comfortable on the tables," the attendant said, adjusting
the lighting on the wall, "your masseur and masseuse will
be in shortly."

As soon as the door closed, Jayla watched Derrick turn
his back to her. She smirked. Respectful indeed.

"What's the matter?" she teased. "You afraid to see me
naked, Derrick?"

He chuckled and glanced over his shoulder long enough to toss a wink in her direction. "No, I'm afraid I won't be able to lie down flat on my stomach."

Jayla laughed as she loosened the belt on her robe. She let the robe slip from her shoulders and pool at her feet. Her breath quickened, and her eyes remained fixed on Derrick's back. He had to feel the sudden spike in sexual tension, which nearly had the room vibrating. She waited.

When his own robe fell to the floor, she sucked in a breath. Damn, the man was cut. She could easily visualize her nails raking over each chiseled area of his chocolate frame, from the defined angles in his back down to those ripped thighs, taut with, Jayla fantasized, enough aggressive power to handle even her wildest orgasm. He shifted slightly, and she eyed the tattoo on his shoulder. The deep black ink magnified the delicate feathers of angel wings. The words *My Sister's Keeper* were written on a banner that coiled around the image.

"What happened to your sister, if you don't mind me asking?" Jayla asked. She watched as Derrick climbed onto the table. Even though he still managed to keep his eyes from gazing in her direction, she saw the crease of his forehead as he tensed, then relaxed.

"She died," he said. "I was young. About seven. She is two years older than me."

Is. Not was. Jayla could almost feel the ache of his distant memory.

"I wasn't there," he went on. "Really don't remember the details. She had spent the night with a friend, and the mother was bringing her home when she had a car accident. Moms hasn't been the same since."

"I'm sorry." Jayla didn't know why she felt the need to apologize. Or the urge to walk over and hold him. Sensing he probably wouldn't delve deeper, she climbed onto the table, lay facedown, and adjusted the sheet to cover her waist and legs.

They rested in silence for a few moments as a soft jazz melody played through an in-ceiling speaker.

A man and woman walked through the door, dressed identically in crisp white T-shirts and white cargo shorts. Her masseur was Jude, a young blond dude with a stocky build and huge hands. She closed her eyes and enjoyed the feeling of warm oil being dribbled on her back. She couldn't be sure if Jude was actually trying to hold a conversation with her, and honestly, she couldn't care less. Instead, she focused on her body, which began to hum with his delicate presses, his fingers gliding over her skin like satin.

She pictured Derrick's hands on her, kneading her back, easing down to squeeze her ass, slap it, then massage the sting with gentle strokes. He would replace his hands with his tongue and would use the tip to coat her skin and lap the oil. Then he would trail down. Down. He would spread her thighs just enough to access her pussy from the back. It would already be glazed with her juices, and he'd moan and lick his lips, prepping to devour. When she wiggled in anticipation, he would dive in, fuck her with his tongue, alternating between feathery grazes and deep penetration to taste her honey walls. She'd moan, grind against his face, allowing him to greedily suckle and swallow every last drop of—

"Ma'am?"

Jude's nudge snatched Jayla from her daydream. She eyed him, curious if she'd made some outward display of the damn good fantasy her mind had played for her.

"You're all done," he said.

Jayla stifled a moan when she felt her clit throbbing between her moist thighs. *Not hardly*.

After they dressed, Jayla and Derrick were shown to the lobby, and Jayla had to admit her body tingled from the bodywork. Derrick brushed his knuckles on her cheek before fingering the hair at her shoulder.

"You look good," he commented.

"That's always," she teased, with a wink. Her smile faded when she read his face: passion had darkened his eyes and had him running his tongue along his bottom lip again.

"For real," he said. "You needed that."

The hunger clawed at her, and after releasing a yearning exhale, she spoke. "So what else do you have planned?" she asked. "Didn't you mention something about me doing my girly thing?"

He had. And Jayla easily complied when he insisted she go and indulge in more of the included spa services. She got some type of milk and honey treatment, and the rejuvenating scrub left her skin throbbing, with a pristine radiance. She allowed the nail technician to talk her into a hot stone manicure, and she went ahead and agreed to the facial, because the idea of a cleansing was very attractive. Plus, the paste left her skin smelling like a delicious ripe fruit.

It was while Jayla was getting her pedicure that she glanced up just in time to see Tracy's sister, Lauren. The woman strolled by the window, a laughing Marcus on her heels. The world had just got smaller and smaller once she had started fucking everybody's man.

Jayla glanced around. Tracy was probably there as well. She quickly stepped out of the jetted footbath, not caring that her pedicure was only half done. She didn't need a scene here in front of Derrick. The nail tech was confused, but Jayla explained that she wanted to hurry up and get back to her "boo thang."

"Feel better?" Derrick asked when she met up with him a few moments later in the lobby.

"Much better," she said. "You're spoiling me."

The nail tech came over and told them both that it was time for their final treatment, the lavender-scented sauna.

While Derrick had waited for Jayla to have her facial and other exotic treatments, he had sauntered off to buy her a little sexy something. He pulled a bag out from behind his back. The spa's logo was printed on the bag. A curious smile tugged at Jayla's lips as she lowered her hand in the bag and pulled out a black-and-gold bikini.

"For the sauna," he explained. "Unless you want to go in naked."

Jayla laughed when he toyed with the belt keeping her robe closed. "I'll wear the bikini. Thank you."

The sweltering room was made of natural hemlock wood and had two tiered rows of benches and recessed lighting that cast a soothing green tint over the space. Jayla climbed onto the upper bench, while Derrick stretched out right beneath her. She let her foot dangle in his face and giggled when he stuck out his tongue, as if he would lick her toes.

"Thank you again," Jayla said when they had relaxed in a cozy silence. "I really do appreciate this, Derrick."

"No problem, sexy."

More silence.

Jayla sighed, not wanting to ask her next question. But curiosity overrode logic. "Derrick, let me ask you something." She readjusted her towel on the hot bench. The sauna already had her sweaty underneath the tied pieces of the swimsuit. "Have you ever cheated on a woman in your past relationships?"

If he was taken aback by the question, he didn't show it. "No," he answered without hesitation.

"You said that a little too fast," she said, and then her lips turned up in a doubtful smirk.

"I can answer fast those questions I know the answers to," he said. "Like if you ask me my name."

"So, never cheated?"

"Never."

Jayla glanced down to see his face and was surprised when she decided he was being completely truthful. "Okay, well, why did you break up with your last girlfriend?"

"Because she kept pressuring me about marriage. She was a few years older than me. So she probably was feeling that itch, and me, well, I wasn't about to be given an ultimatum for that kind of decision."

"So, do you want to get married one day?"

"Yes."

Jayla chuckled. "Also, a fast answer."

"Well, I know the answer," he said, his eyes studying hers. The way he looked at her had her heart faltering. Interesting how a hundred-degree sauna could suddenly feel like a thousand degrees.

He held her gaze for a moment longer. Then his smile spread once more, and she could almost feel the sudden tension melt just as quickly as it had developed.

"Your turn," he said.

"My turn?"

"Yeah. You get the interrogation."

Jayla laughed. "That was hardly an interrogation."

"True. Well, same questions, then. Have you ever cheated on a man in your past relationships? And do you want to get married one day?"

She frowned. More loaded questions. "No." The practiced lie slipped naturally from her lips.

"No to which one?"

"No, I've never cheated."

Derrick nodded. "Okay. And do you want to get married one day?"

Jayla paused. Years ago, she would've said, "Of course." Now, she couldn't be sure.

"You didn't answer that one at all," he said and had her shrugging.

"That's because I really don't know." She felt him staring at her, and she glanced down and watched the sweat beading on her thighs. He was getting entirely too personal for her comfort.

"Why not?" he asked, pressing.

Jayla opened her mouth to respond, then shut it again. "Why are you asking so many questions?" she asked instead of answering him, her eyebrows creasing in a playful frown. She didn't like the way Derrick continued to stare, as if he was searching for something.

"I'm trying to get to know you," he said. "I thought that is what we agreed on."

"Okay. Well, ask me my favorite color. Ask me if I have ever been to Paris. Ask me if I eat sushi."

Derrick's lips curved, and his eyes glinted.

"Fair enough," he said. "What is your favorite color?"

Jayla narrowed her eyes. So now he was being a smartass. "Red," she answered.

"Have you ever been to Paris?"

"Yes."

"Do you like sushi?"

"No."

"Are you happy now?" Derrick's question was loaded, and Jayla's eyes gleamed at the insinuation. She lowered her eyes to the subtle bulge against the swim trunks and eyed him with a sneaky smile. She relaxed when she saw his grin and the bulge tighten in welcoming response.

"Do you want to make me happy, Derrick?" she flirted.

This time, he laughed out loud. "You are funny," he said as he rose. "Let's go before you melt, sexy." He extended a hand to help Jayla to her feet.

She smiled. At least she had deflected the personal questions. For the moment.

***

Jayla felt the brush of fingers on her hair, her neck, and her lips curved. She moaned, arched her back toward the touch, encouraging more.

"Jayla," Derrick called. His voice seemed distant and hazy. He repeated her name, each repetition gaining volume and strength. She felt the pat on her leg, and her eyes flew open.

Shit, how many times was she going to doze off? That thirty-minute or so drive had her slumped in her seat after the busy spa day. She looked around, realized they were parked in the lot. Yawning, she leaned up to stretch and glanced over at Derrick.

"What were you dreaming about?"

His knowing smile had her narrowing her eyes. "You're a little cocky over there, aren't you?" She watched his eyes fall to his lap, then come back up to meet hers. Jayla yawned.

"A lot," he said and winked,

She giggled. The man was a trip. She peered through the windshield and frowned when she recognized Spades.

"What are we doing here?" she asked, sitting up straighter, on alert now.

"I just thought we'd come here and have a drink." He got out of the car, not bothering to wait for a response.

"I think I'm just ready to get home," she said once he'd come around and opened her car door. It would be just her luck that they came across Joi tonight.

When he leaned in, she held her breath, braced for the expectant explosion. But this was different. He pressed his lips against her forehead first before using his finger to lift her chin and angle her face to meet his.

The kiss was gentle, coaxing. He didn't bother with tongue. Just let his lips linger for a moment or two before he pulled away. The tease worked. When he broke contact, he had her mouth tingling from the brief touch and silently begging for more. *Damn.*

"Just one drink," he promised, tugging her arm.

Still dizzy from the kiss and unable to formulate another excuse, Jayla allowed him to pull her from the car, and she placed her hand in his as they strolled up to the building. All the while, she held her breath, praying Joi was off work tonight.

The place was just as crowded as before. Sure enough, there was Joi, along with another bartender, juggling plates and mugs of beer in the U-shaped bar. Almost as if she'd been expecting her, Joi glanced up in their direction and smiled.

A lump formed in Jayla's throat. How the hell was she going to explain this one?

Derrick propelled her through the crowd, and once they were at the bar, he motioned for her to take the one available stool while he stood behind her. "Be right back," he said directly in her ear. He disappeared back into the crowd just as Joi moseyed up, a flirtatious smile already in place.

"Hey, Cherry Popper," she greeted, licking her lips. "Back for more?"

"Listen, Joi," Jayla said, raising her voice so she would be heard over the music. "Now is not a good time."

Joi boldly reached forward and dipped her hand into the neckline of Jayla's shirt.

Jayla snatched herself back before Joi's fingers could grope her titties. "Joi, I'm serious," she said, nearly pleading, her frown firm. She glanced behind her toward the restroom area but didn't see Derrick. "Not tonight. I'm on a date."

Joi shrugged her shoulders nonchalantly. "So? He can join if he's down for that freaky shit." She laughed and turned to tend to a customer who was calling.

Jayla let out a sigh and swiveled on the stool, just in time to see that Derrick was coming back.

"Hey, baby." He kissed her cheek. "Everything okay?" He was frowning at Jayla's worried expression.

"I think I'm getting a little sick," Jayla admitted.

"Damn, I'm sorry. You need me to take you back to your car?"

Jayla heard someone sit a drink on the counter, and she looked up and met Joi's eyes once more. Even without looking at the glass, she knew Joi had mixed up her signature Cherry Popper just for her.

Joi's eyes slid to Derrick, and to Jayla's confusion, her face lit up in a surprised smile. "Hey, D. What are you doing here, love?"

Love? Oh shit! They know each other? Are they ex-lovers? Jayla thought.

Derrick leaned over the bar and hugged Joi and gave her a peck on her cheek. "I know it's been a minute. Working. You know how it goes."

"Yeah, I know how it goes." Joi motioned toward the crowded bar before sitting her hand on one of her hips. Her eyes slid back to Jayla. "She with you?"

"Yeah. Joi, this is Jayla. Jayla, this is my sister, Joi."

Jayla felt like she'd swallowed a brick. *Sister?* She remained quiet, her eyes wide, at the recent news. She made no move, and she wondered if Joi was about to lay all her shit bare.

Joi extended her hand. "Pleasure to meet you, Jayla," she said with a bright smile. Her eyes seemed to twinkle in amusement.

Jayla accepted the hand and glanced at the drink in front of her. Shit, she needed some shots after this one.

"I wanted to stop by and speak, but we're probably about to bounce," Derrick said. "Jayla's not feeling well."

"Oh, that's too bad." Joi's voice carried exaggerated sympathy. She fixed her eyes on Jayla. "Feel better. I hope to see you again soon."

Jayla nodded and quickly headed to the door, not caring to see if Derrick was following behind. She needed air. Shit was getting nauseating fast.

"So, your sister, huh?" she said as soon as they'd gotten back in the truck. "She's nice."

"Yeah, I need to keep my eye on her." Derrick grinned as he started his truck. "She was all up your ass."

The joke had Jayla's heart quickening. "What are you talking about?"

"She's gay," he answered, clarifying matters, as he pulled out of the Spades parking lot. "Or bi. Hell, I don't know, really. But you are most definitely her type."

He didn't know how right he was. And what the hell would he think if he knew she'd been riding his sister's face like a bronco? "Are y'all pretty close?"

Derrick shrugged. "Not as close as we used to be. Joi's sneaky. She's tried to get at a few girlfriends of mine in the past. Then I caught her sucking my homeboy's dick once. I really don't know with her, honestly. I can't trust her. And I can't be around nobody I can't trust. So we're just cool."

Jayla nodded and fell silent as they drove. By the time they had pulled back up to her truck, she had determined that she damn sure couldn't be trusted, either, so she couldn't fault Joi. The issue was, What the hell was she going to do about her now?

After kissing Derrick goodbye and thanking him for a wonderful day, she slammed the passenger door and solemnly walked to her vehicle. Not paying any attention to her surroundings, she climbed behind the wheel. Then she pulled out of the parking lot, breathing a sigh of relief for how the day had ended, as she knew it could have gone either way.

Just as she pulled in her driveway, she looked in her rearview to see Derrick had followed her home. He parked behind her and sprinted toward her truck.

"You didn't have to do that," she said as he helped her out of the truck. "It's not like I've been drinking or anything." She held her hand in his as they walked to her door.

"I know. But you said you weren't feeling good. I was a little worried."

Jayla opened the door and stood back to let him in. "Well, I appreciate it," she said, closing the door behind him.

"Feeling better now?"

"Yes."

Derrick took a step closer. "Sure?"

"Um . . ." Jayla felt uneasy, as he was studying her like a textbook. Was it guilt he read on her face? "Yes, I'm fine."

"Good." He eased closer, pressed his cheek against hers, and his breath stroked her ear. "I want to make love to you, Jayla," he whispered.

She was surprised she moistened at the comment. *Make love?* Hell, had she ever made love? Leave it to him to make her feel like a shy virgin with just a whisper and a touch.

She felt his large arms circle underneath her legs and around her neck as he hoisted her into his arms. She kept her eyes closed, felt herself being carried to her bed. Then she felt his knuckles gently grazing her skin as he pulled the jumper set down from her shoulders, over her breasts, down her stomach, her hips, her thighs, and the length of her legs. She hadn't bothered to put on anything apart from the jumper, so she lay there, completely naked, feeling his eyes soaking her up.

The bed sank under his weight as he straddled her, and her breath caught when she felt the first dribble of the warm massage oil hit her stomach. Then his slick hands began to knead her skin in a gentle massage. First, her shoulders, then her breasts, his hands moving as gracefully as those of an experienced masseur. She had to admit, she was all the way turned on by the time he made his way back up to her head and tangled his fingers in her hair.

"Turn over," he instructed, lifting slightly to allow her to do so.

She did, and her body began to ache when more oil hit the small of her back and he began massaging again, applying gentle pressure as he worked his way up first, then back down. Part of her wanted to open her eyes, but the other part was loving the element of surprise. She felt him shift again, heard him slipping from his shorts. Then he was on her again, and she felt his large dick rubbing against her leg. She braced herself, but he merely leaned forward and replaced his hands with his tongue. It was thick, wet, and gentle as he slowly caressed her skin. She felt the first pool of cream dampen her thighs, and she moaned, unable to control the pleasure coursing through her body. This entire sensation was so foreign, she didn't know what to expect. But damn she was loving it.

"Derrick," she whispered.

He nudged her shoulder for her to turn over so she was faceup once more. He then sucked each breast tenderly, his tongue tracing the outline of her nipple before he inserted it in his mouth. He didn't move until he'd paid the same amount of attention to each breast, and then he slowly began working his way down. She felt his tongue flick over her clit, and the sudden burst of the first orgasm had her nearly screaming out loud. She felt his lips curve on her pussy, heard him take a deep whiff, as if he were savoring his favorite dessert. Then he took her clit in his mouth and began sucking on it as he'd just done her nipples.

She gasped and tried to catch her breath. *Too much, too much.* She felt like she would explode. She gripped his head as he used his tongue to trace each pussy lip, each neat pink fold, before inserting it in her hole to lick on her walls. Her thighs clenched his face, and the next orgasm left her shaking. When he continued to feast, she gripped the sheets, had a bunch of fabric balled in her fists. She bucked and arched her back against his lips.

"Please." Her voice came out in a desperate whine, and she wasn't sure what the hell she was begging for. *Stop? Keep going?* But she continued to moan, "Please, please, please," as he sent her climbing again.

Then he pulled away, gave her just a second to catch her breath as he put on the condom. He slid in, gentle and deep. She gasped at the thickness, and her breath caught again as he slowly inched his way the entire length of her pussy. That was all it took. She felt her pussy muscles clenching to catch the orgasm, and she gripped his body and yanked him to her.

"Yes, babe," he huffed in her ear as he quickened his pace.

She heard mumbling, didn't realize it was her own voice. The orgasm left her feeling like she'd been strangled as she let his name fall from her lips and flood her heart with pure ecstasy.

CHAPTER ELEVEN

Jayla struggled to ignore the tug of guilt as she sank to her bed to begin applying lotion. It wasn't like Derrick was her boyfriend. Well, hell, not really. Sure, they had been talking every day for the past few weeks and fucked like teenagers whenever they saw each other. Sure, she could admit she liked him . . . a lot. But she still had a job to do.

The LCD displaying the time showed she was already running behind, so putting all thoughts of Derrick out of her mind, she got to her feet and headed for her closet.

When she came downstairs a few minutes later, she spotted Jocelyn on the couch, her swollen feet propped up on the ottoman, her hand shoved in a bag of sour cream and onion chips. She looked as if labor was a contraction away, that huge belly bulging from beneath a long T-shirt and maternity leggings.

She glanced over as Jayla entered the living room. "Going out again?"

Jayla sighed. "Joce, what have I told you about eating all over the house? Why couldn't you stay in the kitchen?"

Jocelyn smacked her lips and, licking her fingers, crumpled the bag closed. "Well, excuse me," she grumbled. "It's just crumbs, damn. I'll vacuum."

Jayla ignored the smart remark and crossed into the kitchen. Those damn hormones had Jayla counting down the minutes until Jocelyn dropped the baby and went the hell on about her business.

The phone rang, and Jayla scooped up the cordless phone on the kitchen counter.

"How is our patient?" Jackie greeted and had Jayla nearly rolling her eyes. Of course, her ass would sound cheerful. She didn't have to deal with the stank attitude.

"Fine," she answered. "Grumpy as hell."

"That's to be expected," Jackie assured her. "She's walking around with a rough little boy tearing her up from the inside out. Plus, she's as big as a house and peeing and eating all the damn time. That's enough to make anyone grumpy." Jayla's doubtful grunt in response had Jackie adding, "No one expects you to understand. You've never been pregnant."

That you know of. Jayla hesitated to pose the question on her mind, then finally asked, "How is Jasmine doing?"

"She's fine," Jackie answered. "Still staying out all times of the night, running in and out of my house. Plus, she's gotten some tattoos or something. I don't know what has gotten into her, but I'm starting not to give a damn. She's grown."

Jayla nodded. She hadn't talked to Jasmine in weeks. Lord knows what, or who, she was doing.

They got off the phone, and Jayla headed toward the front door. "I'll be back later," she announced.

Jocelyn glanced up from the TV. "Where are you going?"

"Out."

"Out where?"

Jayla sighed. *Here it comes.* "My business, Joce."

Jocelyn's eyes glittered with excitement, and her lips drew back in a mischievous grin. "Out with ole boy you've been talking to on the phone all day and night?" Her grin widened. "Girl, don't act stupid," she added when Jayla made no move to answer. "I hear you up there giggling and shit all night. Who is he?"

Jayla struggled to hide her own smile. "Nobody."

"Listen, I am your sister," Jocelyn said. You know I love you, right?"

"Joce, what are you talking about?"

"I'm just saying. You quick to confide in Tara, like she's your sister."

"That's not true," Jayla said, shaking her head.

"Feels like it sometimes."

Was Jocelyn jealous? Yeah, this chick was crazy. Jayla sighed. "Yes, it's a guy I met that works with Tara's husband. Remember, he came to Jackie's barbecue?"

Jocelyn lifted an eyebrow. "Oh really? You said y'all weren't together then."

"We weren't."

"Uh-huh. But now you are?"

Jayla remained quiet. She didn't know what she and Derrick were.

"You think he's your Mr. Right?" Jocelyn asked, pressing.

Jayla had to frown at the thought. It had never crossed her mind before, but it surprised her when she didn't immediately reject the absurdity.

Apparently, Jocelyn was equally surprised. "Wow. Dead silence. There may be some element of truth there."

The thought of it, the mention of it, Jayla had to admit, brought her subtle excitement. Then disappointment. If that were the case, then she was a fucking idiot.

"I'll be glad when I find me a man," Jocelyn continued. "Someone who can love and appreciate me and my son. Alex has been calling me left and right, but I haven't talked to him since I saw those damn pictures."

Again, Jayla saw in her mind's eye Jasmine's juicy ass bouncing on Alex at the hotel. The image was sickening, and she wished she could unsee that shit. She opened the door to leave. "Will you be all right for a few hours?"

"Yes, I'm fine. Tell your Mr. Right, I said, 'Hello,' and 'I can't wait to see him.'"

Jayla nodded. She couldn't wait to see him, either. It just wouldn't be tonight.

Jayla nearly laughed out loud when she followed Reggie into the parking lot of K. Sutra. She remembered Tara dragging her here when the strip club had first opened. Overpriced liquor and a variety of women—white, black, old, young—doing everything short of fucking right there on the stage. But she had to admit, the food was damn good.

She found a place to park in plain sight of the front door. Reggie was with his same group of friends from before. He seemed relaxed, and by the way he stumbled a bit, it was obvious he had done more than work, as he had told his lady. But the way they slapped hands, backs, and shared a laugh, it was obvious these men were dead set on enjoying themselves tonight.

Jayla waited about ten minutes before stepping from her vehicle and strutting up to the door.

"You must be here for amateur night." The bouncer had apparently spent more time lifting weights than anything else. Unfortunately, the massive biceps bulging underneath the black T-shirt didn't distract from the sagging belly. Or the musty odor. He licked his lips and smiled at Jayla.

She frowned. "What?"

"Amateur night. It starts in an hour."

She hadn't thought about it, but the idea was definitely genius. Especially for Reggie. She glanced down at the fitted purple minidress and nude Gucci heels she wore. Way overdressed for amateur night.

"Is there a clothing store or something in the area?" she said. "Somewhere I can get lingerie or something?"

He nodded. "There's one inside, actually. Just go to the bar and sign in, and they'll show you where it is."

Jayla thanked him and ignored the slap on her ass as she walked by. She would have to assume the role tonight. She had work to do.

They had definitely upgraded since her last visit. The large space, the neon lights, the deafening music reminded her of places on the Sin City Strip. Crowded glass high-top tables and barstools peppered the open area, and a T-shaped stage occupied the center of the space, with poles at each corner. Plush circular booths lined one side of the room; they were slightly elevated to ensure unobstructed views of asses and titties from any angle. In the corner, a spiral staircase led up to, Jayla assumed, the VIP rooms on the second level.

People were everywhere—leaning on the marble bar, nursing shots; stretched out in the booths, with strippers lying in their laps; and all throughout the common area, using dollar bills to stroke pussies of varying shades, licking nipples, and watching juicy asses bouncing to the rhythmic beats of Luke.

Jayla walked past two naked strippers, caught the smell of hot wings suffocated by weed, perfume, and muted cum. It was an interesting environment, and she was glad it wasn't appealing to her.

She leaned on the bar and lifted her voice over the bass of the music. "Excuse me. I need to sign up for amateur night," Jayla said.

The woman at the bar nodded and laid a sheet of paper and a pen in front of her. Jayla thought for a minute and scribbled a stage name on the list. Next to it, she wrote a brief introduction. This was going to be fun.

"The guy at the door also said you had a store," Jayla said, and the woman nodded toward a curtain behind the bar.

Jayla went behind the curtain and found that they had arranged several racks of skimpy outfits in a small space. Packages of fishnet stockings and garters were organized in plastic bins, and wigs and shoes were displayed on shelves.

Jayla picked out a mesh see-through minidress, a matching bra and thong set, and a blond wig. As she headed out of the small store, she watched twin strippers breeze through the curtain. Both wore nothing but eight-inch clear heels and long streaked wigs, the dangling hair brushing their ass. Jayla eyed their identical caramel skin, which was riddled with suggestive piercings and tattoos. She smiled at a sudden idea.

"Excuse me, ladies."

They turned in unison.

"Would you two mind going up there onstage with me? I would love to do a routine with you. You can have all the tip money, and if we win, we can split the winnings."

One of them grinned. "Absolutely. I'm Nikki. This is Lexi. And you are?"

"Kitty Lick," Jayla said, and the twins both exchanged a sexy grin.

"We'll listen out for you, Kitty," said the other one, Lexi, then licked her lips.

Jayla nodded, blew each of them a kiss and gave them each a wink, and then headed to the bar to pay for her items.

A man who looked clearly old enough to be her grandfather offered to buy her a few drinks, and she accepted the gesture, then knocked back shots until she had achieved a comfortable buzz. She scanned the room for Reggie, saw he was being thoroughly entertained by some white chick in one of the booths. *Good.* Keep him occupied for now. As long as he didn't leave before she gave him what he needed.

When they finally announced that amateur night was starting, Jayla sat back to enjoy the show. Some of the women were so uncoordinated. A few nearly stumbled in their high heels as they tried to keep up with the music. Some were embarrassed, standing in the glaring lights amidst a stream of boos as they struggled to cover their exposed body. Still, some went out there and ate up the attention, hitting splits and spread-eagle handstands, and gliding their pussies up and down the pole until the metal was slick with juices. Very entertaining.

When the bartender tapped her shoulder and motioned to her that she would be up next, Jayla headed for the back room to change. If this didn't get Reggie all up in her goodies, nothing would. Ten minutes later she was ready to hit the stage.

"All right. Now coming to the stage is a sensual delight for you all."

Jayla listened as the DJ added his own spin to the description she had written on the paper.

"This next one here loves a juicy tongue. She's anxious for someone to eat her from the inside out, complete with a good clit sucking, and don't forget to swallow her sweet juices. Damn. Everyone, please give it up for Kitty Lick."

Jayla had requested a slow song, and when she heard the beginning bars of a slow mix, she smiled, did one last adjustment to make sure the wig was on properly, and slipped from behind the red curtain and onto the stage.

The spotlight was blinding, so all she could make out were shadows in the darkened room. But that was okay. She remembered exactly where Reggie was sitting, and she made her way in that direction as white, red, and purple lights hit her body from different angles. It felt more natural than before. She licked her lips as she began an impromptu routine, gyrating her body to the music, rubbing on her breasts, her stomach, her thighs. She zeroed in on Reggie, saw the recognition hit his face, then saw his friends whisper to him and gesture toward her. Oh yeah. It was *her*.

Jayla squatted with her legs spread, used her fingers to play with her pussy lips before turning and stretching her legs so her ass was in the air right in his direction. The mini she'd chosen had risen to bunch at her waist with the movement, and she bounced her ass cheeks, making each one jump separately before making them clap together. The bills were flooding the stage; the cheers were loud. She even felt the stroke of someone's hand on her leg. Jayla lay down flat on her stomach, spread her legs, and sat up until she was in a split. Then, using her upper-body strength, she lifted her ass from the floor and bounced it to the beat. She caught the eye of Nikki and Lexi and blew a kiss, signaling that they were up.

Nikki walked up to the edge of the stage, where Jayla continued to do her split twerking trick. She felt the feminine touch of Nikki's hand on her ass as she massaged it and then the sting as she slapped it. The cheers and whistles nearly blocked out the music as Jayla let Nikki crawl between her legs and maneuver that agile body over hers and onto the stage. The woman purposely let her kitty hover over Jayla's mouth, and for dramatic effect, Jayla kissed it and used her teeth to pull at the silk panty material separating the goodies from her mouth. At least she was clean, so Jayla didn't mind the subtle taste of her juices. More bills hit her face as Lexi did the same thing, and then Jayla stood to finish the show. She was fueled by the attention, by the applause. She then allowed the twin strippers to take off her clothes, leaving her fully exposed.

Jayla stood completely naked in all her glory and threw her head back, gripping the wig, while one twin licked her from her neck to her breast and the other licked her leg up to her thigh. As the music ended, Jayla grabbed one of the twins—which one she didn't know— gripped her by her neck, and began kissing her wildly, letting her tongue dart in and out of her parted lips. The other twin slapped Jayla's ass, and then all three posed as they were showered with applause.

"Damn," the DJ said, barely audible over the cheers. "I know all of y'all came after that routine. Give it up for Kitty Lick and our girls Nikki and Lexi."

Jayla sashayed off the stage and left the twins to pick up the money. They could have that. She had much bigger fish to fry.

Jayla changed back into her regular clothes and took off her wig, then snuck back into the main area as other amateur dancers took the stage. She had to admit, no one tore the floor up like she and the twins just had, but they got an A for effort. She ignored the men gawking at her as she made her way over to Reggie's table.

"Hello again, gentlemen," she greeted, eyeing each one before settling on Reggie.

The one she remembered as Bruce spoke up first and scooted over, making room for her to sit down. "Damn, Slim. Yo' fine ass ate that stage up. You ain't no damn amateur."

Jayla pretended to blush. "My first time," she lied, smiling at the compliment. "What are y'all doing here?"

"*Shit*, we came for the show," Mike said, laughing. "And I think I'm broke after your routine. The hell are you doing here? Stripping and shit?"

"The twins are some friends of mine," Jayla said with a shrug. "Nikki and Lexi. They told me about amateur night and asked if I wanted to come out. You know. Just get out of the house. I don't do that much lately."

The men gave a few more approving comments before she turned her attention to Reggie. "How have you been?" She lowered her voice so only he could hear her.

He nodded. "I've been good. And you?"

Jayla glanced around, making sure no one else was paying attention and also hoping she didn't see anyone she knew. Sure enough, Reggie's friends had left the table to throw money at the stage for the next dancer.

"Good. I feel kind of bad. You know, with how things went down last time. It's funny you're here, because I've been wanting to call you . . ."

"Call me to say what?"

"I've been thinking about you," she said, casually resting her hand on his arm and giving it a gentle squeeze. She made the gesture appear innocent, and he didn't bother moving his arm. "Plus, I felt I needed to apologize for my behavior before. I just can't help how I feel, but I shouldn't have forced myself on you." She watched Reggie's face soften, and he lifted his hand to brush at her hair.

"You don't owe me an apology," he assured her with a smile. "I feel the same way." He used his thumb to brush Jayla's cheek, and her lips turned up in an accomplished smile. "And trust me. You didn't force me to do anything I didn't want to do." His finger lingered on her lips, and Jayla kissed it before sitting back against the booth.

"Well, that's good to know." She began to shimmy out of the booth, and Reggie's hand slid down to grip her arm. *Too easy.* "Where are you going?"

"I was just going to get back to my friends and let you get back to yours."

"They're busy," he said, gesturing toward Mike, who was putting some bills in a stripper's ass with his mouth. "Let's go upstairs."

Jayla thought about the details of the contract she had on this assignment. Heather wanted a full-fledged evaluation. She recalled Heather's words. *The works. Let him do any and everything he wanted. No boundaries. Just a detailed report afterward.* Jayla nodded and let him take her hand, and he led her to the spiral staircase and guided her upstairs.

Another bouncer stood at the top of the stairs, and he raised his hand to stop them from going down the hall. "What the hell do you think you're doing?" he asked.

"Come on. She's going to give me a private dance," Reggie said.

"Only the real dancers use the VIP rooms. Not the amateurs."

Jayla ran her finger up her neck before slipping it into her mouth and giving it a seductive suckle.

"Did I look like an amateur?" she said. The bouncer ignored her, and Jayla thought he wasn't going to acquiesce, until she saw the bulge growing in his pants. She tried again. "Listen, I'm friends with Nikki and Lexi, and they're working on trying to get me a job here. I promise, we won't be long."

The bouncer looked her body over and threw a hesitant glance down the stairs. "Make it quick," he growled. "Room B."

There was a huge bed in the middle of the room and a picture of a naked woman mounted on the wall above the headboard. The room even had a TV with a DVD player and a stack of pornos. Off to one side, there was a small bar area with a sink. The room was illuminated by a red light, and it cast a crimson glow on the neat comforter.

Jayla immediately came out of her clothes and stood naked at the foot of the bed, waiting for Reggie to make the first move. He did, lifting her up until her legs were wrapped around his waist and yanking her head back by her hair to ravage her neck. When she felt the nip of his teeth, the sensation was both pleasure and pain all at once. She raked her nails up his back as he moved to devour each succulent breast.

When he laid her back on the bed, he yanked his shirt over his head and stepped from his jeans. "Turn over," he commanded.

Obediently, she flipped onto her stomach. He grabbed her waist, and his fingers tightened as he snatched her body back toward him. She heard him fumbling with a condom, heard the latex crinkle as he slid it on his dick, and felt his fingers rub her pussy and slither through the crack of her ass before spreading her cheeks. She didn't even have time to brace herself before he shoved it in, and she yelped at the searing pain.

Jayla had only done it in the ass once or twice, but both instances were so long ago, she felt like a virgin again. Damn, the shit hurt. She buried her face in the comforter, wincing as he jammed it in hard before easing out slowly and repeating the technique. Eventually, her hole loosened up, and she lifted her head as the pain subsided and the pleasure overpowered her.

"Oh, shit," he murmured, and she felt his thighs slamming into her ass. He gripped it hard, gave it a few stinging slaps. "I've been wanting to get in this ass since I first saw you."

"Oh yeah?" she said, encouraging him. "Well, take your ass, then. It's yours, babe."

He sped up, gripping her waist so hard, she wondered if he'd break the skin. He mumbled some more, and she felt the muscles in his thighs tighten against her cheeks. She braced herself.

"Yes. You feel so good," he groaned as she felt the dick tightening inside her. His yell was high pitched as she felt the explosion against the flimsy plastic. She waited while his body convulsed for a bit, then collapsed on her back.

Her knees gave way, and they slid from underneath her until she lay prostrate on the bed, underneath his weight.

He pulled out and took a step back, eyeing the cum-filled latex. He blew out a breath.

Jayla turned over, lifted herself up on her elbows, and eyed his body for the first time. *Not bad.* She approved. He could use a few more sit-ups, and those shirts he wore made his arms look a lot bigger than they were, but overall, he was not too bad at all.

"So?" she said when he made no move to speak. "Now what?"

He sighed and slid the condom from his flaccid dick. He snatched the wrapper from the floor, where he'd hastily thrown it earlier, and took his time putting the condom back in.

"Now, I hope you got your money's worth."

The words punched her, and she had to shake her head to make sure she'd heard properly. "Excuse me?"

"You heard me," he said, a smile forming on his lips. He began stepping into his pants. "I hope you got your money's worth. I found that shit between you and my girl, Heather. Now, I hope I've given you something to write about in your little *evaluation.*"

Jayla's mouth hung open, and she felt torn between embarrassment and anger. How the hell had she let that happen? That stupid bitch Heather.

"What's the matter?" He was rubbing it in, looking so damn smug, so damn accomplished. "Don't know what to write?" He yanked the shirt over his head. "I'll tell you exactly what to write. You tell Heather I *loved* her. You tell Heather I am a faithful man, but you tell her I'm done with her trifling ass for being so hell-bent on setting me up with a . . . a prostitute to get me to cheat."

The words stung and seemed to resonate in the room. Jayla shook her head. It was weak, she knew. Even while they were in a strip club VIP room that reeked of sex.

"You knew," she whispered. "When . . . ? How?"

"Shortly after that night we kissed," he said. "The idiot left the contract out on the dining-room table, with her notes and other shit from your meetings, her payments, everything. At first, I was so beyond pissed, I didn't know what to do. Then I knew exactly what I needed to do to get back at her, and at you for setting me up. Baiting me."

He rubbed Jayla's leg, and she kicked his hand away. Hell, she didn't even know how to take the news. She was angry at both of them. Mad at herself too.

His smile was victorious as he headed for the door. It made Jayla nauseated.

"I figured, well, since she paid for my prostitute," he was saying, "I might as well get something out of the deal. Get her money's worth, you know? So it seemed like a win-win-win for everyone involved. She got what she wanted, I got what I wanted, and you got what you wanted. Mission accomplished." He blew Jayla a kiss and opened the door. "Pleasure meeting you, Slim," he said and left her alone.

Jayla cringed. Never in the ten years she'd been in this business had she ever felt more degraded, disgusted, and downright pathetic. She stood to put on her clothes and whirled around when the door opened again. She'd thought it was Reggie returning, and she frowned when the bouncer entered the room.

"I'm leaving," she said quickly, snatching her clothes off the floor.

The bouncer closed the door behind him, and Jayla's heart stopped as he slid the lock into place. "What's your hurry, Kitty Lick?" he asked, walking toward her.

Jayla backed up in a panic as he began undoing his pants. "Wait a minute." She struggled to find her voice but could only manage a frantic whisper. "I don't know what you think is going on here . . ."

"Oh, I know what's going on here." Bouncer man let his pants fall to his feet, his thick dick bouncing free like a springboard. "You're the new girl here, right? Well, every new girl needs to be approved." He lifted his hands to his dreads and pulled them back into a low ponytail with the rubber band around his wrist.

"No, I'm not." Jayla was desperate as she backed into the wall. "I was just here for amateur night. I lied."

"Did you now?" Bouncer man didn't seem to care about the information as he stepped from his pants. "What about your friends Nikki and Lexi?"

"I've never met them before tonight. I swear."

"Well, that's too bad." He crept closer. "Because those greedy bitches just offered you to me. Said I could fuck you rough, like you like it, if I gave them six hundred dollars." He was towering over her now, but Jayla could barely make out his face through the haze of tears. "So now, let's see how good your kitty is, bitch."

Jayla didn't have time to run before he backhanded her. His knuckles felt like rocks against her cheek, and she fell to the bed from the force. Her earlier orgasm with Reggie had left the sheets slick with cum, and now she lay face-first in her own juices as Bouncer man snatched her legs open and shoved it in raw.

The shit was painful, and Jayla could only cry into the bed as he power drove her, stabbing her swollen pussy until it was sore and throbbing. With one hand, he held her head against the bed and with the other, he clutched her ass so tight, she thought he was going to take a chunk of it off. Over and over, she felt like complete filth, even more so when he shot his seeds up in her with the force of a cannon. He pulled out, and his cum flowed from her like a waterfall, tinted pink from a bit of blood.

"'Preciate that," he said, laughing. "You're hired."

Jayla didn't bother opening her eyes. Just cried softly into the folds of the sheets while she listened to him put on his clothes and leave.

Fear had her not wasting any time once he'd closed the door behind him. For all she knew, those grimy twins could've been racking up downstairs, auctioning off her pussy to the highest bidder.

She threw on her clothes, ran down the hallway, and nearly stumbled as she flew down the stairs and headed toward the exit. Embarrassment had her keeping her head down as the music blared and the lights swept the stage and the audience. Everything was a blur, but she did notice Tara's husband, Kevin, perched at the bar, grinning into a glass of cognac.

What the hell was he doing there? she wondered.

CHAPTER TWELVE

Jayla's ass and pussy were still on fire the next morning, but she quickly turned over, snatched the cell phone from her nightstand, and punched in Heather's number. She was surprised when the girl picked up almost immediately.

"Denise, I—"

"You stupid-ass bitch!" Jayla didn't even bother thinking, just let loose, her rage fueled by last night's combination of embarrassment and anger and today's shooting daggers of pain from the waist down. "I ought to come over there and choke the shit out of you for that stupid shit you did!"

"I'm sorry . . ."

"Reggie played me because of you! How the hell do you leave the papers out on the table for him to see? What the hell were you thinking?"

"I'm sorry," Heather said through muffled sobs. "I don't want to lose him. Please don't let him leave me."

Jayla scoffed. The girl was sick. "Look, I don't give a damn about you and Reggie." Her tone was deadly calm. "But I know you better pay me the rest of my money, bitch."

Heather's response was indistinct as dramatic cries resonated through the phone. Jayla heard only snippets, like "I love him!" and "What have I done!" between labored breaths. She shook her head, unfazed.

"My money," she said and rattled off the address to her studio apartment. "Mail me the rest of my money, because I'm afraid if I see you, I would try to kill you." She stabbed the OFF button on her phone and, exasperated, pushed her hair back from her face.

She needed painkillers.

She figured Jocelyn was still asleep. It was pretty early. So when she made her way to the kitchen, she was shocked and surprised to find, not Jocelyn, but Jackie making herself busy over some pots and pans on the stove.

"Good morning," Jackie greeted. "I hope you don't mind, but I figured you wouldn't think to make anything for my sister and nephew except cereal."

"Probably," Jayla agreed as she slid onto a barstool. "Where is she, anyway?"

"Girl, she let me in and took her ass back to sleep." Jackie laughed as she put some pancakes on a plate and started cracking eggs for an omelet. "You slept late," she said, tossing a look over her shoulder. "Late night?"

"Something like that." Jayla couldn't care less about a damn conversation. She was pissed. Not to mention sore.

"Now you're starting to sound like Jasmine."

Jayla rolled her eyes in response.

After a moment of silence, Jackie turned to face her, crossing her arms over her chest. "I've been meaning to talk to you about her."

"What about her?" Jayla's voice reflected her lack of concern. She shrugged. "You said she was grown and doing her own thing."

"Yeah, but I figured you would know what's going on. You two were talking damn near every day at one point."

Jayla shrugged again. "Well, I don't know," she admitted. "I haven't talked to her in a while. I thought I told you that."

Jackie nodded and reached over to turn the eye on the stove down a few notches. "Well, do you think you can talk to her for me?"

"Jack, leave that girl alone." The thought of Jasmine's behavior was irritating Jayla to no end. The bitch needed a leash. "Damn. Stop babying her and stay out of her damn business."

"Excuse me?" Jackie whirled around, her eyes blazing from her own attitude about the comment. "The least you can do is care, Jaye. She is your family. What if something happened to her?"

Jayla smacked her lips. "Fuck her," she mumbled in the worst attitude she could muster.

Jackie charged forward so fast, Jayla was prepping herself for a punch. She shrank back as Jackie leaned forward across the counter, her face coming so close, Jayla felt the anger like a bolt of electricity between them.

"Fuck *her*!" Jackie was yelling, even though her nose was pressed against Jayla's. "No, fuck *you*, Jayla! I figured you would've grown the fuck up by now, but you're the same selfish, nonchalant bitch you were when you gave her up for adoption!"

Jayla blinked, knowing she hadn't heard what she thought she had heard.

"Yeah, you heard me," Jackie affirmed, nodding her head. "Jasmine is your daughter. I adopted her."

When the shock wore off, it was instantly replaced by denial. "That's not possible." Jayla jumped to her feet, needing space between herself and the apparent truth. "You were pregnant with your own baby when you came home that summer from college, and I placed my baby up for adoption."

"I had a miscarriage." Jackie's words had tears seeping from her eyes. "No one knew but Mama. I called her, crying, and it was Mama who suggested I adopt your baby. Ya know, the one she was raising? Hell, you were only fourteen. Everyone knew damn well you weren't in no mind to raise no baby. And me, well, I was in school, but Quentin and I were planning our wedding, and I was talking suicide. The miscarriage put me in a depression."

Jayla shut her eyes as the pieces clicked together. No, the pregnancy hadn't been planned, and she'd wanted an abortion. It was, indeed, her mother who had encouraged her to have the baby and later give it up for the adoption. It all made sense now. Jasmine was her mini me.

Feeling dizzy, she lowered herself onto a dining-room chair. She tried to wrap her mind around all of it, searching, wishing for something that didn't line up.

"I'm sorry, Jaye," Jackie said. "I didn't plan on telling you. I can't imagine how this must feel, finding this out after all this time. Quentin, Mama, and I swore we'd keep it a secret. Jasmine doesn't even know."

Jayla sucked in a greedy breath as she remembered how she'd turned Jasmine out. Damn, she hadn't wanted that for her *daughter*. What the fuck had she done?

Jackie stood in the kitchen, not sure how to handle Jayla's tense silence. "Do you know who the father is?" she asked.

Jayla squeezed her eyes shut. "No," she lied. She didn't know whether to be hurt or angry, but she suddenly felt sick.

Without another word, she ran back upstairs and into her bedroom, slammed the door, and buried herself under her covers. She didn't know she was crying until her pillow was completely drenched.

Jayla's phone rang a few hours later. She didn't budge. The ringing stopped; then it started once more.

Jayla turned to lie on her back and covered her ears with her hands to drown out the incessant ringing for the second, then the third time. Her tears had long since stopped, replaced by a sharp headache and a heart that felt as heavy as lead. How could she not have known? How was that even possible?

The phone stopped ringing, and then it started up a fourth time.

Jayla pictured Jasmine's face and had to admit they favored one another. But hell, Jasmine favored her sister, too, so Jayla had had no reason to think Jasmine was hers. Nothing as wild as the shit she'd just heard downstairs had ever crossed her mind.

The phone had fallen silent, but now the ringing began again, for the fifth time, and Jayla found the noise almost deafening in the silent room. Groaning, she picked up the phone and answered, not bothering to look at the caller ID. She heard a slight whimper, then hesitant sobs.

"Auntie . . ." Jasmine's voice was dripping with fear, and tears had reduced her speech to a mere whisper.

Jayla bolted upright in the bed. "Jasmine? What's wrong?" *Oh God, please don't tell me something has happened to this child! My child. Not over some foolishness I have gotten her into.*

Jasmine's voice hitched, so Jayla could barely make out her words. "Can you come pick me up, please?"

"Baby, what's wrong? Come pick you up?"

"I . . . I'm sorry," Jasmine said, pleading. "I fucked up. I'm sorry." Jayla strained to hear the soft words. She swung her legs over her bed and grabbed some shorts from her dresser.

"Jasmine, baby, where are you?" Jayla slipped on the shorts and ran to the closet for some flip-flops.

Shit, shit, shit.

Jasmine managed to relay the address, and Jayla felt the color drain from her face.

"The abortion clinic? You're pregnant?"

"I'm scared," Jasmine said through sobs. "I came to do it, but I'm too scared. I don't want to kill my baby. Please come get me."

Jayla held her breath, afraid to ask the next question. "Is it by Alex?"

"I don't know," Jasmine wailed. "Shit, I don't know. Maybe. I just . . . Auntie, I'm sorry. I fucked up so bad."

"I'm on the way," Jayla said and hung up. She'd refrained from saying what she had wanted to say. *That's what your grown ass gets.*

She flew down the stairs and nearly collided with Jocelyn. Jayla pulled up short and frowned as her sister intentionally blocked her way. Damn, had she heard the conversation? she wondered.

"Joce, what is it? I have an emergency," Jayla said, attempting to sidestep the woman.

Jocelyn moved into her path once more.

Jayla let out an exasperated sigh. "What is it? Where is Jackie?" Her eyes swept the empty living room.

"Gone." Jocelyn's clipped tone was a chilly twenty degrees. "What kind of shit are you into, Jaye?"

Jayla narrowed her eyes at her sister, who stood with her feet shoulder width apart, like a heavyweight boxer, but with a stomach and all. "What the hell are you talking about?"

"Don't 'What are you talking about?' me, like I'm crazy!" Jocelyn snapped back. "What kind of business are you into? What do you do?"

Jayla frowned, still unsure what her sister was getting at or how she had deduced that something was off. "You know what I do . . . Chill out."

"Don't lie to me." Jocelyn's eyes were nearly piercing hers, and Jayla froze, unsure how to react. "I'm your sister. I thought you could come to me with anything, and you hide shit from me like we're strangers."

The fuck was she talking about? Jasmine being her daughter? Jasmine at the abortion clinic? Hell, the shorter list was what Jayla *wasn't* hiding.

Jayla paused, taking her time to respond. "Listen." Her voice was calm. "Can you please tell me what's going on? Because I'm really confused right now."

Jocelyn turned and stomped over to the coffee table. She swiped at a magazine, sending the glossy pages flying across the room. Remaining on the table, where it had obviously been hidden under the magazine, was a card. The last card Jayla had received. Just seeing the eerie teddy bear and the sharp red lettering sent a shiver up Jayla's spine once more.

"Who sent you this?" Jocelyn pointed at the evidence, her head whipping back. She stared her sister dead in the face. "Someone is threatening you. Someone wants to kill you."

Jayla tore her eyes from the teddy bear's menacing snarl, once again envisioning the harsh words inside. *This much.* Someone wanted to kill her. *This much.* She remained silent, hoping the fear wasn't transparent.

"Jaye." Jocelyn's voice had softened as she took a step forward. "Please, talk to me. Who sent you this?"

Jayla let out a shaky breath and shut her eyes. "I don't know," she said. That was partially true. She had some inkling. That crazy bitch Tracy came to mind. But she couldn't very well tell her sister that.

"All right," Jocelyn said after a pause. "Let me ask you this. Do you know why?"

Jayla debated answering the question truthfully. She couldn't very well tell her baby sister it was probably some vindictive ex-client who had paid her to sleep with her husband or boyfriend. "I have some idea," she said evasively. "But I don't want you to be worried. It's not a big deal."

"Not a big deal?"

"Joce." Jayla crossed to Jocelyn and gently sat her hands on her shoulders. Hopefully, she could convince her sister everything was fine, even if she didn't believe it herself. "Please don't worry about me. This is the only one I've received," she lied. "And that was months ago. I had forgotten all about it."

Jocelyn cast a doubtful look at the card. "Yeah. I still think you should get the police involved." She was upset and had every right to be.

Jayla leaned over and snatched the card from the table. "And tell them what? 'Oh, excuse me. There's some psycho out there who sent me a strange note. Oh no, I don't know who it could be. Oh no, I don't know what the person looks like.' Really, Joce, what are they going to do?" Jayla ripped the card in half, then placed the two halves together and ripped them again. She let the shredded pieces flutter to the floor and pulled her sister into a comforting hug. "Listen, if I felt I had something to worry about, I would do something. But I'm not worried. I'm fine. Okay?"

She could tell Jocelyn was somewhat appeased, and she nodded, turning her lips up in a slight smile.

"Okay," Jocelyn said. "I just panicked. I'm sorry. I shouldn't have been all up in your business. I just stumbled across it when I was in the kitchen, and I was worried."

Jayla nodded and headed toward the front door.

"I noticed how you conveniently didn't answer me," Jocelyn added.

Jayla sighed. "What didn't I answer?"

"What do you do? You're not doing anything illegal are you?"

Jayla stood by the steps, her hand on the bannister. "Not necessarily." She paused, and when Jocelyn made no move to speak, she went on. "It's not drugs or any- thing like that, Joce. I promise. But I do have my own business."

Jocelyn nodded and gestured toward the card pieces scattered on the floor. "A business that would prompt someone to want to kill you?" she whispered, her eyes downcast. Bitter silence.

"Jocelyn, I would prefer you keep this between us," Jayla said, instead of answering the question. "I don't want Jackie or anyone all in my business. Just know that I'm very successful, I've done it for a long time, and everything has been fine." She paused. "In fact, I may be getting out of it soon," she revealed, even as the thought crossed her mind for the first time.

Jocelyn nodded. She stood, stoic, her face unreadable.

Jayla studied her. "You're not judging me, are you?" she asked, not realizing she needed an answer.

Jocelyn shook her head. "Of course not," she assured her. "I just love you. I want what's best for you. And I definitely don't want to see you in any trouble."

"Don't let those hormones get you all stressed about me," Jayla teased. "I'm three years older than you. I got me. You just worry about my little man in there. He is plenty."

Jocelyn nodded and turned to sit on the couch. Jayla watched her pick up the remote, flick the TV on and, without a word, begin flipping through the channels. She wasn't really satisfied with the way the conversation had ended, but at least it had ended.

Jayla stepped outside. It was a gorgeous day. Sunshine and blue skies. She almost could hear the birds chirping. But damn it if she wasn't upset. And now frustrated, thanks to Jocelyn.

***

Jasmine was standing outside the clinic, her arms crossed over her flat stomach, her eyes swollen from crying. Jayla immediately noticed how different her niece—well, daughter—looked from the past few times she'd seen her. Jayla immediately thought about Derrick. Knew she needed to call him. But there was no way in hell she could tell him she had a child.

Gone was that dramatic weave, the heavy makeup, the skimpy clothes. Hell, now Jasmine looked basic in some jeans and a sweatshirt, despite the seventy-five-degree weather.

Jasmine squinted at the truck when Jayla pulled up to the curb, and her grateful smile bloomed as she trotted to the passenger-side door. She got in and closed the door, then immediately turned to hug Jayla. "Thank you," she murmured against her hair. "I'm so sorry."

Jayla patted her back and pulled away, putting the truck in park. This was her daughter. Damn, the shit was surreal. "Have you told Jackie?" she asked, not quite able to refer to her sister as Jasmine's mom anymore. It just wouldn't be the same.

"No," Jasmine answered on a sigh. "She would kick my ass. I know I fucked up. That's why I was trying to get the abortion." She glanced out the window at the clinic. "I went in there and got sick, Auntie. I just couldn't bring myself to do it."

Jayla nodded and took a breath. "I know," she said, remembering her own abortion the second time she got pregnant. "I understand. But you have to do it, Jasmine."

Jasmine's eyes were desperate when she turned to gaze at Jayla, and she had a look of horror on her face. "Wh-what?"

Jayla sighed her regret. It had to be done. "I'm sorry, Jasmine, but what the hell do you want me to say? I'm trying not to be angry, but you damn sure can't think you'll be able to keep this baby. You don't even know who the damn daddy is."

"I . . ." Jasmine struggled to formulate the sentence. "I know, but it's probably Alex . . ."

"Alex!" Jayla spat. "Well, then, you damn sure can't expect shit is going to be sunshine and rainbows. What will Jocelyn say? *She* is about to have his baby. Let alone you tell her you drugged him and slept with him, so she'll leave him. Now you're pregnant by him. Really? Don't be stupid."

Jasmine drew back as if she'd been slapped.

"And what about Jackie and Quentin?" Jayla asked, pushing, wedging the knife in deeper. "How do you think they'll feel, knowing you're about to make them grandparents? And you know Alex ain't about to do *shit* for that baby, so you'll be a single mother."

"I got money." Jasmine had let loose another bout of tears as she clung to shreds of hope.

"Okay. And how long do you think that'll last?" Jayla shot back, lifting her eyebrows as she posed the question. "You damn sure can't do evaluations anymore. Or are you going to be doing that afterward, with a newborn baby? So where is your income stream, because it damn sure won't be child support. And school. Have you thought about that? You're supposed to be headed back for your third year in a couple of months." Jayla lifted her hands, not at all expecting Jasmine to answer any of these obvious questions.

Jasmine just remained quiet. Her sobs had been reduced to sniffles once more.

Jayla shut the car off. After getting out, she rounded the hood and opened the door for Jasmine. "Let's go," she prompted, perhaps a bit too forceful, when Jasmine didn't budge.

Obediently, Jasmine climbed from the truck and dragged her feet back up the stone walkway toward the building.

Jayla followed behind. She was glad she'd made her point. Jasmine had fucked herself up, but Jayla would be damned if she'd let her daughter fuck her shit up too.

Story of my life.

CHAPTER THIRTEEN

Jayla could barely contain her excitement as the plane began its descent. Of course, she had been to the Bahamas before. But the thrill of the spontaneous vacation with Derrick had had her nearly bouncing out of her seat the entire two-hour ride. Derrick had dozed off shortly after they took off, and that had allowed Jayla to relax in her first-class window seat, sip her complimentary champagne, and assess the increasing seriousness of her feelings for this man. As she had watched him sleep, she'd had to admit one thing. She was, indeed, falling for him.

The wheels touched down with a quick jolt, stirring Derrick awake. Jayla smiled as his eyes fluttered open and his lips curved in response. "Hey, sexy," he murmured as he stretched.

"If I'd known you were going to sleep, I would've suggested we stay home," she teased, with a wink.

"Just getting it out of the way."

His smirk had the color rising in her cheeks. No words. Only emotions. Damn, what had he done to her?

"I'm glad you were able to come with me," he added. "I just had to spend a little more time with you before I left town."

Jayla nodded her appreciation and ignored the tug of disappointment. He'd be gone nearly four weeks, overseeing his company's branch in California. She was never one to get into her feelings, but she would damn sure miss him.

The beautiful rooftops and the palm trees outside the plane's window, coupled with the gorgeous weather, had the couple looking forward to a few inviting days.

Jayla waited patiently as Derrick maneuvered their carry-ons from the overhead compartment. She then followed him from the aircraft, nodding her gratitude to each of the smiling flight attendants, into the crowded airport. He'd apparently called for a car to meet them. As they emerged into the blazing sun, he gestured toward the stocky chauffeur gripping a sign that said derrick lewis.

"Welcome to Nassau, Mr. Lewis," the chauffeur greeted, his words thick from his Bahamian accent, when they made their way over to where he was standing. "Mrs. Lewis." He nodded to Jayla, and she smiled in response, not bothering to correct him. The man took their bags from Derrick and placed them in the trunk of a glistening silver Infiniti. He then opened the back door, and Jayla slid onto the plush seat. Derrick stepped in after her.

As the chauffeur drove, Derrick's hand loosely gripped her thigh, and he had his other hand thrown around her shoulders. Jayla felt good speeding down the island streets, observing the vast array of tropical foliage, listening to some reggae mix blaring through the speakers. She could even smell the beach, as the scent of salt water wafted in through the open car windows. All her problems felt like they were miles away, back in Atlanta, and she welcomed the peace.

Since she had promised to touch base with her baby sister when they landed, Jayla pulled her phone from her purse and punched in Jocelyn's number.

"I'm here safe and sound," she informed Jocelyn after she picked up.

"Good."

Jayla frowned. Her sister sounded preoccupied. "What's wrong? What are you doing?" she asked.

Jocelyn took her time responding. "Nothing. Just a little tired. I'm fine."

"Are you sure? Do you need me to call Jackie?"

"Please don't. I'm good. I can manage by myself for the weekend." She paused. "Besides," she added, "Jackie said she would come over and spend the night tomorrow, so I'm fine."

Jayla still felt slightly uneasy, but she didn't know why. Once Jocelyn assured her she would call if she needed her, they hung up. She didn't realize she was still deep in thought until Derrick rubbed her arm.

"Everything okay?" he asked.

Jayla smiled, remembering she had promised herself she would relax and have fun. "Just fine," she said. "I'm all yours all weekend."

She looked down when her phone rang. It was the hospital again. They called so damn much, she could recognize the number. Always the same message. *Give us a call.* . . . Whatever it was, she knew she wouldn't want to hear it. Ignorance was bliss. Jayla swiped the screen to reject the call.

They checked into a gorgeous beachfront hotel, and Jayla was nearly floored by the beauty of the room. Cushioned area rugs had been placed strategically across the glistening mahogany hardwood floor. Two queen-size beds adorned with red and beige pillows and patchwork linens dominated the airy room. Someone had taken the time to spell out *Welcome* in carefully arranged rose petals on one of the beds. Two large, dark wood shutter doors were open, revealing the furnished patio overlooking a manicured lawn with hammocks and palm trees. A little farther, but still within walking distance, Jayla saw the white sand and the crystal-blue water of the ocean.

"This place is like heaven," she said after the bellhop had wheeled their bags into the room and had left them alone. "Thank you so much. I needed this."

Though they both had polished off the complimentary champagne served during check-in in the lobby, Derrick gently tapped his empty glass against hers, anyway.

"We did," he said. "So how about we get started enjoying each other?" He fingered the strap of her baby blue bohemian dress. "Was this expensive?" he asked.

Jayla frowned. "No."

"Good." In one swift motion, he snatched the strap from her shoulder and ripped the dress damn near in half.

Jayla giggled as he backed her up to the bed and lifted her by her legs, sending her tumbling backward onto the plush comforter and rose petals. Derrick licked her thigh as he guided her legs around his neck. He nuzzled her kitty first, taking a long sniff and sighing from the aroma.

"Damn, I love your juicy, sweet-ass pussy," he murmured.

"Oh yeah? Well, show me how much."

As if he was on a mission, Derrick dove in, burying his nose and mouth in her pussy folds, and used his tongue to lick her from the inside out.

One thing was becoming clear.

As Jayla lay out on the lawn chair, the sun kissing the bits of her skin revealed by the skimpy red bikini, she stared at Derrick from behind her big-frame sunglasses. Yes, the man was absolutely enticing, both mentally and physically.

She could not believe how much this man was getting to her. Even now, just thinking about him tugged on her heart, some deep place that hadn't been touched in years.

Damn, it was dangerous, she knew, but she couldn't deny that this man was irresistible. Funny. She had always considered herself as a man's weakness. Now she had found her own. And she didn't know what the hell she was going to do about it.

On a sigh, she pulled the strings loose on her bikini top, and holding the top to her chest, she turned to rest on her stomach. She could get used to this. Maybe Patricia was right. She needed to sit back and enjoy the fruits of her labor. Especially when she had someone to share them with. What was he? Her man? Her boyfriend? Hell, she didn't know. Neither of them had spoken about labels, and Jayla figured it was for the best. That way, she could still do what she wanted without reproach. But how long would that last? And worst of all, what would she do when he declared that he wanted more? She didn't want to lose him. . . . She frowned at the thought. Lose him? Was he considered hers to lose?

The hands on her back had her eyes fluttering open, and then she glanced over to see Derrick sitting down beside her on the lawn chair. "You'll burn if you keep sleeping out here, sexy," he murmured, but Jayla didn't bother budging. His hands felt good. This felt good. Felt right.

She grinned when she felt his lips gently replace his hands on her skin.

"Are you hungry?" he said.

"Yes."

"Why don't we change and get some dinner?" He was already retying the strings on her bikini top. Then he helped her up and, still holding her hand, led the way back up the beach toward their hotel.

They never did make it to dinner. After a round in the shower and on the bathroom counter, Derrick suggested they order in instead.

After room service had wheeled in a cart of covered dishes and left, Derrick maneuvered the cart to the patio door and began unloading the dishes on the patio table and uncovering them.

Jayla accepted the glass of wine he poured from the bottle in the chilled bucket, and made herself comfortable in the chair. Derrick set a dinner plate in front of her, and she took a deep inhale of the large lobster tail, peas and rice, and baked macaroni and cheese. The distinct island spices that enhanced the food nearly had her mouth watering. Derrick placed his own dinner plate close to hers and took a seat.

Both of them ate in peaceful silence, lulled by the crashing of waves and the distant chatter as people continued to play on the beach. Occasionally, a seagull shrieked overhead.

Jayla sighed wistfully.

"I can get used to this," Derrick murmured, as if on cue. "Traveling, enjoying each other, having fun together." He gazed at the ocean in the distance. "Why have you never been married?" he asked suddenly and had Jayla's fork pausing in midair over the food. She laid it down and stalled some more by gently patting her lips with the cotton napkin and taking another sip of her champagne.

"That just wasn't a priority for me before," she finally said.

He nodded, seemed to be thoroughly evaluating her answer. "And now?" he prompted.

She eyed him. The look in his eye indicated that he was completely serious. "Why do you ask?" she said, instead of answering his question. "You trying to marry me or something, Derrick?" She smirked, but she was halfway surprised when he didn't chuckle at the small joke.

She heard her phone ringing inside the room, and grateful for the interruption, Jayla tossed her napkin on the table and darted inside. She grabbed her phone out of her purse, which lay on one of the beds, and one look at the caller ID had her groaning. She hadn't had to deal with this issue, and she damn sure wasn't trying to deal with it now. She made a mental note to power off her phone at some point so she could really relax.

Jayla swiped her screen to reject the incoming call, but she was not surprised when the phone rang again in her hand. "Hello?" she answered. Better to face the shit head-on.

"Cherry." Joi's voice breezed through the phone and annoyed the hell out of Jayla. "I've missed you, oh, so much," she cooed, lathering her voice with sugar.

"Have you?" Jayla said simply. A pause. She glanced at the patio door, saw Derrick had walked out a bit toward the beach.

"Why you acting like that?" Joi now had an attitude. "Does this have anything to do with my brother?"

"Joi, stop. We weren't in a relationship or any kind of shit like that, so what difference does it make?"

"*Shit like that*, huh?" Joi smacked her lips. "It wasn't *shit like that* when I was slurping that pussy like a milkshake, huh? Or when we were bumping coochies in the stockroom, right?"

Jayla cringed.

"So you fucking my brother or what?" Joi asked, pushing.

"Joi, don't call me anymore," Jayla snapped and hung up. She waited, not really expecting Joi to comply. When her phone didn't ring again, she tossed it back in her purse. *Good.* Maybe that clingy bitch could take a hint.

She glanced back at Derrick just as he fished his own cell phone out of his pocket. *Shit.* Jayla could tell by the way he was frowning at the screen that it was Joi. She ran back outside and headed across the grass.

"What's wrong, sweetie?" she said, attempting to sound casual, when she reached his side. She froze when Derrick frowned at her.

"Did you know my sister before I introduced you to her?"

"What?" Jayla replied in an effort to stall as she plastered a look of confusion on her face. "What are you talking about?"

"I just got some random, bullshit text from Joi about you," he said. "I told you I don't trust her, so I'm asking you, what the fuck is she talking about? Do you know her?"

Jayla turned up her lips in disgust. "The fuck? Are you kidding me?" she said, feigning sincerity. She threw up her hands and shook her head, really selling that shit. "I've been to Spades a few times with some friends, and one particular time, she tried to talk to me, and I refused. That was it. What the hell is she saying about me, Derrick? I can't believe she's trying to pull some ratchet shit like that." Jayla thought a moment and then laid it on extra thick. "Damn, and you said she was sneaky too." She sucked her teeth, peering at Derrick through narrowed eyes.

She licked her lips nervously when he started pressing buttons on his phone. "What are you doing?"

"I'm about to get to the bottom of this shit," he said, putting the phone to his ear. "My sister's pulling that same bullshit like she used to. Lying and shit. That's why I stopped dealing with her before." Anger had colored his eyes with something Jayla had never seen before.

Fuck. The next thought came like a life jacket, and Jayla grabbed it desperately, letting the lie fall free. "This is fucked up," she sputtered. "Got me all upset, and I'm pregnant and shit."

"Hello, Derrick?" She heard Joi answer the phone with a triumphant tone, but Derrick was already pulling the device away from his face as he stared at Jayla.

"What did you say?" he whispered.

Jayla licked her lips again, her eyes quickly darting to the phone, which he clutched in a vise grip. At least he had hung up. She took another breath to calm her nerves. "I didn't want you to find out this way," she confessed, struggling to read his face. "I took a test. And it was positive."

His face split with the smile as he dragged Jayla toward him. "Why didn't you tell me?" he said, but he didn't bother waiting for a response before crushing his lips against hers.

Damn, she hadn't expected him to *want* the baby. She had just needed a brief distraction. Something. Anything to keep him from speaking with Joi. She had expected the initial shock. Followed by the "I'm not ready to be a father," "We're not married" type of bullshit excuses men were so quick to throw out. Then maybe a tentative abortion suggestion, which she would quickly agree to. This was damn sure not what she had expected. But then, Derrick hadn't been what she expected from the moment she saw him.

"Please don't let her come between us, babe. Plus, we have only this short weekend together, so let's enjoy it." Jayla angled her head to look him in the eye as she spoke.

"No, babe, I'd never let her do that," he said and then kissed her deeply to reaffirm his promise.

It wasn't a total lie, she reasoned as she wheeled her luggage to the Atlanta Airport parking lot. She hadn't taken a test, so she very well could be pregnant. Hell, when was the last time she'd taken her birth control, anyway? Jayla scrolled through her cell phone calendar and frowned when the dates didn't jog her memory. She had been so busy, she couldn't even remember.

As Derrick had made his way to California, Jayla had headed back to Atlanta with one thing in mind . . . slowing down her business so she could spend more time with Derrick. She had racked her brain on the solo plane ride back and had finally settled on one of two options. Either get pregnant or fake a miscarriage.

Option B had had Jayla shuddering. She didn't know how Derrick would react to news of a miscarriage. Her mind had immediately flashed back to the last time she'd pulled this stunt: The guy had beaten her so damn bad, she'd been in the hospital for two weeks. It was her fault, he had insisted. Her fault she'd had a miscarriage. Part of her knew Derrick would never go that far. Part of her. The other part had decided option A was the only viable one.

She finally found her car in the parking lot. After stowing her luggage, she climbed behind the wheel and left the lot. Then she turned her truck in the direction of Chris's house. Maybe she could test her luck. She didn't know why, but she couldn't lose Derrick. Not to the truth. Not to a lie. Maybe, just maybe she could fashion a fairy tale out of the hell she had built for herself.

Jayla parked across from Chris's house. She eyed the master bedroom window, felt satisfied when she saw a light on. Chris would never raw dog her. He was much too careful for that. Keeping that in mind, she pulled a condom out of her glove compartment, and gently made a small tear in the wrapper, then removed the latex glove. Next, she found a safety pin in her armrest compartment and began placing strategic holes in the condom. Satisfied with her handiwork, she placed the condom back in the wrapper and stepped from the truck.

"What the fuck are you doing here, Jayla?" Chris yelled as soon as he opened the door.

"The fuck you think you talking to, Chris?" She met anger with anger, just like he liked it, and shoved him backward into his living room. "I did what you asked. I gave your pussy ass some space. Now I want my dick. I hope you ain't got no bitch in here, because she about to get a front-row seat."

"You a crazy-ass bitch," he mumbled, grabbing Jayla's arm to shove her back toward the door.

Jayla snatched her arm from his grasp and slapped him. She smirked when his eyes darkened. "Yeah, I hit you," she taunted. "The fuck you gone do about it, pussy?"

He slammed her back against the door, briefly knocking the wind out of her. His hand was around her throat, and Jayla kept her grin in place, even as he tightened his grip.

"You want to beat me," she breathed. She lifted the condom wrapper for him to see. "Or you want to beat this juicy-ass pussy, huh? You want to make me squirt like you used to, don't you, Chris? You want to shove that thick-ass dick deep in my cervix, huh?"

"You stupid-ass, fuck-ass bitch," he growled, snatching the wrapper from her hand. He used his teeth to tear it all the way open and expertly maneuvered the condom on his rock-hard dick through the slit in his boxers.

Jayla wrapped her legs around his waist and gasped when he shoved it in so deep, it felt like it ripped her walls. He kept his grip around her throat as he pounded her, the force of each thrust slapping her ass and pushing her back against the plaster wall. She moaned through the delicious pain, his breath roaring in her ears, as he increased his speed.

"Damn, I missed this pussy," he whispered.

Jayla felt the wall crack just as he erupted and his cum slithered through the puncture holes in the condom to lather her insides. She smiled. Hell, between Chris, the bouncer at the strip club, and even Derrick, she damn sure should be pregnant by somebody. Maybe her thinking was skewed, but damn it, she would get the life she wanted with Derrick. If she got pregnant and he found out the baby wasn't his, well, she would handle that shit like a boss too. But first, she would make damn sure the truth never came out.

Afterward, Jayla was able to sneak the condom out of Chris's house, and she was nearly gloating as she trotted back to her truck. For some reason, the prospect of a life with Derrick excited her. Was it love? She giggled to herself as she climbed back in her truck. She didn't give a damn. She just didn't want it to end.

The muffled jingle of her ringtone had Jayla frowning at her purse. Her eyes slid to the digital clock on the dashboard. It was 2:17 a.m. Who the hell could that be?

Jayla saw the cell phone's light illuminating the darkness inside her purse, casting an eerie glow on its contents. She saw Jackie's number on the caller ID, took the call, and quickly placed the phone to her ear.

"Jaye." Jackie's voice was thick with tears and laced with fear. She was in an obvious panic.

"Jackie, calm down. What is it?"

"It's Jocelyn," she said. "Jaye, you have to get to Regency Hospital fast. There's been an accident."

"What?"

"Just hurry!" Jackie pleaded, and then the line disconnected.

Jayla held the phone in her hand and felt rising panic. *Accident?* What the hell had happened to Jocelyn? She prayed the baby was okay.

CHAPTER FOURTEEN

The air in the hospital was tainted with the faint odor of antiseptics and lemon Pine Sol. Jayla burst through the emergency room's automatic doors and immediately felt nauseated from the smell. Though it was only close to six o'clock in the morning, the waiting room was packed. Couples, children . . . some holding their stomach, pressing ice to their head, or fiddling with the gauze on their arm.

They were all a blur as she ran to the registration desk. "Excuse me," she said, speaking even though the woman on duty held a phone to her ear. "Can you please give me the room number for Jocelyn Morgan? She's pregnant, and there's been an accident." The woman cupped the receiver with her hand and motioned to a set of double doors. She then touched a buzzer under her desk, and the doors swung open to let Jayla through.

Jackie was in the small hallway, pacing like a caged panther. She looked distressed, her eyes downcast, her normally kempt hair tousled from nerves, lack of sleep, or both.

"Jack," Jayla called as she trotted up, nearly breathless. She looked frantically at her sister for answers. "What happened? Where is she?"

Jackie enveloped her in a desperate hug, and Jayla felt the tears dampen her pullover. "I should've been there." Her voice was muffled by Jayla's sleeve. "Something told me to go over there tonight, but she swore she was okay."

Jayla pulled back, grabbing her shoulders. "Calm down. Tell me what happened. Where is Joce?"

Her eyes reddened by tears, Jackie tossed a look at the double doors behind her. "She's in surgery. They're having to do an emergency C-section to try to save the baby."

Jayla felt the gut punch of the words. Her knees grew weak from the reality of the situation. She lowered herself onto a bench against the wall.

"Surgery?" Fear had Jayla's voice lowered to a whisper. "To try to save the baby?"

Jackie nodded and slid on the bench beside her. "They are hopeful, but they don't know."

Jayla shut her eyes against the threatening tears. Oh, Lord, please let her sister and nephew be all right. "Did you call Aunt Bev?" she asked.

"Yeah, but she's not feeling good, so I tried not to make it sound so bad, so she wouldn't come."

"Start from the beginning, Jack. What happened?"

When Jackie took her time responding, Jayla braced herself. "Well, after you left for your trip, I asked Joce if she wanted me to come spend the night. You know, cook her dinner and make sure she was okay. I didn't think she needed to be by herself. She swore she was fine. Said that she was tired. Said you had left some cooked spaghetti in the house, so she would probably eat that and go to bed. Said the baby had been kicking like crazy." Jackie paused, and Jayla's heart quickened as she waited.

Hospital staff moved about with the same steady urgency they felt on any given day. Some even smiled at Jackie and Jayla and murmured a cordial greeting in passing, clearly oblivious to the fact that the two women were about to have nervous breakdowns right there on the emergency floor. With the exception of a distant alarm sounding in the sterile hallway, Jayla wouldn't have known anything was wrong.

"So, I said okay and left it at that," Jackie continued hesitantly. "Well, the next day I was supposed to go over there and stay with her, anyway. She told me not to worry about it and that she would be okay. So I didn't go. I should've, but I didn't. Today I decided to check on her again, even though I knew you were supposed to be back. You know, see if she needed anything. Her phone kept going to voicemail. I figured she had just turned it off, but then I wondered why she would do that, knowing you were out of town, I was at home, and she was over at your place alone. Hell, anything could've happened. So I drove over there . . ." Jackie trailed off, and Jayla saw the flicker of fear and the restrained panic play on her face. "Jaye." Her voice had lowered to a whisper. "Someone had broken in."

"What?" Jayla felt the fear snake up the back of her neck. "Broken in to my house?"

"The front door was open. Just wide open. When I went in, I saw Jocelyn at the bottom of the steps." Jackie's voice cracked with the words. "She was bleeding, Jaye." Jackie began screaming so loud now that nurses headed in their direction to quiet her down. But then she composed herself. "Shit, she was bleeding so bad. It was so much blood, and she was just lying there on her stomach. She was unconscious. I thought she was dead." Jackie buried her face in her hands, and Jayla shut her eyes, struggling to erase the image her sister had just painted.

Jayla couldn't speak. She immediately pictured one of her disgruntled ex-clients attacking anyone who was at the house. The thought sickened her, and she felt a wave of nausea bubble in the pit of her stomach.

Jayla opened her eyes as Quentin and Jasmine dashed up. Quentin quickly enveloped his wife in a hug. "What the hell is going on? Are you two okay?"

Without thinking, Jayla threw her arms around Quentin. She felt comforted when he brought his other arm around to grip her shoulders. Just like old times.

A couple of hours later, they were still waiting for a doctor to provide an update on Jocelyn's condition. Having exhausted herself by crying every ounce of tears she had in her, Jayla sat slumped in the stiff hospital chair, waiting for news. All that could be heard was the occasional intercom call for this doctor or that doctor, and the slight squeak of Jackie's sneakers on the linoleum floor as she paced in front of her.

She was grateful for Derrick. She had called him to relay the night's events, and he had called Tara and Kevin for her. He had listened to her cry and had comforted her with words of encouragement and support. It felt like he wasn't even thousands of miles away. She hated appearing weak, but she didn't have the time or the energy to care.

"Jack," Jayla mumbled, her voice slightly hoarse. "Please sit down."

"I can't sit still," Jackie responded. "Where the hell are the doctors? Why hasn't anyone said anything yet?"

Jayla stood. Her leg muscles had tightened from the seated position she'd maintained in the stiff chair. "I'll go ask," she said and headed to the desk in the center of the waiting room.

Two nurses were giggling about something. One sat at the computer, and the other was leaning casually against the counter beside her. They looked to be in their early twenties. Jayla sighed. She wondered how they could be so happy, so carefree in the middle of a crisis center.

"Excuse me?" she said, and both of them looked at her. "I just wanted to get some information on Jocelyn Morgan.

She came in a couple hours ago, and the doctors took her back to do a C-section. We haven't heard anything yet."

One nurse nodded, her lips curved in a compassionate smile. "Yes, ma'am," she said, lifting the telephone receiver to her ear. "Let me get someone down here to speak with you."

Jayla nodded, turned, and started to head back to Jackie, but she stopped when she spotted Tara and Kevin rushing through the doors. She immediately engulfed Tara in a grateful hug.

"Thank you for coming," she murmured, comforted by her best friend's embrace.

"I'm sorry we took so long," Tara said. "I didn't see the missed call until we woke up this morning. How is she?"

Jayla sighed, suddenly feeling the urge to cry again. "We don't know. The doctor's on his way to tell us something." She glanced over at Kevin, caught the strange look in his eye before he looked away. "Hi, Kevin," she said, slightly uneasy about his expression. He looked just like he had at the strip club.

"Hey, Jayla," he said.

Jayla watched the corner of his lips twitch. Was he trying not to smile? She opened her mouth to address this, but Tara spoke up first.

"Sweetie, I'm sure everyone is hungry. Can you go down to the cafeteria to get some food?" she said to Kevin.

He nodded and then gave Jayla another look before strolling off.

Tara turned her gaze to Jayla. "What happened?"

Tara's question brought Jayla's eyes back to hers, and putting Kevin's bullshit attitude out of her mind, she led the way back to her seat in the waiting room. Tara greeted Jackie and then sat down beside Jayla.

"A break-in at my house," Jayla explained. "I don't know. Jackie found Jocelyn at the bottom of the stairs, bleeding. They rushed her into surgery to perform a C-section, and we haven't heard anything since."

"Damn." Tara shook her head, and she immediately grabbed Jayla's hand. "I'm so sorry. Who the hell would do this?"

"I just hope everything is all right," Jackie interjected.

Kevin soon returned with plastic bags full of to-go boxes. Jayla was appreciative, but as he cleared the stained magazines from the coffee table to make room for the food, she didn't know how she was going to eat. She felt nauseated and damn sure didn't have an appetite.

Tara rubbed Jayla's back. "I know this isn't the time or the place." Tara spoke in a hushed tone. "But I did want to congratulate you."

Jayla's head was spinning as she struggled to wrap her mind around Tara's words. "What?"

"Derrick told Kev about the baby," Tara said. She offered a weak smile. "Congratulations. I know this must be extra difficult, considering . . . the circumstances."

Jayla lowered her eyes. She felt dizzy, and another flood of tears was threatening to burst free.

Just then a doctor rounded the corner, a petite man with horn-rimmed glasses and a head full of gray hair. He stopped when he reached them. "Are you the family of Jocelyn Morgan?" he asked, and everyone stood up.

Jayla spoke up first. "Yes. What happened? How is she?"

The doctor's lips compressed in a grim line. "I'm Dr. Patel, by the way," he said, introducing himself, but he did not bother to extend his hand or wait for a response. "I performed Ms. Morgan's surgery. She is out of surgery and still in recovery. She lost a lot of blood. She also suffered a slight concussion, but she's going to be all right. We're going to keep her here for a few days for observation."

Jayla didn't realize she'd been holding her breath until she felt a slight cramp in her chest. Relieved about her sister, she let it out. Thank God she was all right. For a brief moment, Jayla felt her heart lift and her tense muscles relax inch by wonderful inch. She had to get to Jocelyn. Needed to see her. To see for herself, to hug her, something. The threat of losing her had almost been too much to bear.

"What about the baby?" Jackie asked.

It was as if the news was broadcast on the doctor's face. Jayla felt every muscle tighten.

"I'm sorry," he said.

Jayla shut her eyes as the tears erupted once more. Her body felt dense and hollow. The doctor kept murmuring apologies, but his voice sounded so distant. She pictured her nephew, a nameless, faceless shadow, whom they had shopped for, prepped for, and waited for. And who had died before he had even had a chance.

Jocelyn was curled up in the fetal position, her back toward the door. Her face was half hidden, but Jayla could see her sister's hands fisted against white cotton sheets. Her complexion wasn't the usual caramel with that recognizable pregnancy glow. No, that was long gone. She looked more ashen then anything, a cross between gray and pastel brown, as if she'd been watered down. The hospital gown she wore was a crisp white, and it seemed to underscore the change in Jocelyn's complexion. Jayla shuddered. The woman was like a ghost. And her anguish permeated the small hospital room.

Jocelyn remained motionless even after the door's quiet click echoed off the walls. Jayla would've thought she was asleep if not for her fingers' subtle caressing of the empty bassinet at the side of her bed. A tray of food sat on the table beside her, the lunch completely untouched.

Jayla had requested privacy, but now that just she was alone with Jocelyn in the room, she felt claustrophobic, as if she was choking.

"Hey, Joce." Jayla took another tentative step toward the center of the room. "Do you feel like talking?"

"No." Joce's one-word answer, delivered in a low voice, was harsh.

"Why don't I help you sit up and come out from under the covers?"

"Get the hell out, Jayla," she said.

Jayla sighed and ignoring the command, sat a gentle hip on the side of the bed. "Maybe it'll help if you talk about it." She shut her eyes against the guilt that was exploding in the pit of her stomach.

When Jocelyn made no move to answer, Jayla pressed on. "I'm sorry, Joce." Pause. No response. Jayla opened her mouth to speak again and then closed it on a frown when the door swung open and two police officers entered the room.

The dark-haired one introduced himself first. "Good afternoon, ladies. I'm Lieutenant Torres." His fluid Spanish accent wrapped around each word. "And this is my partner, Detective Morrell. If you don't mind, we'd like to ask Jocelyn Morgan some questions."

Jayla stood and crossed her arms over her chest. "Yes, I do mind."

Detective Morrell frowned. "And you are, ma'am?"

"I'm her sister Jayla. Jocelyn has been through a very traumatic experience. Don't you think this should wait?"

Lieutenant Torres spoke again. "We understand the delicate situation, but given what happened, we would like to collect as many facts as possible to help with the investigation. It's best while the details are still fresh in her mind."

Jayla narrowed her eyes. The logic made sense, but she still didn't like the idea of these two badgering her sister.

"It's fine," Jocelyn said, sitting up for the first time.

Jayla grimaced when Jocelyn crossed her arms over her flattening belly.

The officers didn't wait for any invitation. Just took out their notepads and sat on the stiff hospital converter couch underneath the window.

"First off, Ms. Morgan, on behalf of the entire precinct," said Lieutenant Torres, "we would like to apologize for your loss. Our condolences go out to you and your family during this trying time."

Jayla rolled her eyes. The speech had sounded completely dispassionate and rehearsed.

"Now," he continued, "please, in your own words, give us the details of what happened last Friday night."

"I was doing laundry," Jocelyn began. She didn't bother looking at the cops. Merely stared ahead at the blank wall across from her, as if she were in some sort of daze. "I heard someone come upstairs. Not sure how they got in."

"Is there an alarm in the house?" Detective Morrell asked.

Jayla spoke up first. "Yes, there is. The place actually belongs to me."

"Please give us your entire name for the record," Detective Morrell stated.

"Jayla Morgan."

"And your relationship to the victim?"

Jayla rolled her eyes once more and let out a frustrated sigh. "I told you before, I'm her sister."

"And where were you, Ms. Morgan, at the time of the incident in question?" Lieutenant Torres eyed her as he posed the question.

"I was out of town," Jayla answered. "The Bahamas," she added when he made a move to open his mouth once more.

"What happened next, Ms. Morgan?" the lieutenant asked, his gaze on Jocelyn.

"Like I said, I heard someone coming up the stairs," Jocelyn continued. "I panicked, because I didn't think I had left the front door unlocked. I couldn't remember if I had turned on the alarm, but either way, I knew I should've been at home alone, so I immediately freaked out. So I hid in the hall closet. I heard the person walk by, headed for Jaye's bedroom. When the intruder did, I ran out of the closet and tripped going down the stairs. Then I blacked out."

"So you didn't see the perpetrator?" Detective Morrell said.

"No."

"Okay. Do either of you ladies know someone who would try to harm you?"

Jocelyn didn't speak, so Jayla volunteered to answer the question. "No," she said.

"No enemies?" Detective Morrell asked, pressing. "No disgruntled coworkers, no neighbors, no one you can think of that could possibly have done this?"

Jayla's thoughts fell to Tracy, and she rolled her eyes. No, she planned on handling that personally when she saw her next time. "Nope," she said.

Lieutenant Torres produced a card and handed it to Jayla. "Please call us if you two think of something else."

The officers left, and Jayla sucked in a grateful breath as she sat back down on the edge of the bed. Things were already bad enough without the police getting involved.

Jayla grimaced at the thought. *More than just bad.* She had managed to sneak into the house in the wee hours of the morning, before the police had barricaded it with crime-scene tape and a forensics team had arrived. With the amount of blood at the scene, it was a wonder her sister was still alive. Lord knows how long she had been lying there before Jackie showed up. Hell, the large bloodstain on her carpet didn't even begin to tell the story of the horror that had occurred.

"You can see yourself out too," Jocelyn prompted when Jayla continued to sit in silence on the edge of her bed.

Jayla sighed. "Listen, Jocelyn, I'm sorry how all of this went down," she said. "But damn, I feel bad enough as it is. Can you get rid of the attitude?" She looked at her sister and was nearly shocked when she saw the raging resentment burning in her eyes. *If looks could kill.*

Jayla stood and headed to the door, the burden of the guilt like a huge lump in the middle of her throat. She couldn't swallow it, couldn't throw it up. It just sat there. She left the room without another word.

As Jayla headed back to the waiting room, she caught Jasmine walking toward her, her fists balled, like she was ready to throw some punches. Jayla glanced around, unsure whom she was coming for.

"You're such a fucking bitch!" Jasmine hissed and shoved Jayla so hard, she collided with the nearby water fountain.

The pain cut like a dagger in her back and had Jayla's breath catching.

"I heard about your pregnancy," Jasmine snapped. "You force me to get an abortion, and now you're pregnant?"

Jayla shook her head. "It's not true . . ."

"I fucking hate you!" Jasmine all but screamed. "If I could cut that shit out of your stomach myself, I would! Trust me." She stepped closer and emphasized every word when she said, "You will regret crossing me."

The comment shocked Jayla, but even more shocking was the fact that Jasmine then spit at her. The spit hit Jayla's cheek and slid down the side of her face.

Jasmine turned and stalked off, her arms now folded over her own flat stomach. *Jayla's child.*

CHAPTER FIFTEEN

Jayla parked outside the bank and waited. It seemed like she'd been crying for days, and this had left her eyes a bloodshot, puffy mess. They were now shielded by thick sunglasses, despite the overcast sky. She caught movement in the corner of her eye and turned to looked at the gray Impala parked across the street. Had that been Jasmine? Jayla narrowed her eyes, observed the Impala's empty seats through the windshield. She hadn't seen her since the hospital encounter, but she easily remembered how the chick had been on some other kind of lunacy. Jayla glanced back at the bank, kept her eyes steady on the glass doors.

When she saw Heather emerge from the building, Jayla rolled down her window. "Over here," she called, motioning for the woman to come over to the car.

Heather was at her side in an instant, clutching an envelope. "Denise, I—"

"Miss me with that bullshit, Heather," Jayla interrupted, snatching the envelope from her fingers. "You were supposed to mail this before. You lucky I don't stomp your stupid ass right here in this parking lot."

Heather looked frazzled. "I know. I just wanted to see you face-to-face to tell you I'm sorry."

"You can lick my ass with that sorry," Jayla snapped. "You don't know what the fuck I went through that night. All for you. For your crummy ass! And for what? To walk right into a fucking setup!"

Heather normally pale face was now pink from emotion. "Please listen to me. I'm sorry. I had no idea. This is all my fault for putting you through this. But please help me get my Reggie back," Heather said, almost pleading, as tears spilled down her cheeks. She sniffed, but snot kept leaking from her nose. "Oh, God, I love him so much! Don't you see that's why I came to you? I'll kill myself without him!"

Jayla narrowed her eyes behind the sunglasses. "Use a razor, bitch," she snapped. "And don't get blood on the carpet. It stains." Jayla revved her engine, and fear had Heather jumping back as she sped off.

Jayla glanced in her rearview mirror and watched Heather crumple to her knees in the street.

When she got home, Jayla stripped out of her clothes, tossed her money on the coffee table, and sank onto the leather couch. This "home" felt awkward. She had moved in to the second "work" studio apartment she owned across town. It had seemed like the best idea, but the place didn't feel the same as her real home. In the past, she had brought client after client through here, had sucked and sexed in every inch of the nine hundred square feet, had even sprinkled the space with a few of her things to give the impression of an actual lived-in place. It had been a week since she'd moved in, and she had even managed to unpack every single box, but she still found herself lying awake at night.

Jayla snatched her cell phone from the coffee table and punched in her sister Jackie's number. Jackie picked up on the second ring.

"How is she?" Jayla asked.

"Not good," Jackie admitted and released a deep sigh, as if to prove her point. "She's not eating, not sleeping. All she does is sit up in that spare bedroom and cry. I'm worried."

"Maybe she needs to see somebody."

"Jaye, you know she is not going to go for that."

Jayla sighed. It was her fault. Damn, she couldn't swallow the guilt. Whoever it was that had attacked Jocelyn, they were clearly after her. Her sister had just so happened to get caught in the crossfire.

"How's Jasmine?" she asked tentatively.

Jackie sighed. "I don't know what's going on with her, either, Jaye," she murmured. "It's like the world has turned on its damn axis. She doesn't go out anymore, but she does the same thing as Joce. Sitting up in her room, listening to music. I don't know what's gotten into her, either, but they're both scaring the hell out of me, honestly."

Jayla squeezed her eyes shut. She had figured as much.

"Do you think I should tell her? About . . . the adoption?" Jackie asked.

"No," Jayla answered quickly. "She's going through her own thing right now. Let's all talk to her when we feel she's ready."

When Jackie remained quiet, Jayla went on, before she broke down right there on the phone. All she could manage to say before she ended the call was, "Tell them both I called. And I love them." The words were completely genuine, but they did nothing to soothe the pain. Not wanting to think, not wanting to feel anything, she immediately dialed another number. She needed a distraction.

When Derrick didn't answer, she groaned, willing herself not to be frustrated. She tried again, left an absent message for him to call her; then she called Tara.

"How are you?" Tara asked as soon as she picked up.

"I'm okay. What are you doing?"

"Probably about to go out to dinner with Kevin. Why?"

Jayla swallowed her disappointment. "Oh, okay."

"You should come, Jaye," Tara suggested. "You need to get out of the house."

"No, I'm not trying to be a third wheel. Y'all go ahead and have fun."

"Well, call Derrick."

"I think he's working late," Jayla said, trying to keep the pout off her face.

"Fine. I'm dumping Kevin so I can go out to dinner with you instead."

"No!"

"Jayla." Tara's voice was laced with impatience. "I'm on my way there to pick you up. I don't give a damn what you say. You need to be with your best friend now. So get dressed."

The click echoed in her ear, and Jayla pulled the phone away from her ear, frowning. Tara was right. She did need to be with someone right now. The mere thought of spending another night in this lonely place had her feeling fearful. She needed to get out. If only for a few hours.

She was surprised to see Kevin had decided to come along. But there he was, neatly folded in the back seat of Tara's silver Nissan.

"Hey, Jaye," he greeted. "I hope you don't mind if I tag along."

"Um, no, not at all," she said. She glanced at Tara, who shrugged. Apparently, the idea of his company didn't seem as awkward to her.

The ride to the restaurant consisted of Tara holding a conversation with Kevin, and Jayla wishing she had made up some bullshit excuse to stay home. Her stomach hurt. Her head hurt. Everything hurt.

Even when they got to the table, Jayla remained quiet, babysitting a glass of water as Tara chatted about work.

"So . . ." Tara turned to her and had Jayla lifting her eyes. "We never got a chance to talk about the Bahamas."

Jayla's lips curved at the memory. Too bad she hadn't even had time to marinate on their little vacation.

"It was good," she answered. "Wish it could've been longer, but it was fun."

"That's it?" Tara seemed disappointed by the skimpy details. "It was *good*? It was *fun*?"

Jayla's eyes shifted to Kevin, who seemed to be gloating about something. What the hell was wrong with this man? "I really don't feel like talking about it," she admitted.

Jayla couldn't pinpoint the exact cause, but she felt lost. How her life had managed to wither and crumble through her fingers, she couldn't be sure. But between the craziness with her sister Jocelyn, the psycho bitch Tracy, Derrick and whatever the hell was going on with him, she felt like a fucking zombie. Or maybe she was on autopilot, and she was hovering overhead, like some ghost watching the mess of her life play out like a terrible movie. Not to mention her business. "Hell, what business?" was more like it. She couldn't very well keep it going. Not after what had happened to her baby sister. And her nephew. Oh God, her poor nephew. Just thinking of the events had tears stinging the corners of her eyes.

"I understand." Tara gave Jayla a comforting smile and a pat on her hand before she rose. "Let me go to the restroom. Be right back."

Jayla watched her friend sashay through the restaurant's booths before she disappeared around a corner. With a sigh, Jayla slid her eyes to Kevin, who was giving her that disgustingly eerie smile, like he was sitting on a million-dollar lottery ticket but didn't wish to share the news.

"Kevin, what is supposed to be your problem?" she asked, trying to keep from sounding too snappish.

"What are you talking about?"

The fact that he was feigning innocence had Jayla rolling her eyes. "You really want to act like that?"

Kevin took his time responding, taking a leisurely sip from his Coke and tossing a casual glance over his shoulder. "You were at K. Sutra a while back," he said, and Jayla sucked in a breath.

Shit, shit, shit. How could she forget?

Kevin continued. "Saw your little performance with the twins. I didn't know you had a birthmark on your thigh." He stopped and stared at her.

Jayla waited, her heart rate quickening as he dragged out each lazy minute, apparently relishing his knowledge.

"Did you have fun in the VIP room?" he finally went on, and pierced by the memory of that painful experience, Jayla shut her eyes. "Oh, no need to be ashamed. I saw the whole thing. You up there acting like a slut. I can't believe Tara is friends with someone like you."

"Okay, wait a damn minute!" Jayla did snap at him this time. His rude comment had felt like a dagger. "You don't know anything about my friendship with Tara. I've known that woman for years. I was in her life well before you came into the picture. So don't act like you know me, because you damn sure don't."

"I know what I saw." He leaned over, lowered his voice. "I know you were up there fucking some other nigga, and you supposed to be with Derrick. I know you let that bouncer nigga fuck you too. And I know Tara don't know nothing about your little alternative lifestyle, because you know as well as I do that she would have a problem with it." When she remained quiet, he added, "I do know this little . . . fiasco can remain between us. For a price."

"*Price?*" Jayla scoffed. "The hell kind of price? And how the hell do you know what I was doing in VIP?"

She watched his eyes trail down her body, linger on her heaving breasts, before returning to meet her gaze.

"I can't believe you!" Jayla felt numb. "Tara is my friend—no, my *best* friend—and you're supposed to be cool with Derrick. How can you ask me to do something like that?"

When he leaned forward to rub his fingers on her arm, she snatched her arm away.

"Don't worry about how I know. You, well, you seem to enjoy giving it away, so I figure, why the hell not?" He grinned, and Jayla turned away in disgust. "Or would you rather I pay you, like the others?"

"I'm pregnant, and what you think you saw is not what really went down." Jayla said it like a plea, hopeful that the lie would untangle her from this mess. It didn't.

Kevin smirked. "I actually was kind of turned on by that," he said. "Just picture my dick stroking Derrick's fetus. Like rocking it to sleep."

Jayla gagged. This man was a fucking sick lunatic. She glanced over her shoulder, caught Tara making her way back to the table. "It's not like either one of them will care," she insisted, trying to convince herself. "Tara damn sure won't, and it's not like me and Derrick are a couple. So this blackmail shit won't work." She watched his nonchalant shrug.

"Do you want to find out?" he taunted.

Tara eased back into her seat, tossing a casual glance from Kevin to Jayla. "Everything okay?" she asked, and Jayla frowned when Kevin put his arm around his wife's shoulders.

"Just fine," he assured her before kissing her cheek.

They ate in awkward silence, and Jayla was grateful when Tara called for the check afterward. She needed to get home. To get away from this bastard and figure out what the hell she was going to do. *Shit, what to do? What to do?* Tara would probably look at her like she was some prostitute if she found out, and Derrick . . . he wouldn't go for that kind of lifestyle. Jayla's heart felt heavy from just thinking about Derrick. If he ever found out . . . No, he couldn't. He couldn't find out.

"You gone be okay, girl?" Tara asked once they had pulled back up in Jayla's driveway.

Jayla didn't bother looking back, but she could tell Kevin's eyes were on her as she opened the car door.

"Yeah," she lied. "I just have a headache. Just need to get some rest."

"Okay. Call me tomorrow if you're not feeling better," Tara said.

Jayla could only nod and lift a weak hand to wave as the car pulled away. Maybe, just maybe, Kevin would chicken out on his own fucked-up deal. Maybe she wouldn't have to worry about any of it.

All the wishful thinking flew out of her mind as soon as she heard the muffled jingle of her phone. A text message. Jayla took her time going inside, and she sat her Coach purse on the table. She just looked at the purse, already dreading the text message.

Finally, Jayla pulled her cell phone out and swiped the touch screen to view the text.

I'll be back in an hour.

Jayla shut her eyes on the simple statement. He knew. He knew as well as she did that he had put her between a rock and a hard place. She couldn't bear the thought of losing Derrick. Not now. Not when she'd found a little sliver of happiness. Hell, her life was in shambles, and he was the only thing keeping her sane right now. She needed him. She sighed, realizing she had no other choice.

Okay, Jayla responded.

Jayla felt the tears sting her eyes as she lay on the bed, not bothering to move as her best friend's husband rammed himself inside her. His dick was small, so his efforts to overcompensate translated into load moans and a consistent knocking of her headboard against the wall. She wasn't even wet. Hell, she wasn't even fully naked. But he didn't seem to care, and she didn't stop him as he gripped her thighs and dirty talked himself into an orgasm.

When he was done, she still didn't move as he shuffled about, putting on his clothes and putting his barely filled condom and wrapper in her bathroom trash can.

"Damn, girl." He blew out a breath as he reentered the bedroom. "You got some good pussy. I see why you got niggas crawling all up and through there. You know you sitting on premium."

Jayla turned over, pulling the sheets with her. "Get the fuck out of my house," she mumbled. This was the second time she felt low, used, and soiled. The griminess had her skin crawling.

"So, if I need you again, I'll call."

Horror had Jayla sitting up. "Oh no. One time. That is it. I'm not doing it again." She struggled to make her voice firm, even though she felt completely weak and vulnerable.

Kevin grinned and blew her a kiss. "Well, let me get home to Tara," he said, making sure to dig the knife in further. "I told her I had to run out to the store. Say hi to Derrick for me, will you?"

Jayla cringed as he left, and she held her breath until she heard the front door slam shut. She saw the indicator light on her cell phone blinking, and already dreading

who it could be, she picked up the phone from the nightstand.

Derrick had called. Twice. She put the phone to her ear
and felt the disgusting sting of tears as she listened to his
message.

*Hey, sexy. Sorry I missed your call. I was actually
trying to surprise you. I just touched down back in
Atlanta. I was worried about you and the baby, so I
arranged to come back a little early. Hope you're doing
okay. I want to see you if you feel up to hanging out, so
call me back. Miss you.*

She caught her reflection in the mirror: her hair was
disheveled from sex, and her body was still sore from
Kevin's rough grip.

Jayla couldn't stop the flow of tears as she dragged
herself to the kitchen. She needed something. Some
sort of relief. Something to take her mind off the hurt. It
wasn't even her body. Her heart was aching. *Bad.* She
had fucked up. She knew, even as she had allowed her
best friend's husband to fuck her dry, she knew she had
fucked up.

Her numb fingers pushed through snacks in the cabinet until they landed on the popcorn. She wasn't even
hungry, but she just needed to keep moving. So she
ripped open the packaging and put the popcorn in the
microwave. She even willed herself to come up with some
sort of song to the hum of the microwave motor as it
filled the tiny kitchen. Maybe this was what insanity felt
like. Jayla allowed a laugh to bubble up and spill out at
the thought. The delirious noise seemed to confirm just
that.

When the timer went off, Jayla pulled the bag from the
microwave. Not caring that the heat stung the tips of her
fingers, she opened the bag quickly with bare hands. She
poured the popcorn into a bowl and just concentrated on
the inviting smell as it permeated the kitchen.

Bowl in hand, she headed into the living room and plopped on the couch. Flicking on the TV with one hand, she shoveled a handful of popcorn into her mouth with the other. She jabbed at the channel button until a familiar scene from *Sex and the City* filled on the screen. *Perfect*. She could get lost in the appealing sexual lives of other women.

So Jayla sat in the dark, eating popcorn, illuminated by the show, for a moment allowing herself to forget. Forget everything for a second. Her daughter, Jasmine; her unborn child; her sister's dead child; her sexcapades for cash; and her sexcapade with her best friend's husband. It was all too much. Sure she had built an empire. But the shit was crashing, and she was sure there wouldn't be anyone left when the dust settled.

CHAPTER SIXTEEN

Jayla lifted the slender stick to read the results. "*Fuck!*" she screamed and flung the pregnancy test across the bathroom. It landed against the wall, results side up, displaying the clearly visible words *not pregnant*. Ninth one in four days, and nothing had come of it but a waste of damn money. She leaned against the counter and eyed her reflection. Maybe she should just fake a miscarriage at this point to save face.

Derrick was starting to ask a shitload of questions that had her panicking. "When is your appointment? Can I see an ultrasound picture? Are you taking your vitamins? Why aren't you showing?" He'd rubbed her flat belly so many times, straining to feel a heartbeat. He'd even gone out and purchased a high chair because it was on sale. Now he was talking about selling his condo and was even spending his weekends house hunting, looking for a spacious house with a large backyard.

Jayla didn't know why she'd let the lie linger on for so long. Maybe part of her hoped she was pregnant. Especially after seeing how proud he was at the news. Then the several times she'd opened her mouth to divulge the truth, he'd slipped into some discussion about baby names or day cares. It was killing her to keep her mouth shut, but it would kill her to tell the truth. She felt like complete shit.

Without thinking, Jayla ran into the kitchen and snatched her keys off the counter. She felt like there was only one person she could turn to.

"Puma. What a pleasant surprise." Patricia leaned on the doorjamb with a welcoming smile. Her eyebrows creased when she saw the distraught look on Jayla's face. "What is it? What's wrong?"

Jayla let out a breath. "Everything," she murmured.

Patricia nodded her understanding, turned, and led the way into the spacious kitchen. The strong aroma of spices wafted in the air, and various pots simmered on the stove. "You hungry?" Patricia asked, lifting the top on a sizzling skillet of sautéed shrimp.

Jayla slid onto a barstool at the marble island, set down her purse, and absently brushed invisible dust from the countertop. She noticed the wineglasses, plates, eating utensils, all arranged in pairs, and immediately regretted her decision to stop by.

"I'm sorry," she said. "I should have called. You're having company."

Patricia waved away the apology with a flick of her wrist. She adjusted the temperature on the stove, leaned into the oven to gauge if the garlic toast was ready, and turned to Jayla. "So, what's the matter?" she asked.

Jayla sighed and started from the beginning. Patricia listened attentively, her eyes patient and completely nonjudmental, which Jayla appreciated.

"There's more," Jayla went on after a brief moment of silence. She took a breath. "I think someone is after me. I believe it's this girl Tracy. One of my previous assignments. I've been getting strange packages in the mail, and when I went away for the weekend, whoever it was broke into my house. My sister was there. She fell down the stairs and lost the baby." Her voice cracked with the last statement, and she felt Patricia's hand cover hers.

"You feel responsible," Patricia concluded.

"Patricia, I *am* responsible. The person, Tracy, or whoever did it, was after me. My sister just happened to be there, and she was trying to run away when she had the accident. And now she's lapsed into some kind of resentful depression, and hell, I can't blame her." Jayla sounded desperate. "Patricia, I've never thought about this so long and hard before, but I want out. I can't do this anymore."

Patricia sighed and sat down on the stool next to her.

Jayla watched her sink deep in thought, as if struggling for the right words to say. "Do you know why I went around the world?" she asked after a long silence. "I went around the world because I felt I was drowning, and I needed to get away. So, I went away for a year, gave myself time to breathe, and now I'm back." She patted the short stack of plates next to her. "I'm back, making jambalaya." She tapped her fingernails lightly on one of the wineglasses. "Serving wine. Business as usual." She forced a smile and brushed Jayla's hair behind her shoulder.

"So . . ." Jayla shut her eyes. She could almost hear the click as the puzzle piece snapped into place. "There is no getting out."

Patricia stood on a sigh, circled to the refrigerator, then pulled out a wine bottle. The sexy red teddy she wore peeked out from underneath the matching sheer, thigh-length robe. The material hugged her curves as she moved to pop the cork and pour the red liquid into one of the glasses.

"You know, sometimes I wonder if I was right to introduce you to this lifestyle." She picked up the glass she'd filled and took a sip. "This life—*my* life. My world. It comes with a lot of sacrifice, as you now know."

"But it makes you stronger." Jayla murmured the familiar phrase.

"Yeah." Patricia nodded. "But it can also break you if you let it."

Too late.

"Come here," Patricia said with a sensual smile. "Let me make you feel better."

Jayla slipped off the barstool, made her way over to Patricia, and allowed herself to be tongue kissed. Patricia expertly used her tongue to massage her lips while caressing Jayla's nipples through her shirt. Jayla felt completely numb. Even her pussy seemed to be nonresponsive.

Patricia kneeled between Jayla's legs and nuzzled her kitty through her jeans. "Let me make you feel better," she whispered again, then planted kisses all over the crotch area of Jayla's jeans.

Reluctantly, Jayla nudged Patricia's shoulders. "I'm sorry," she mumbled, feeling slightly embarrassed. "Maybe too much is on my mind right now. I can't."

Patricia nodded and stood and gave Jayla another passionate kiss. "I understand," she said, resting her forehead against Jayla's. "I'm here if you need me. Always. You know I love you."

The oven's timer buzzed, signaling that the garlic toast was ready. Jayla picked her purse up off the kitchen island and adjusted the strap on her shoulder. "I guess I'll let you get back to work," she said.

"I'm sorry. You came for a way out," Patricia said, giving her back a gentle pat. "Think about leaving. For good."

Jayla pulled back, with a frown. "Like, *leave* leave?"

"I came back," Patricia said. "That doesn't mean you have to."

As if on cue, the doorbell rang, signaling that Patricia's assignment had arrived.

They walked arm in arm to the front door, and Patricia pulled it open. Jayla glanced at the visitor, mildly surprised it was a woman who was standing on the porch, silhouetted by the afternoon sun. If she had been paying attention, she probably would've recognized the distinct features of her soft face, the gray-streaked hair, which the woman had placed neatly in a bun at the nape of her neck.

"I'm sorry," The woman glanced from Patricia to Jayla. "I hope I'm not interrupting."

"Not at all." Patricia smiled and stepped aside to allow the woman room to enter the house. "Come on in. My daughter was just leaving."

Patricia leaned in to kiss Jayla's cheek as the woman stepped over the threshold. "You're strong," she whispered. "You wouldn't have made it this far if you weren't. You know what you need to do."

An index card was taped to her front door. Already prepared for a sadistic message, Jayla didn't even assess her fear as she ripped the card off the door and flipped it over to read the back.

Too bad about your sister. Second time's a charm. I won't need a third.

Jayla ripped the card into shreds and tossed the pieces on the grass before stepping in the house. After she locked the door, Jayla punched the wood panel and cried out when pain shot like a bullet from her fingertips to her wrist. "Shit," she hissed, massaging her knuckles.

Her phone buzzed just then, and Jayla ignored it at first, scampering to the kitchen to retrieve some ice and a towel for her wounded hand. Her hand chilling on ice, she turned her attention to her phone and was surprised to see she had a video message from Jasmine. She pressed PLAY.

Immediately, Jasmine's face covered the screen: her mouth was hanging open, and pleasure had her eyes rolling back in her head. She moaned, and Jayla realized she had the camera up in her face while some faceless man was jabbing her ass from the back. Apparently, he was giving it to her good and hard, because her titties were swinging like crazy.

"Oh yeah," Jasmine moaned again and bit her lip. "Yes, fuck me! Fuck me harder, Derrick! Fuck, yes! Take this young pussy! Jayla's pussy ain't got shit on mine!"

Jayla saw red as she tore her eyes from the porno. Still, she heard Jasmine's moans, the man's grunts, and the distinct slapping sound of wet skin against wet skin. As Jasmine's moans grew more intense, Jayla felt her own blood boiling. Finally, her own scream exploded. Ironically, it was in harmony with Jasmine's high-pitched orgasmic scream as Derrick apparently stroked her daughter's G-spot.

CHAPTER SEVENTEEN

"Hey, sexy." Derrick pulled Jayla into his arms, not noticing her icy composure. "You missed Big Daddy? Good dick keeping you up all night?"

Jayla sidestepped him, walked into his living room, and glanced around. She almost expected to see Jasmine still there, ass naked on the couch or something.

"Where have you been?" she asked, her eyes smoldering as they landed back on him.

Derrick frowned. "Um, here. Working earlier, but I've been home all evening. What's up?"

Jayla remained silent, her chest heaving, as she struggled to remain calm. "Home, huh?"

Derrick stepped forward cautiously. "Yeah, home. Why?"

Jayla wanted to bust his ass for looking so damn innocent. She whipped out her cell phone, pressed the PLAY AGAIN button, and shoved the phone in his direction. Once again, Jasmine's desperate moans filled the room and had Jayla's stomach bubbling with nausea.

When Derrick heard his name, he frowned and squinted at the screen. To Jayla's amazement, he laughed. "The hell? Really, Jayla?" He laughed again, which only raked her nerves even more. "You really think she's talking about me? I ain't never seen that girl before in my life."

Jayla rolled her eyes. "Don't fucking play me, Derrick!" she shouted, against her better judgment. "Who the fuck else could it be?"

"How the hell should I know?" he shot back. "Apparently, one of the other twenty million dudes on this planet with the name Derrick. When have I ever given you a reason not to trust me?"

Jayla pursed her lips, not sure what to believe. Hell, Jasmine had pulled some foul shit before with Jocelyn's baby daddy. Why wouldn't she do the same thing with Derrick? Jayla remembered their confrontation in the hospital. Jasmine had been beyond pissed.

"Look again, Jayla." Derrick's eyes were so sincere and his tone so compassionate as he spoke. "I promise that ain't me, baby. You know me. I love you."

She watched the video once more, and his words seemed to shed light on the entire filmed episode. Suddenly, Jasmine's moans seemed exaggerated, her orgasm seemed fake, and the grunts didn't even reach the same depth as Derrick's.

Jayla stopped the video and lowered her eyes, shame and confusion like a rapid wave dragging her under. "I'm sorry," she whispered, shutting her eyes. She felt Derrick's arms circle her waist and pull her in for a hug. She let the tears fall.

He kissed the top of her hair and tilted her chin upward so her face was angled up to his. His kiss was meant to be comforting, but guilt had Jayla deepening the kiss. He was just too damn good to her. And she damn sure didn't deserve it.

Before long, they were naked, and Jayla sat in a chair and pulled him to her, then deep throated his massive dick until it tickled her tonsils. Fueled by Derrick's moans, she flicked her tongue across his tip, using her hand to stroke the length of the shaft.

"Oh shit!" Derrick had a fistful of her hair in his hand, and his grip tightened as she put her lips around him to suck once more. Knowing full well how to take him closer,

she shut her eyes and let a low gurgling moan vibrate in
her throat and pierce the air to comingle with his moan.
She felt his dick tighten in her mouth, and in an expert
maneuver, she pulled off, straddled his lap on the floor,
slid it into her pussy.

Jayla bounced her ass in his lap, letting her juicy pussy
stroke his dick like her mouth had done for the past
thirty minutes. She started fast, using her pussy muscles
to tighten and mold herself against his length. Then she
slowed, letting herself glide up and down at a leisurely
pace, much like a stripper on the pole. She alternated
speeds, huffing his name, leaning forward to press her
titties against his taut chest.

His arms snaked around her back to hold her in
place, and he lifted his pelvis to press harder against her
thrusts. "Damn, baby. I love you. I love you. I love you."
He was nearly singing the words, and hearing them had
the spontaneous orgasm yanking her breath away. She
felt his legs clench her thighs as he joined her, his sexy
moans heightening with the release.

They lay together on the living-room floor, drenched,
and Jayla felt too sedated to think of anything or anyone
else. She sat up when she heard a car horn sound, and
gazed out the window. She saw what looked like Tracy's
car drive by. She started to get up to look closer but
stopped when Derrick gently stroked her back. Sighing,
she lay back down and snuggled in his arms.

"Was that an apology?" he teased.

Jayla laughed. "Yeah, something like that."

"I think I got something to take your mind off everything. I know you have a lot going on with your sister and
the baby. It's a little short notice, but why don't you come
with me to a retirement party at my job this evening? I
didn't want to go, but I feel I have to, and you damn sure
need to relax and have some fun." He slapped Jayla's ass,

and her lips curved in response. "Besides," he went on, "if I have to sit through this boring-ass party, I'm going to need some eye candy."

After driving home from a good fuck session, Jayla showered and started getting ready for the party. She slipped on a dress and turned in front of the bedroom mirror, hands on hips, forgetting all about the video Jasmine had sent and the possibility that Tracy was following her.

The silk fabric of the dress had a bold orange and brown print, and the hem flirted at each knee and flared an inch or so higher on the sides. The halter formed a bow behind her neck, and the excess ribbon cascaded down her bare back, elegantly exposed by the hip-cut backdrop that gathered at her lower back. A handkerchief dress, the saleswoman had called it when she'd seen Jayla pause at the mannequin. Perfect for any formal or casual event.

She did another 360 with a satisfied smile, watching the bend of the material with her movement. She figured she could easily play up the role as eye candy tonight. Hell, she didn't mind being a distraction to the whole damn party. The attention would be fun. And she needed that tonight.

Jayla opened her front door to check the weather. It was uncharacteristically warm out tonight. She eyed the streetlights casting a soft glow on the empty street. Somewhere, a window must have been open, because she heard the faint music of some game show playing on a TV.

As she closed the door, Jayla didn't know why she suddenly felt nervous about this party. After all, it was just Derrick. They were practically a couple, though neither had bothered to voice the label. She absently lifted a hand and fluffed up her hair, gave into the urge to lick her lips moist. She thought of the perfume among the clutter on her dresser, eyed the front door again and opened it in a brief debate. Maybe if she hurried . . . She stopped short when she saw a jet-black limousine cruise to a stop at her curb.

The driver got out. He was a young black man dressed in a crisp uniform. He tipped his hat at her, rounded the back of the limo and, standing to the side, opened the back door. Derrick stepped out with a bouquet of roses in his hand, and Jayla's heart all but melted in a puddle at her feet. She headed toward him, and when she got closer, she easily saw the appreciation in his eyes as he admired how her clingy dress fell over her curves and yet swayed with each brisk step.

"Derrick." His name came out in a sigh as she accepted the flowers. "You didn't have to do all of this."

"I know." He grinned and leaned in to place a soft peck on her lips.

She felt him finger the dangerously low neckline on the dress, felt his lips curve against her when she shuddered in response to the absent brush of his knuckle against her skin.

"Your body is so responsive," he murmured. "I'm starting to think you can't handle me, Ms. Morgan."

Jayla's gaze didn't waiver. They both knew the simple statement was a dare, and damn it if he wasn't right. Her body ached for his; his voice alone could coax her thighs open. She let her eyes fall to his lips before grabbing his collar and dragging his mouth to meet hers. His hand found her arm, and he gripped it.

Peppermint. She savored the flavor of his tongue, used her own to caress the roof of his mouth, and swallowed his moan in response. His grip tightened on her arm, as if he was urging her to give him more or demanding it. She wasn't sure which. But he seemed to be not only reigniting that deep, deep passion she'd long ago buried, but also altering it so that it brought her new sensations, ones that made her feel like a stranger in her own body. He sucked on her bottom lip, and she quivered. His body hummed against hers.

It was Derrick who broke the contact first, pulling his face back to rest his forehead on hers. They remained quiet for a minute, their jagged breaths in perfect unison as they struggled to slow down.

She spoke up first. "Come inside and fuck me, Derrick," she said and let the request hang between them.

He grinned. "Later," he said. The one-word promise sent a tingle coursing through her body. His gaze lowered to her outfit once again. "First, let's get to this party. And I'll work on not fantasizing about you and this sexy dress."

Jayla laughed, torn between relief and flattery, at his statement. "Fair enough," she agreed. She released his shirt collar finally and made a weak attempt to smooth out the wrinkles.

Derrick led her to the limo, and she eased into the back seat first. The thick smell of clean leather and the soft jazz playing created an inviting ambiance. Once the limo pulled away from her house, Derrick poured them both a flute of the complimentary champagne.

By the time the driver had guided the limo through the downtown traffic and pulled up to the curb of the upscale hotel, Jayla was thoroughly relaxed. The mixture of the champagne and her sexy-ass companion had her hazy mind on all kinds of explicit sexual activities she hoped to engage in later.

She stepped from the limo and possessively laced her arm through Derrick's. She inhaled that crisp signature scent of his, a combination of grapefruit, saffron, and redwood. The subtle seduction had her thighs tingling, and she leaned in closer, intentionally rubbed her nipple under the flimsy material against his forearm.

"Down, girl," Derrick teased. "You keep that up and we'll be leaving before we get in here."

The stepped inside the hotel lobby, the concierge directed them to the escalator, and they headed up to the ballroom on the second floor. The planning committee had really gone all out, fully decorating the elaborate ballroom with black and gold balloons, streamers, and banners. Matching centerpieces and tablecloths adorned each of the round tables throughout the room. A DJ was playing some old-school mix, prompting a few people to two-step on the lit dance floor.

A white guy walked up, his scruffy beard, large glasses, and Dynasty cap a glaring juxtaposition to the creased slacks and the button-up he wore. "Hey, Derrick."

"Wilson," Derrick said. "How you been?"

"Good, good." Wilson's eyes grew behind the glare of his glasses when he turned to gaze at Jayla. "Seems you're doing pretty good too, man," he said, gawking.

Derrick grinned and slid his arm around Jayla's waist. "Something like that," he said. "This is my girl, Jayla. Jayla, this is Robert Wilson. He works in the IT department."

Wilson stuck his hand out to shake Jayla's hand. She accepted, and he gave her a flirtacious kiss on the top of her hand. She couldn't help but smile both from Wilson's gesture and the fact that Derrick had so casually tossed out "my girl" when introducing her.

"You sure got you a good-lookin' one," Wilson said, still clutching Jayla's hand. "Would it be too much to leave this one and come home with me, Jayla?"

Jayla pretended to ponder the proposition. "I don't know, Wilson," she said. "It's tempting, but I think I kinda like this one. Better hang on to him for a minute."

Wilson winked and smiled, his curved lips nearly hidden beneath the beard. "Smart too," he commented. He let out an exaggerated sigh. "I guess I'll just have to go through the rest of my life in a depression since I can't have you."

"Or you know you can go home and crawl in bed with that beautiful wife of yours," Derrick said.

"I know," Wilson teased. "That's why I'm headed to the bar now."

Jayla couldn't help but laugh. The man was a character.

Wilson gave Jayla's hand a gentle squeeze before releasing it. "Absolute pleasure meeting you," he said and turned to Derrick. "D, you keep a hold on this one."

Derrick acknowledged a few more people as they made their way to the buffet table lining one side of the room. Trays of wings, fruit, sandwiches, and pasta were arranged on either side of the table, and at one end was a multitiered cake fashioned in the shape of a clock.

"They really go all out for these types of events, huh?" Jayla observed.

"Ronald, the guy who is retiring, is one of the lead executives," Derrick said, handing her an empty plate. "You kind of have to show up. Hell, I think most people are here because they're actually glad to see him go."

Jayla laughed and began filling her plate from the various selections. She spotted Tara first, and the quick moment of confusion gave way to recollection. Damn, she'd forgotten Kevin and Derrick were coworkers. Thankfully, Kevin hadn't reached out to Jayla in the past few days. Perhaps he was really done with their little affair. Jayla forced a grin when Tara spotted them and began making her way through the crowd.

"Hey, you," Tara greeted. She glanced from Derrick to Jayla, unable to hide the amused smirk. "I wondered if y'all would finally come out of the closet, with all the hush-hush."

"Good to see you again too, Tara," Derrick teased. "Where is Kevin?"

Jayla lowered her eyes as Tara threw an absent glance to the crowd.

"Who knows? Probably over at the bar."

Derrick leaned over and pecked Jayla on the cheek. "Let me go find us a table," he said and left them alone.

Jayla felt suffocated by the awkwardness of the situation, but Tara didn't seem to notice her rising discomfort.

"Girl, I feel like we haven't talked in forever," Tara said. "I know you've been busy under Derrick, but damn, you can come up for air for a minute and talk to your girl. How's your sister doing?"

"She's okay." Jayla inched along with the buffet line, not bothering to grab anything else.

"She still upset?"

"Yeah," Jayla said with a shrug. "She's not talking to Jackie. Damn sure not talking to me. We don't know what to do."

More and more people crowded onto the dance floor as the DJ played a steady stream of popular R & B hits. A combination of sweat and too much perfume permeated the ballroom, thanks to the upbeat music and the gyrating bodies. Jayla maneuvered through the throng of people and saw Derrick and Kevin at a table toward one corner. She paused, eyeing Kevin's lips as he spoke, studying Derrick's brow as it creased in reaction to what had been said. Then both men laughed and threw back a shot.

Tara spoke up first when they joined the guys at the table and took a seat. "What are you boys laughing about?"

Jayla didn't look up from her plate, but she felt Kevin's eyes on her.

"Nothing important," he said, grinning. "Hey, Jayla."

Jayla took a sip of the wine from the glass Derrick had placed on her cocktail napkin, and nodded a greeting in his direction.

"I hear you and D here are an item now," Kevin went on. "That's cool. Real cool. You got you a good one, D. How's the baby, Jayla?"

She flicked a scowl in his direction. She saw his eyes gleaming. He was obviously savoring her discomfort. She took another sip from her wineglass, let the tasteless liquid glide down her throat.

Thankfully, she heard her cell phone ring just then. "Excuse me." She forced a smile and, pushing back from the table, pulled her phone from her purse.

As she retreated to the restroom, she took the call. "Hello?"

"Hi. Is this Jayla Morgan?" The voice was clipped and completely monotone.

Jayla frowned. "Um, who is asking?"

"This is Ms. Bennett. I'm one of the nurses here at Regency Hospital."

Immediately, Jayla thought about Jocelyn. The last time she was at Regency was when she'd gotten the news about her sister's accident. And the death of her nephew. "Is it about my sister?"

"Um, no, ma'am. It is about your lab results. We've been trying to reach you for months now."

"Oh." Jayla rolled her eyes as she stepped into the restroom. "Well, what's the problem?"

"Ms. Morgan, we would prefer to speak to you face-to-face, if that is possible."

"What is it?" she asked, panic causing her stomach to turn.

"Uh, we would rather—"

"Bitch, don't call my phone with no bullshit," Jayla snapped as she stood in front of one of the sinks. She cut

her eyes to the woman who entered the restroom just at
that moment. The woman saw Jayla and quickly stepped
back through the door.

"Ms. Morgan, can you please calm down?"

"I'm calm. But you're starting to piss me off. What is
wrong with my lab results?"

The woman paused, apparently unsure how to deal
with the situation. "Your results came back . . . slightly
abnormal," she said quietly. "We just want to retest you
to be sure."

"Sure of what?" Jayla yelled.

"We believe you have a sexually transmitted disease."

Jayla frowned. She remained quiet, waiting for more.

"Ms. Morgan, are you there?"

"Yeah," Jayla said. She began to pace. This couldn't be
as bad as she was thinking. "Can't y'all just give me a shot
or something? I mean, I've had chlamydia and syphilis
before. Write me a damn prescription and call it a day."

"Um . . . um," the woman sputtered. "Perhaps we
should schedule an appointment to discuss things further."

Jayla hung up, not wanting to hear anything else. It
was big deal, or so she thought, so why was the nurse
bitch trying to make it a big deal? *Fuck her*. Jayla pictured Kevin at the table, relishing the fact that she had
caved and broken him off some pussy. *Fuck him too*.

Jayla leaned over the granite vanity countertop, too
embarrassed to look at her reflection in the mirror. How
the hell had she gotten in this deep? And what the hell
was she supposed to do about it? Right then it was as
if Patricia's words echoed off the empty walls. *Take a
break*. If she could start over, she would. She needed
a way out. A sign. A life preserver in the midst of this
deep-sea bullshit.

Kevin swung into the bathroom, that disgusting grin
already planted on his sneaky-ass face. "I came to check

on you."

Jayla didn't bother looking at him, but she heard the restroom lock click into place.

"Derrick's worried. Tara's worried." His fingers brushed her shoulder and trailed up to tangle in her hair. He made sure to rub the bulge of his pants against her hip as he stood behind her. "I'm worried," he whispered.

When he reached for Jayla's arm, she snatched it back in disgust. "Don't fucking touch me," she spat.

Kevin exaggerated a pout as he put a dramatic hand to his heart. "Now, that hurt my feelings. Why are you acting like what we shared wasn't special?"

"Why the fuck won't you leave me alone?" Her hushed voice was sharp. "You were all up in my business, you got what you wanted, and it's done."

"All up in your business?" Kevin circled her. "You had your business all up on that stage, remember?" His voice was nearly a whisper. The stench of the beer was riding high on his jagged breath as he lowered his lips to her ear. "And I would like to get all up in your business again, because it was damn sure hella juicy."

This time, Jayla didn't stop him as he whirled her around and lifted her onto the sink. All she could think about was the nurse's phone call, the words *sexually transmitted disease* echoing in her ears. The nasty, cheating bastard deserved whatever death sentence he got from her tainted pussy. So she didn't stop him when he bunched her dress at the waist, and she spread her legs apart to let him indulge.

She pushed him down by his shoulders, scooted to the edge of the sink to allow him an accessible drink of her kitten. Of course, he obliged and licked and sucked her pussy like a greedy savage, twirling his tongue on her clit and generously stroking the supple flesh inside her plump lips.

"Deeper," she said, guiding his head. He dipped his tongue inside, moaned at the first taste of her honey milk, already caked around her opening.

"Yes," she coaxed as he slurped and drank. "Do it to me, baby. Get it, baby."

Her jumbled emotions had her coming so hard, she felt her juices squirt into his mouth. Kevin moaned and swallowed, smacked his lips at the delicious flavor.

He looked up at her as he began fumbling with his pants, but Jayla put her foot on his forehead and shoved him backward. He fell into a stall, and Jayla took the opportunity to jump from the sink, her dress falling back into place. She watched him struggle to get to his feet and mutter curses when he lost his balance and fell once again.

The smile was in place as she spun on her heel and breezed back into the ballroom.

The DJ had everybody doing some new line dance, the crowd moving in unison as they followed the footwork instructions blaring through the speakers.

Jayla caught a glimpse of Tara and Derrick in the midst of the crowd, laughing as they fumbled through the dance steps.

"Jaye," Tara called and motioned for her to join them.

Jayla lifted her hand to decline and sighed when both headed in her direction.

"What's the matter, girl?" Tara said, her eyebrows creased in concern.

"I'm just not feeling too well," Jayla admitted. That, at least, wasn't a lie.

"What's the matter, babe?" Derrick pressed the back of his hand to her cheek. "Anything I can do? Is it the baby?" His hand instinctively shot out to rub her stomach.

Jayla shook her head. "I think I just need to go home," she said.

She watched Tara and Derrick exchange uneasy glances. "Is something wrong?" she said. Confused, she studied Derrick, who ran his hand from her cheek down the length of her arm to clasp her hand. The realization hit her like a gut punch even as he slowly descended to one knee, his hand already reaching in the pocket of his black dress slacks.

The engagement ring glistened like a teardrop from the black velvet box. The large round-cut diamond was set in an elaborate band encrusted with side stones. Jayla didn't realize her hand was shaking as she desperate clutched his. She didn't hear anything, though the music had stopped and the crowd had gathered around to witness the romantic moment. Hell, she didn't even hear him speaking. Only heard the roar of her breath as she struggled to see through the tears blurring her vision. She couldn't think. Couldn't feel.

Only saw the gentle movement of his lips curling around each syllable of each word. "I love you, Jayla. Marry me."

CHAPTER EIGHTEEN

Jayla did a slight spin on the pedestal, her fingers rubbing the diamond embellishments on the corset bodice. It felt pleasantly awkward.

"It really is gorgeous," Tara said, verbalized everyone's thoughts, with a genuine smile.

"I like it too," Jayla agreed with a wistful sigh. "But you don't think it's too much? Too fancy?"

Jackie fluffed the generous tulle skirt. "I don't know your budget, but Derrick is going to hit the floor when he sees you in this."

"So will I when I shell out the money to pay for this thing."

Jayla smiled as she eyed the dress once more. It was an elaborate empire-waist dress, so it left her arms and shoulders completely bare. The beaded corset cinched her waist just right and lifted her titties. It gave way to layers upon layers of tulle to create the skirt, which was embellished with small diamonds and led to the huge train that cascaded in the back. Yes, absolutely gorgeous.

"What do you think, Joce?" Jayla turned to her baby sister, who was sitting in one of the cushioned armchairs near the dressing room.

Jocelyn smiled and nodded. "I love it," she said.

Jayla smiled. She was thrilled her sister was doing much better.

"So," Tara said, beaming as she clapped her hands together in excitement, "is that a yes to the dress?"

Jayla sat her hands on her waist. "I think so," she said, and all four women began clapping and cheering. She really could not believe this was happening; it was like something out of a fairy tale.

Jayla had to admit, she was genuinely happy. She had her man, her fiancé, her lifeboat, and she felt like she was soaring. She had never even thought of marriage, or love, for that matter, because she had honestly figured no one would be able to love her for the type of person she was. Hell, she hadn't even thought she deserved to be loved. So she had filed away any idea of a "happily ever after" and had settled for money and sex. Thank God Derrick had swooped in and proved her wrong, or else she would have never known what she was missing.

Of course, she was still conflicted over of the pregnancy. Or the lack thereof. Not to mention whatever STD she had. She had denied Derrick sex repeatedly, always blaming it on the busy wedding planning or the "baby." And Derrick was so damn loving and understanding, he had never pushed the issue. She had already put him and a lot of others in harm's way. No telling what she had or how long she had been carrying it. She had felt trapped and confused. The only way to avoid the feelings had been to start with wedding planning, as crazy as it all seemed.

After the dress fitting, they piled into Jackie's car and dropped Tara off first, then Jocelyn, at her new townhome. It had only been a month, but she had finally decided to move out of Jackie's house. Probably had been sick of all of Jackie's hovering.

The two sisters in the car waved at Jocelyn. Jackie tooted the horn and then headed toward Jayla's place.

"I never thought I would see the day my sister got married," Jackie teased.

Jayla laughed, lifting her hand in the air to smile at the engagement ring glittering on her finger. She damn sure had never thought it herself.

Jackie's phone rang as she drove, and she clicked a button on her steering wheel to answer it through her speakers.

"Hello?" she said.

"Mom."

Jayla frowned upon hearing Jasmine's voice. She had never brought up the false sex video to her, because she had wanted to kill the sneaky bitch over that. The whole thing still left a bitter taste in her mouth.

"Hey, baby," Jackie said. "What's up?"

"What are you doing?"

"Finishing up some shopping. Everything all right?"

Silence.

Jayla's eyes fixed on one of the speakers. She could almost see Jasmine's low-down ass concocting something.

"Mom, Aunt Jaye made me have an abortion," Jasmine blurted before she began sobbing like a baby.

Shit. Jayla's eyes bulged as the news had Jackie nearly swerving into oncoming traffic.

"The hell are you talking about?" Jackie asked. Her eyes flew to Jayla, but fear had Jayla trained on the speaker. She held her breath as Jasmine rushed on.

"Aunt Jaye offered me a job earlier this summer. As a Heartbreaker," she revealed. "I didn't know what the hell that meant, but she started sending me on assignments where I had to go sleep with men to say they were cheaters. I got pregnant, and when I told Auntie Jaye, she made me get an abortion."

Jayla felt deflated and exposed, her private life on display for everyone to judge. She pursed her lips when Jackie's eyes turned to her. "She's lying," Jayla whispered, wishing like hell it was true.

Only the sound of the muffled traffic outside the car could be heard, the background to the tension.

Jackie spoke first. Her speech was slow, as she seemed to articulate her words to ensure she would be better understood. "Jaye, please tell me that none of this is true."

Jayla opened her mouth, almost choked when nothing came out. She sighed and leaned back on the seat, rested her head on the headrest. She felt like several pounds of weights rested on her chest, and the sensation seemed to intensify with each passing second.

Jackie's lips were turned up in utter disdain, and her deep-set frown seemed etched on her face. She narrowed her eyes. "So wait a minute." Jackie's speech was still slow and calculated as she tried to process the information. "You forced Jasmine to have an abortion after making her sleep with men for money? And is that what you do? Sleep with men for money?"

Jayla opened her mouth to respond, then closed it again. She covered her face with her hands to fight the threatening tears. All she felt was utter and complete shame. Never had she planned for everything to come to the surface.

"Bitch," Jackie snarled. The word clasped the air in a desperate grip and resonated like a lingering song note. The verbal epitome of everything she felt.

"Get your nasty ass out of my car." Jackie's voice was a frightening whisper.

Jayla frowned as the car picked up speed. "Pull over at the—"

"No, you trifling-ass bitch!" Jackie screamed and punched Jayla so hard in the face, she heard her teeth rattle. Jackie kept one hand on the wheel and leaned over, pulled the handle on Jayla's car door. The movement had her swerving. The gush of wind flung the door open on its hinges, and outside the road whizzed by in a blur.

"Jackie, no!" Jayla screamed as Jackie shoved her shoulder, forcing her toward the open air.

Jackie didn't listen. She continued to push her sister and drive the car, while Jayla struggled backward in the seat. Jackie elbowed Jayla in her ribs, and seizing the opportunity, gave her sister one final thrust, which sent her catapulting sideward out of the car.

Jayla landed on her side in the street and skidded across the scalding pavement, the pain searing her arm and shoulder. It felt like someone was ripping the flesh smooth off her bones. She rolled a ways before settling on her stomach, took greedy breaths to slow her racing heart. Jackie had just tried to kill her.

She heard a car coming in the distance, and ignoring the shards of pain, Jayla scrambled to her feet and scurried to the grassy bank of the road just as the car flew past. Nobody stopped to help her or assess the situation. Jayla was on her own in this battle.

Defeated, Jayla sat on her couch, cradling her now bandaged arm. Even after Tara had picked her up, interrogated her on the way to the hospital, and dropped her off at home, Jayla still couldn't digest how everything went down.

Tara hadn't been happy about Jayla's lack of responses, and she had finally left her alone to wallow in her thoughts. Jayla couldn't believe Jasmine had stooped so low. She had pulled the fucking trump card. All the cards were laid out on the table now, and Jayla had no choice but to fold. She couldn't even cry anymore. Her head was throbbing. The hospital had given her something for pain and sleep, but both bottles lay untouched on the kitchen counter. The entire scene replayed in her head, and once again, seeing the rush of road coming up to greet her scared her shitless. Jackie, her sister, so consumed by anger, had pushed her from a car flying down the road at fifty-five miles an hour. It was a wonder she hadn't broken her face, or anything else, in the fall.

Jayla rose and headed for the front door. She couldn't stay there, or she would damn near go insane.

She didn't know where she was going until she pulled up to Jocelyn's townhome. Maybe that was it. She just needed the comfort of family. Maybe then she wouldn't feel so alone. So hollow. And so utterly broken. She hoped like hell that Joce hadn't caught wind of what just went down.

Jayla walked up the walkway and lifted her hand to knock on the door. She glanced at the knob and, without thinking, turned it and pushed the door open. It gave way easily. She frowned, stepped over the threshold into the dark living room. Her hand felt along the wall for a light switch.

"Joce, are you—" She flicked the light on, turned to scan the room, and screamed.

She couldn't stop screaming. Even when a neighbor ran in behind her and folded her in his arms, then shifted his body to block her view. Jayla still saw Jocelyn dangling from the banister, an overturned chair below her suspended bare feet, her body swaying like a gentle pendulum from the extension cord connecting her neck to the railing.

CHAPTER NINETEEN

The funeral was gorgeous. Cream and lavender, her sister's favorite colors, adorned the tiny church, and Jocelyn was nestled among velvet cushions of the same hues. She looked as if she were sleeping.

Jayla rubbed the faint line around her sister's neck like a lingering trail. They'd taken care to cover it with makeup, but Jayla could see it, as if the cord was still there.

She's with her son now. The phrase had been murmured over and over during the service. As if that made it easier.

Jayla took a steadying breath. She had no more tears left. Her heart, what was left of it, had grown completely numb. Her baby sister was gone. She turned and followed the rest of the crowd outside. It was time to lay her sister to rest.

Despite the sheets of rain pelting the churchyard, people grieved together under umbrellas, waiting to follow the body to the cemetery. Jayla stood on the covered porch of the church, nodding in response to the people who shared their condolences.

Jackie's husband, Quentin, walked up and stood beside her. "How you holding up?"

Jayla shrugged. "I'll live," she mumbled, not really sure how true that was.

Quentin nodded and started to head down the stairs.

"Wait, Que," Jayla called, stopping him in his tracks. She stepped closer to him, then glanced back through the open door of the church, saw Jasmine sitting quietly alone on a pew. "Why didn't you tell me that you had adopted our daughter?"

Quentin lowered his eyes and sighed. "I didn't intend on you finding out," he admitted.

Jayla nodded. She understood. Their brief affair had happened when she was fourteen and he was seventeen, a year younger than Jackie but still Jackie's boyfriend nonetheless. The fling hadn't been planned, and neither had the pregnancy. And he was her first love. She'd been young and foolish, but she would kill to return to those moments in life.

"I've fucked up my life in so many ways, Que," she said, turning back to face him. Her eyes carried a heavy sadness. "I almost fucked up Jasmine's. Thank you for being the better parent."

Quentin leaned down to kiss her forehead, and his lips lingered in tender encouragement. He then walked back into the church, slid on the pew beside Jasmine, and wrapped his arms around her protectively.

Jayla tried her best to stay busy. Derrick had already cleaned his place from top to bottom, and back to the top again. But nerves had her dusting the already pristine coffee table and sweeping the kitchen for the fourth time since he'd left. His mother. She hadn't realized she would be this nervous to meet his mother. It had come as a shock when he mentioned she would be in town for a few days to visit. Of course, she had expected to meet her eventually, but the uncertainty had been somewhat of a comfort. Now the meeting was too much of a reality. She hoped he hadn't told his mother about the pregnancy.

Jayla hadn't told Derrick anything about her sister throwing her from a car, because frankly, that left room for way too many questions on the source of Jackie's anger and why she would be willing to do that in the first place. Instead, Jayla had mentioned she was in a little car accident, and she planned on using that to drop the news of her "miscarriage." It would devastate him, she knew, so she really was stalling at this point. Now at least she had a means for losing the baby. But she didn't want to put that on him today. Let him enjoy his mother, she decided. She'd be here for a week, and when she was gone, Jayla would drop the bomb. And pray he still wanted her.

From the way Derrick had praised his mother, Gloria seemed like a nice woman, but all women, she was sure, had some reservation about meeting the other woman in their son's life. Which made Jayla feel like a target.

She separated the blinds, eyed the empty street on an anxious sigh. How long did it take to get to the airport? Shouldn't they be back by now? Jayla was tempted to call Derrick, just to make sure he was on his way, and had to shake her head at her absurd behavior. She felt compelled to impress Ms. Lewis. Even down to her choice of attire. Jayla fingered the frill adorning the cream blouse she wore. Not too low cut. Very casual. And the gray slacks were a perfect complement. She didn't realize she had placed such weight on the woman's acceptance, but that was to be expected. After all, the woman would be her mother-in-law once she got married.

Jayla's cell phone rang and, fully anticipating Derek's number on the caller ID, she had to ignore the slight disappointment when it wasn't.

"Hey, girl," Tara greeted when Jayla answered. "What are you up to?"

"Hey, T. Remember, I told you Derrick's mother would be in town today?"

"Um, no, not really."

Faint amusement had Jayla rolling her eyes. "Well, yeah, she's here in Atlanta, so Derrick went to pick her up from the airport. They should be here any minute."

"Awww. Are you nervous?"

"Yes," Jayla admitted, then released a staggered sigh. "I just hope she thinks I'm . . . I don't know. Good enough for her son. You know how mothers can be."

"Girl, you'll be fine," Tara said. "Derrick adores you, so I'm sure he's raved about you to his mom."

"See, that's the thing. I don't want to have to try to live up to some crazy expectation. I don't really know what she is expecting."

"Jaye, she is expecting the woman her son wants to wife. Now, she raised her son right. I'm sure she trusts his instincts."

Jayla frowned, slightly discouraged by the last comment. Were Derrick's instincts right about her? What about her lifestyle, which she'd managed to keep hidden? She felt as tainted as if she were wearing the scarlet letter. But, both fortunately and unfortunately, Derrick's mom wouldn't be exposed to all that.

"Thanks, Tara," Jayla said. Restlessness had her moseying back over to the window to peer out again. "I really do appreciate the encouragement. This is my first time with this."

"And your last. So after today, it's all downhill from here." She paused. "Listen," she added, "when you get a free moment, I need to talk to you."

Jayla froze. Tara couldn't be talking about the affair with her husband. Her tone was much too calm for that to be the case. A car door slammed and had Jayla glancing through the blinds. She saw Derrick already rounding the hood of his car to assist his mother.

"Is that okay?" Tara was saying, pulling Jayla back to the conversation.

"Sure, that's fine. I got to go, T. They're here." She glanced through the blinds again. "But, yeah, you should come over. We can talk and pack my stuff," she added with a laugh.

"Pack?"

"Yeah, Derrick and I agreed to move in together."

Tara groaned. "I wanted to have a girl chat with you. Not you trying to put me to work. I should've kept my mouth shut. Call me later."

Jayla clicked the phone off and, after doing one final primp in the mirror, trotted downstairs. She opened the front door just as Derrick walked up, clutching his mother's arm. Jayla stopped in her tracks.

Yes, this was the woman from the picture, but this was the same woman she'd run into at Patricia's house. She was aging gracefully, with soft wrinkles and huge eyes round with warmth. She'd cut her hair: she now had huge black and silver-streaked curls, and some of them looped around to touch the diamond studs resting in her ears. Derrick looked exactly like her, all the way down to the dimples, so how the hell had she not recognized the woman before? Shit, she'd been so engrossed in her issues, she hadn't even realized Derrick's mother was Patricia's client. She held her breath, silently praying the woman wouldn't remember their chance encounter.

Derrick wasted no time making introductions as he helped the woman into the house. "Mom, this is my fiancée, Jayla. Jayla, my mom, Gloria Lewis."

Jayla held out a shaky hand. "It's an absolute pleasure to meet you, Ms. Lewis," she whispered, averting her eyes.

"Same here, dear," Gloria said. "And please call me Gloria."

Jayla nodded and took the suitcase from Derrick. She needed to move. Needed to keep busy. Needed to think. "Would you like me to get you something?" she offered. "Tea? Juice? Water?"

"No, dear, I'm just fine. I need to get these old bones to a chair, that's all."

Feeling helpless and still uneasy, Jayla set down the suitcase and stood in the middle of the living-room floor while Derrick helped his mother to the sofa.

Gloria sighed as she lowered herself onto the cushions. "That is so much better." She smiled. "This old body ain't what it used to be."

Jayla eyed the crisp linen skirt suit Derrick's mother wore, the flesh-tone stockings, and the three-inch heels. She wondered why in the world she would choose to take a two-hour flight in church clothes, but she decided it was best not to ask. Derrick had warned her that his mother was exhibiting symptoms of the early stages of dementia. The last thing Jayla wanted to do was offend her.

And maybe, just maybe, Gloria didn't remember her. But that begged the question, What the hell was Gloria doing at Patricia's? This was just too much.

"Jayla is it?"

"Yes, ma'am." Jayla walked over and took a hesitant seat on the recliner opposite the sofa. Shit, maybe she did remember. . . .

"Do you cook?"

Jayla opened her mouth and shut it again, slightly relieved at the innocent question. "A little," she admitted. "I don't cook as often as I would like, but I know how."

"Mom, it's fine," Derrick said with a smile as he sat down at the other end of the sofa. "Jayla has so many positive attributes. That wasn't really a top priority for me."

"But, Derrick, I can cook," Jayla insisted.

Derrick's absent nod had Jayla feeling slightly of-
fended. What the hell was he trying to say?

"I understand," Gloria went on. "I guess I just figured
after a flight in from Chicago, she would've cooked a little
something. That's what I would've done."

Jayla's heart sank. Apparently, she had flunked that
little pop quiz. She rose. "I would be happy to put something together real quick."

"No, dear." Gloria waved her hand and gestured for her
to sit back down. "I'm not saying you're supposed to cook
because I said so. Don't worry about it. I want to talk to
you, anyway." She turned to her son and gestured toward
her suitcase. "Son, can you take my bag upstairs? I want
to have a little talk with your fiancée here, if you don't
mind."

Anxiety had Jayla's forehead creasing with the frown.
Damn, she remembered. The secret was out.

"Sure." Derrick stood and grabbed Gloria's bag. He
leaned forward and placed a kiss on the top of Jayla's
head, gave her arm a reassuring squeeze, and headed
upstairs.

Gloria waited patiently until she was sure her son was
gone, then dove in. "Tell me about yourself, Jayla," she
said. "Derrick doesn't really give me any details. Says it's
none of my business and that I will get to know you later."

Jayla nodded. "Well, there is not much to tell, really. I
absolutely adore your son. He is . . ."

"No, dear." Gloria's tone was laced with slight agitation.
"Like, what do you do? Have any kids? Ever had an STD?
What number of sexual partners have you had? That sort
of thing."

Jayla's eyes widened at the questions, and she quickly
glanced to the stairs. *Damn.* Where the hell was Derrick?
"I'm sorry," she said. "I think those are private questions."

Gloria's lips curved. "That's usually a sign that the answers aren't good, dear," she said. "See, my son doesn't ask those types of questions, and that concerns me. Now, don't get me wrong, I completely trust his heart and his intentions. It's yours I'm not so sure about."

"Ms. Lewis, I assure you—"

"You can assure until hell freezes over, dear," Gloria said. "Didn't he tell you about his last fiancée? Ran off and left him at the altar."

"Yes, ma'am."

"Well, my Derrick didn't see that coming. That little bitch tried to pull a fast one. Excuse my language, but she really was a little bitch. I never liked her."

Jayla pursed her lips, unsure how she was supposed to respond.

"After his sister passed . . . ," Gloria went on, "I don't know. Derrick is so hell-bent on protecting and providing for the women in his life. Even if they don't deserve it. Not sure where he gets it from, because it's damn sure not from his father." She paused and turned curious eyes on Jayla. "So, tell me, Jayla. Do you deserve my Derrick?"

Jayla sighed. Another loaded question. Like mother, like son. "Ms. Lewis," she said, her words slow with sincerity, "I love Derrick. I really do. I've loved only one other man in my life, and that was many years ago." She thought of Jackie's husband and sighed. Of course, she would always have a special place in her heart for Quentin. "Since then," she continued, "I didn't think I could love again, honestly. So when Derrick came into my life, I have to admit, at first, I resisted. But he makes me feel things I didn't know I could feel. Does that make sense at all?"

Gloria pursed her lips. "I understand, dear. But the question bears repeating. I'm happy you love him. I'm happy he loves you. But do you *deserve* him?"

Jayla remained quiet.

Gloria shook her head at the affirmation. "Exactly my point," she said.

Jayla watched Gloria study her face, as if seeing her for the first time. Then Gloria glanced away. "I think I know you, dear," she said, and Jayla shut her eyes.

"Do you?"

"Patricia. Patricia is your mother, right?"

What to do? What to do? Maybe she could play off the dementia, make this woman second-guess her own memory. Maybe she could tell the truth and pray the conversation didn't go any further.

"I think I met you," Gloria went on. "It's been a while, and you have to forgive me, child, but my mind isn't as sharp as it used to be. What is it that you said you do again?"

It was obvious she was fishing, despite the innocent look on her face. Jayla swallowed the lump in her throat.

"I'm a marketing consultant."

"For who?"

"I work for myself."

Gloria's response was a doubtful grunt. "Yes, Patricia is a lovely woman. Absolutely lovely. I don't know what I would've done without her . . . ," she said, her voice almost intimate as she uttered the simple statement. What the hell was going on? Was Gloria a client? Hell, was she a Heartbreaker herself?

"Patricia isn't my biological mother," Jayla said, hoping some of the truth would shed a more positive light on the chaos. She toggled so much between the truth and lies, the line differentiating the two was blurry. "She's more of a friend. She used to be my professor in college, and when my real mother died, I started to look up to her as a mother figure."

Gloria's face widened in what appeared to be genuine surprise. "Oh, I'm sorry, dear. I didn't know."

Jayla nodded. She would lay it on thick. "Patricia convinced me to finish school, get my life together, start my marketing business. I will always love her for that."

"So, you're not a Heartbreaker?"

Jayla struggled to answer quickly, but not too quickly, where it would seem like an obvious lie. "I'm not sure I know what you're talking about," she answered, her face displaying mock confusion.

Gloria just stared, and Jayla couldn't be sure if the woman believed her. The last thing she needed was Gloria to know the truth or, worse, reveal it to Derrick. The shit would most definitely hit the fan.

"You don't know what I'm talking about," she echoed, as if she were trying to translate from a foreign language. She paused a moment. "I can't read you, Jayla," she admitted. "I don't know if you're being serious with me, dear. And when I'm not sure about a person, I can't trust them."

Jayla frowned. *Dementia, my ass. This bitch was sharp.* She opened her mouth and shut it once more. How was she supposed to respond to that?

"So, let me ask you again." Gloria leaned forward, her eyes piercing. "Do you deserve my Derrick?"

"Yes," Jayla said, the pain of the lie stinging her throat. "I deserve Derrick." Then, in an effort to divert attention away from herself, she said, "Do you deserve your husband?"

The question clearly caught her off guard. Gloria's lips dropped in surprise, and her eyes widened in sheer shock. Jayla couldn't be sure, but she could've sworn the woman paled a few shades as well.

Gloria cleared her throat and pursed her lips. "Why do you ask anything about my husband?"

Jayla lifted a shoulder, the shrug meant to seem careless. "I'm just asking," she said. "I haven't heard you mention him."

Gloria frowned. "I don't think that's any of your business."

"It's not? You sure were in my business a moment ago." Jayla's voice sliced the air with renewed confidence. *Good. Let her squirm a little.* "You asked me about Patricia and her line of work, remember?" Gloria remained silent, and Jayla pressed on. "That must mean you know what Patricia does for a living, and considering you were over at her house, I hardly think that was a social call."

Another pause and Gloria's lips turned up in what appeared to be a sneer. "You don't know what the hell you're talking about."

"Yeah, right," Jayla responded. She was glad her voice held strong, despite the continuing discomfort she felt. She hated this. All of this. But, damn it, this woman wasn't about to jeopardize what she'd worked for. "Listen, I'm not trying to blackmail you or anything," Jayla went on. "I don't care that you hired Patricia to sleep with your husband. But the way I see it, we both need to stay out of each other's business. I won't tell if you won't." She waited, watched Gloria's eyes glaze over for a moment.

Gloria pulled out a cigarette, took her time lighting it, and finally put the stick to her lips. She blew out a stream of thick smoke, eyeing Jayla through the haze. Her eyes seemed to be dancing as she shook her head.

"Like I said." Gloria took another heavy drag on the cigarette and exhaled another puff of smoke between them. "You don't know what the hell you're talking about. I wouldn't waste one damn dime on hiring anybody to sleep with my husband. He could keel over dead right now, and I still wouldn't give a damn. You young girls think you're so smart, but you don't know a damn thing. Shame." She tapped the edge of the cigarette, sprinkling a few ashes on the carpet.

Jayla watched the woman stare her down through the cloud of smoke. "So, what were you over there for?" she asked. But then confusion had her feeling like an idiot. And certainly so when Gloria chuckled to herself and didn't respond. Jayla remembered Patricia's lingerie, the dinner she had interrupted, the wine . . . all for what she thought was an assignment. Jayla's lips turned down from shock and disgust as the realization crystalized. "You're *sleeping* with Patricia?" Her voice was nearly a whisper.

Gloria licked her lips moist, as if she were reliving the sexual moment. "Don't underestimate me, child," she responded with a grin. "I know all the ins and outs of Patricia. You would be surprised what I know about *you*."

Damn. It was the truth, she knew. Jayla lowered her eyes as she recalled that visit with Patricia, heard herself spilling everything to Patricia that day. She heard Derrick coming back downstairs, and she took a heavy breath. The tension in the room was about as thick as Gloria's cigarette smoke. She was nearly trembling, pissed that Gloria had laid her shit bare.

Derrick coughed and fanned the air. "Mama, I thought I asked you not to smoke in my house?" he said, rushing to open the windows. "You know Jayla is pregnant."

Gloria's eyes slithered over to Jayla's flat tummy before she met her eyes again. Smiling, as if to prove her knowledge, she took another pull on her cigarette before blowing the smoke in Jayla's direction. Then she stood to her feet and headed toward the kitchen. "I'll make dinner," she offered. "If you want, you can watch, so you can learn a thing or two, Jayla."

***

"She hates me." Jayla bit off each word with a pout as she began taking off her jewelry. She met Derrick's eyes in the mirror.

"She does not hate you," he said. "My mother can be somewhat difficult. But she wants me to be happy all the same."

"I know she does." Jayla turned and sat her hands on her hips. "But she doesn't think I deserve you."

Derrick rounded the bed, and after taking one of Jayla's hands, he pulled her into his embrace. "Yes, you do," he assured her. "Don't you deserve to be happy?"

"Yes."

"Don't I make you happy?"

"Yes."

"There you go. We deserve each other." He kissed her and popped her on her ass.

Jayla frowned. For some reason, that didn't do anything to soothe the uneasiness she felt. Especially because she didn't know what Gloria was going to do with the information she had on her.

"Another thing, I wanted to mention," she said, watching as Derrick shrugged into his basketball shorts and T-shirt. "What was all that earlier about me cooking?"

"What are you talking about?"

"Your mom was going on and on about me not cooking for you, and you said it wasn't a priority."

Derrick shrugged. "It's not."

"But you know I don't mind cooking for you."

Derrick laughed. "I know, sexy. And I appreciate it."

"I just . . ." Jayla sighed. The conversation with Gloria had her so frustrated. "I don't want you to not expect those things of me. I want . . ." She rolled her eyes at her own confusion. "Nothing. Never mind." She wanted to ask Derrick about his father, about his mother and her affair with Patricia, but then, she would have to tell him everything.

Derrick sat on the bed and patted the empty space beside him. "Come here."

Obediently, Jayla lowered herself to the mattress and allowed his arms to pull her to his chest.

"Is the wedding stressing you out, babe?" he asked, concern creasing his forehead. "Do we need to put it off? Especially after what happened to Jocelyn. You got a lot on your mind right now, and I don't mind waiting."

Jayla sighed. Of course, she hadn't told him about the falling-out with Jackie. Yeah, her guilt over Jocelyn's suicide was weighing on her extra heavy. And to date, she still wasn't pregnant. As far as he was concerned, she was just getting those bridal jitters. "No," she said. "No, we don't need to push it off. I guess I was just sort of disappointed when your mom didn't like me. I really wanted to impress her. Now I feel like that may affect your feelings about me." She felt his lips press against her temple.

"Of course not, beautiful," he said. "I love my mom. I believe she has my best interest at heart. But I can't live by my mom's feelings. And remember, my mother has early dementia. Half the time, she doesn't even know what she's saying. So please don't let that stress you, babe. I just know I need my Jayla."

Jayla smiled and, before she could think, blurted, "Tell me about your father."

The question obviously caught Derrick off guard. "My father?" He shrugged. "He's like a normal father, I guess."

"Are you two pretty close?"

"Somewhat," he admitted. "My dad was a hard-ass, so he scared me, to be honest with you. We didn't do the typical stuff, like fish and play basketball, but he was there for me just the same."

"Does he travel a lot?"

Derrick laughed. "What are you getting at, Jayla?"

Jayla shut her eyes. She knew she was acting strange. How was she supposed to tell him? How the hell did she get so heavily involved in this? And how the hell was she going to get out? "You're right." She forced a smile. "I don't know where that came from. I think I'm just tripping a little. I really wanted your mom to like me."

Derrick gave her another kiss. "She'll come around, babe. And if she doesn't, that won't change my feelings for you."

They leaned back on the pillows stacked against the headboard, and his hand rubbed her slightly bloated, but empty stomach. Jayla relaxed in his arms, but she still wanted to say more on the subject. But she didn't want to open that can of worms, either. Gloria had been right on certain levels. For one, Derrick had never asked her about her sexual partners. Hell, she didn't even know the number. But she had to admit it was strange they had never discussed it.

So part of her could agree in that regard. Even though she wanted to deserve Derrick. Needed to. But she'd felt targeted before Gloria had even stepped through the door. And Gloria had been right about something else. Jayla couldn't be trusted.

Jayla wanted to cry. It was a shame. Though Derrick was sure his mother had dementia and spoke from the deep recesses of her subconscious, the reality was that she was completely aware. And Jayla was stuck.

CHAPTER TWENTY

"I'm pregnant too."

Jayla's hand paused over the box of plates and bubble-wrapped wineglasses. She started to ask her friend to repeat that statement. But the way Tara stood at the counter, the knowing smile planted on her face, the hand on her flat stomach, her pregnancy was self-evident. Jayla continued emptying the cabinet and wrapping each dish in newspaper before arranging it neatly in the box.

"You're not going to say anything?" Tara asked, her face betraying her slight surprise.

Jayla opened her mouth. Shock had her closing it again abruptly.

"Wow." Tara's face fell as she eased onto the barstool. "Gee, thanks for your support."

Guilt came first, followed by regret. It wasn't Tara's fault she was married to a cheating asshole. Hell, it wasn't her fault Jayla had entertained the infidelity. She was simply having a baby with her husband of three years. Jayla sighed. She'd already fucked up everything with Jackie and Jasmine. She couldn't lose Tara too.

She skirted the counter and wrapped her arms around Tara's shoulders. "I'm sorry," she said. "I think I was just surprised. I'm going through a lot, and this whole wedding thing has got me all over the place. I'm sorry." Jayla leaned over and placed her cheek against Tara's. "You're right. Congratulations, girl."

Tara's cheeks warmed with the smile. "Thank you, girl."

"How far along are you?" Jayla moved back to the cabinet to resume packing. Numerous boxes had already been stuffed, taped, and labeled, and now they cluttered the linoleum floor and spilled into the hallway.

"About eight or nine weeks. I've known for a minute now, but I wanted to be sure."

Jayla nodded. "How are you feeling? Nauseated or anything?"

"A little, sometimes. Having to pee more, that's for sure. And I feel like I can smell every damn thing."

"And is Kevin excited?" The question sounded innocent enough, but Jayla hated that she had felt compelled to even ask about that bastard.

"Oh yeah. He's wanted a kid for forever. I didn't think we were ready, but . . ." She looked off in the distance, the hint of a smile touching her lips at some memory. "Yeah, we're in a good place now. We both have great jobs, and we're happy. It's a good time to have a baby."

Jayla didn't bother to respond as she finished packing the box and began closing the flaps.

"What about you, Jaye?"

"What about me?"

"Your baby," Tara said with a slight laugh. "You've been tight-lipped about it, so I wasn't sure what was going on. Have you been going to your appointments and stuff?"

"No," Jayla admitted, frowning down at her fists.

"Why not?"

Jayla sighed. The need to tell was so urgent, there was no other way around it. "I'm not pregnant," she said and heard Tara's sharp intake of breath. "I never was. Damn, I fucked up bad. I told him that so he wouldn't leave me, and I didn't have the heart to tell him I had lied. And he started doing the 'proud daddy' thing. I didn't know what to do."

Tara could only shake her head, trying to keep from judging her best friend. But her heart twisted in disgust at the sickening confession. "What are you going to do?"

Jayla leaned back on the counter. "I'm going to have to tell him I had a miscarriage," she said.

"That is fucking crazy," Tara snapped. "Just tell the truth."

Jayla opened her mouth to rebut the statement, then closed it again. She didn't know why she had thought Tara would understand. "You're right," she lied, nodding. She lathered sincerity on so thick that Tara actually smiled. "I will. Next time I see him."

Part of her, a small part, felt obligated to tell Tara everything. She would even admit her own transgressions. But she ignored the nagging feeling and put on an encouraging smile as Tara lapsed into another one-sided conversation.

Jayla toyed with the idea all afternoon and halfway into the night. Tara had helped her finish packing, and now she lay in bed, the satin sheets feeling cold and lonely on her bare skin, her cell phone like a glaring reminder in her open palm. She hadn't told her mentor. Of course, she hadn't told her mentor. Patricia wouldn't be receptive to the idea. She'd probably try to talk her out of it. Jayla grimaced, already envisioning the disapproving conversation. Her heartbeat quickened as she punched in each digit with a tentative thumb. She'd put it off long enough.

"I was just thinking about you," Patricia greeted. "I was going to call you in the morning to see what you decided. I know our last conversation couldn't have been sitting too well with you."

"Not at all," Jayla admitted. "Shit has been crazy." She shut her eyes at Patricia's warm laugh. She would miss that. She would miss her.

"When is shit not crazy in this business?" Patricia said. "So tell me, Puma. What are you going to do? Do I need to help you with anything?"

Jayla blew out an uneasy breath and opened her eyes. "You're probably going to hate me for it, Patricia. But I have to do what's best for me."

"And what is best for you?"

Jayla paused again. "My business is over," she said, delivering the words she'd practiced earlier. "I've stopped. The email, the phone. Shredded everything. I'm going to start over. With someone. My fiancé. He loves me. He wants to be with me, despite everything."

"Despite *everything*?" Patricia's voice seemed distant, and the condescending tone was evident as she repeated the phrase. "This man probably doesn't even know *everything*, Jayla." She paused, allowing Jayla's silence to confirm the assumption. "This man doesn't even know you. You think you can just marry him to escape all the shit you've gotten yourself into?"

A combination of shock and anger had Jayla sitting upright. "Excuse me? The shit I've gotten *myself* into? How about the shit *you* put me up to, Patricia?" She was surprised to hear the laughter.

"Please. When you were nineteen, you came to me, hurt, broken, and weak, looking for something more. Do you remember that?"

Jayla shut her eyes at the vivid memory. Struggling to put herself through school, student loans piling up, watching her grades diminish because she was busting her ass working at the campus bookstore and a local diner. And when she'd caught her boyfriend cheating with her roommate . . . Patricia was right. She'd been broken. Beyond broken.

Jayla opened her eyes. "You're right." The admission was as painful as the memory. "You helped me. You were there when I had no one, Patricia."

"I've loved you like a daughter." Patricia's voice had softened. "Always have. I've never tried to steer you wrong. Even with this whole business." Her sigh was heavy. "I mean, yeah, it looks bad. You try to explain to people, and they judge you. But you've helped so many women escape some real assholes, have you not?"

"I have."

"And the ones who stay, at least you've made them aware they're with an asshole, right?"

"Yes."

"So, it's not all negative, like people say. But I told you years ago you would make enemies. You will be hated. But what?"

Jayla sighed. "But I will be stronger."

"Exactly."

"But how long, Patricia?" Jayla needed her to understand. "Am I supposed to do this until I'm forty, fifty? Am I not supposed to be happy? Be loved? No marriage, no kids?"

"Do you see the irony there?" Patricia's tone was harsher now. "Marriage? Happiness? Can you trust this man?"

"Yes."

"How do you know? Seriously, Jayla?"

"Stop, Patricia." Jayla nearly yelled the desperate plea.

"No, I want to know," Patricia said, pressing. "You've spent the past ten years proving that all men are no-good dogs as soon as they get an attractive piece of ass throwing themselves their way. So, you think this man is any different?"

"You don't know him."

"And neither do you. Hell, you probably need to get his ass evaluated."

"Oh, do I?" Jayla smacked her lips. "Maybe you can do it for me when you're not licking his mom's pussy. How about that?"

She heard Patricia's scoff. "What?"

"Yeah, Gloria. Your jambalaya lover is his mother. Now, what kind of sick shit is that?"

Silence. Jayla was fuming, but she hoped she had gotten Patricia just as mad.

"How did you find that out?" Patricia finally asked.

Jayla felt numb. She closed her eyes as the betrayal snatched her breath away. "You *knew*," she whispered. "You told her about me."

"Well, what the hell was I supposed to do?" Patricia snapped in satisfaction. "I didn't know shit about no Derrick until I started sleeping with her. She started telling me all about what she had heard from Derrick about y'all being in love and all that bullshit. I couldn't let you make that kind of mistake."

"Mistake?" Jayla fumed, her voice stronger from a sudden surge of confidence. "He loves me. And you know what? I love him. And do you know what I've realized after years of evaluations and years of throwing myself at men and women and years of bad sex and infidelity and deception? A man will be a dog if a woman lets him. And I was that woman. Letting men cheat. So, it's not just their fault. Hell, it's mine too. I was that prostitute, slut, bitch that everyone made me out to be. So, I am done." Jayla felt tears of relief touch her cheeks at the finality. "I am going to start over. I am going to be a wife. I am going to trust him, and if he cheats, then hell, we'll cross that bridge if and when we get to it."

"*When* he cheats," Patricia replied, clarifying matters.

"*If,*" Jayla repeated. "I'm not going into this thing as if he's guilty until proven innocent. That's not trust, and that's not love. I am done with everything associated with the old Jayla Morgan." The insinuation was all too clear, and Jayla heard Patricia suck in a breath.

"So, you're done with me," she said.

The words left a bitter taste in her mouth, but Jayla felt overwhelming relief once Patricia had said them. "This is how I'm starting over. You did what was best for Patricia. I'm not running away."

"Yes you are." Patricia was cold and distant again, the hurt as clear as if she'd written it on her face. "You are running away. From your past. That's still running. And you know, after twelve months traveling across the world, I'm still right back where I started. And do you know why? You can't run away. Your shit is out, Puma. It's only a matter of time before you realize that it's not going anywhere. So I suggest you tell your little side piece before his mother does. See if he loves you like you say."

The click was quiet. Jayla wasn't sure Patricia had hung up until she looked at her phone and saw the call had been disconnected. With a sigh, she leaned back against her pillows and eyed the boxes stacked like pillars throughout the room. She couldn't shake Patricia's words. She was right. Derrick didn't know her. Well, not the woman she had grown from, who was relevant to the woman he'd fallen in love with today. She didn't want to tell him. She couldn't even bring herself to tell him. But it would be easier coming from her than from Gloria.

Sighing, she punched in his phone number. "Hey," she said as soon as he picked up. "I think we need to talk. Can I come over?"

CHAPTER TWENTY-ONE

"I'm so glad to see you, wifey." Derrick had Jayla in a hug before she even stepped through the door. "I figured you would be packing all night. Otherwise, I would've asked you to come over hours ago." He shifted to let her step into the living room.

"Yeah, well, Tara came over, and we knocked most of it out." Jayla shrugged out of her jacket and tossed it on the back of the recliner. She felt Derrick's arm around her waist, his lips on her shoulder, and his excitement through the slit of his boxers. She faced him and put her hands on his chest.

"Babe, wait," she said, but he was already tugging on her leggings. He covered her mouth with hers, coaxed her lips apart with the tip of his tongue. "Sweetie," she murmured against his mouth.

"Shhh." He pulled back long enough to lift her T-shirt over her head. "I've missed you. Let me show you how much."

Jayla lowered her lids, already feeling the tears building up. She loved this man, and damn, she didn't want to lose him. She would need to be selfish. Just this one last time. So she lost herself in his delicate strokes, his passionate lips, and she didn't bother thinking anymore as her body took over.

Derrick guided her to the floor, and the carpet felt like silk beneath her skin. He used his knuckles to shift her pink silk panties to the side, then massaged her kitty to life until her juices flowed on his fingers. "Oh, babe," he moaned. "Do you know how much I love you?"

Tears dampened her cheeks as Jayla nodded. "I love you too." It was an odd sensation: her heart throbbing from pain and her body singing from overwhelming pleasure.

He lowered his mouth to suck her nipples, and she gripped his head. *Yes, love me*, she thought.

Jayla didn't know when he'd worked himself out of his boxers, but she lowered her hand, felt his thigh muscles ripen as he used his knee to nudge her legs apart. When he eased in, her pussy molded to his dick in a desperate clutch. She sighed, almost hypnotized by the delicate massage against her walls, his absent stroke of her hair, his gentle suckle on her outstretched neck.

She felt his dick tighten, and he quickened his pace, going deeper and harder with each thrust. The faint smell of candy perfumed his heavy breath as he moaned. He whispered her name over and over, and Jayla wrapped her legs around his waist, held him, held this moment in place. His tip kissed her G-spot, and she felt the ascent, prepped herself for the stimulation.

"Oh, babe, I love you," Derrick whispered, and she felt the explosion of cum erupt as he released. Jayla felt the warm liquid, felt every ounce of his love saturating her inside and out, and she soared, the intensity of the orgasm weakening her and sending her into fitful sobs.

Jayla didn't move. She would relish this moment, snuggled up to her fiancé at the foot of his couch, surrounded by discarded garments. She felt herself drift into a comfortable daze, and she was taken to a place where she and Derrick shared rich lives of love, even disappointment, but always of mutual trust and passion. Kids that had her expressive eyes and Derrick's deep-set dimples. Spontaneous family trips to Disney or couple getaways to Vegas or Paris. Jayla grinned at the thought. She hadn't seen as clear a future before. Now she couldn't see one at all without Derrick.

"What are you smiling at?"

Jayla jumped, slightly startled, and she felt Derrick's reassuring hand caress her arm. "I thought you were asleep," she said.

"Halfway." He yawned, as if to prove it. "We should go upstairs and get in the bed."

"Can we just lie here for a little bit longer?"

Derrick squeezed her arm, and she found security in the innocent gesture. She heard his cell phone ring somewhere upstairs and smiled when he made no move to answer it.

"Derrick." Jayla lifted her head to rest her chin on his chest. "How long do you want to live in Georgia?"

"Never thought about it. Why?"

"I don't know. Just thinking that maybe it would be nice to move somewhere else. Another state." Jayla struggled to make the suggestion sound innocent but, she hoped, convincing enough to warrant consideration.

Derrick chuckled. "Oh really? I thought Georgia was home? I thought you wouldn't dare leave your precious Atlanta."

Jayla's lips curved when he recited her own words. It felt like so long ago. Another time. Another person. Before fake pregnancies and real STDs.

"I know that's what I said before." She sighed, turned, and rested her head on his chest. She found reassurance in the sound of his heartbeat, which was like a muffled thumping, against her ear. "I guess, I'm more open to the idea now."

"What about your family?" Derrick's voice sounded like he was on the edges of sleep. "And your job? Jayla, you got a lot going on here."

"I have you," Jayla said. "That's all I need."

"Well, I'm not totally opposed to it," he said with a smile. "So we'll see."

The doorbell had both of them frowning and jerking themselves into a sitting position. It wasn't so much the doorbell itself, but the multiple rings in rapid succession, followed by fierce banging on the door.

"The hell?" Derrick was on his feet in an instant and almost tripped over a table leg as he glanced at the digital clock on the cable box. It was 10:34 p.m. Derrick's phone rang again, the urgent jingle piercing the air.

Jayla grabbed her shirt and bunched it to her chest. "Babe," she whispered, fear lacing her voice. She didn't know why her mind immediately turned to Tracy and her damn threatening notes. How the hell had she found her over here? "Should I call nine-one-one?" she asked.

"I got it, babe. Hold on." Derrick shoved on his boxers and basketball shorts and was at the door in one long stride. He peered through the peephole, and confusion had him looking at Jayla.

"Who is it?" she asked.

"It's Tara," he said, and he was already sliding the locks out of place.

"Where is that trifling-ass bitch!" Tara's voice was menacing as she stormed into the room. Her hair was wild and her eyes were glazed over with pure hatred as she locked in on Jayla, huddled on the floor.

Jayla felt the rounded knuckles of Tara's fist, the sharp ridges of her princess-cut wedding ring before she could even process that the woman had crossed the room. The punch knocked her sideways against an end table and left her with searing pain in her jaw. Tara's steady stream of curses did not let up, and Derrick attempted to calm her down. Jayla's whole face stung, and a hesitant touch to her cheek had droplets of blood staining her fingertips.

She felt dizzy, and as she tried to pick herself up off the floor the toe of Tara's boot hit her in the stomach and had her recoiling once more. Jayla gasped, struggled to take a breath.

"Tara, what the fuck is your problem!" Derrick yelled, and Jayla looked over to see Tara struggling in his arms. "She's pregnant!"

"Get the fuck off of me, Derrick!" Tara was beyond frantic, apparently fueled even more by his tight grasp. "This shit ain't got nothing to do with you. I'm gone kill that bitch."

Jayla's arm was weak as she lifted it in surrender. The pain was nearly unbearable. "Tara . . ." she managed to choke out between gasps.

"Don't 'Tara' me. How could you, Jayla? You were my fucking friend!" Exhaustion managed to calm her down, and she stopped struggling, the tears coating her face.

"What are you talking about?" Derrick asked as he let go of Tara, and Jayla shut her eyes.

"Ask her, Derrick." Tara turned to face him, gesturing wildly at the limp body on the floor. "Ask her how she fucked my husband a few weeks ago."

Jayla said nothing. She heard Tara's ragged breaths in the tense silence, but she couldn't bring herself to open her eyes.

"He told me everything," Tara went on. "Said he saw her stripping at K. Sutra with some twins, and then she took some guy upstairs to the VIP room to fuck. She paid another guy to fuck her. Then, when he confronted her, said she offered him sex not to tell me or you."

Jayla winced at the mistakes, but she was too weak to bother correcting her. It wasn't like the truth was any better.

"And get this." Tara was clearly on a roll. "I talked to Jackie, trying to see what the hell was up, and apparently, this nasty bitch has been prostituting herself for years. Sleeping with men and women for money."

Jayla fought to sit up on her elbows as the first few tears fell. "It wasn't like that," she said, still not bothering to look at either of them.

"Oh, really?" Tara's voice was closer, and Jayla braced herself for another hit. "It wasn't like what, Jayla? You didn't fuck my husband? You weren't caught stripping and fucking niggas in the VIP room? Or you ain't been fucking everybody for money? Which is it? Because I must be confused!"

Confusion had Derrick's face creased in a heavy frown, and the emotion expressed in his eyes verged on anger as he stared at Jayla, who was crumpled on the floor. He couldn't see her anymore, just saw a soiled mess, someone used up and completely filthy.

"Even tricked her own niece out, Derrick. Yeah, that's what kind of woman you are about to marry. Oh, and get this bullshit! The bitch ain't even pregnant! She lied to you, boo-boo. Told you that so you wouldn't find out what the hell she was up to, and instead of the truth, she was just going to tell you that she had miscarried. Ain't that some shit?"

Jayla remained quiet but for her sobs. Her quick intakes of breath were harsh and jagged. No words. No explanation. She had nothing.

"You are pathetic." Tara's words sliced the air once more. "A nasty, fucking, pathetic-ass bitch. If it wasn't for my child, I would kill your trifling ass. I probably need to get checked for STDs."

Her muffled footsteps faded, and then came the sound of the door opening and closing with a violent slam. Then silence.

Jayla managed to open her eyes and ease a look at Derrick.

He just stood there. She expected anger; she expected upset. She even expected hurt. Sure, somewhere deep down, he felt all of the above. But the prominent glare on his face reflected pure disgust.

"Get out."

She didn't see it on his face, but she heard the menacing hatred in the two words. "Derrick."

"Get your ass out." He paused between each word, letting the threatening command linger.

Obediently, Jayla stood, grimacing in pain, dragging her clothes with her. She dressed as quickly as the pain would allow, feeling his eyes like daggers on her body. When she was dressed, she shuffled across the floor, willing him to say something, anything. She turned, opened her mouth to speak again, but let out a scream when he rammed his fist in the wall beside her head.

The sound of cracking plaster echoed in her ears, and she looked at the hole from the impact. Jayla's heart skipped several beats from the punch. She turned, and after quickly opening the front door, she stepped into the night air. She didn't bother turning around or even flinching when she heard the harsh slam at her back and the click of the lock, like a signal of finality, as it slid into place.

Where would she go now? Whom could she turn to?

CHAPTER TWENTY-TWO

The distant hum of a vacuum pulled Jayla from a distorted sleep. She pulled the comforter from her head, had to squint at the sun coming in through the open blinds.

Jayla hadn't thought loneliness would make her ache. Leave her feeling like a forgotten memory, so hollow inside that it was a wonder she didn't cave into herself. She didn't even realize she'd been crying again until she touched a finger to the damp pillow. Numb. That was it. She felt completely numb.

It probably didn't help that the room was so stuffy, so unfamiliar. Not that it wasn't nice. Patricia had decorated every room in her mini mansion with rich colors, abstract art, and elaborate furnishings. This one had walls painted a deep teal and a canopy bed accented with purple and mustard linens. The room was big enough to accommodate a full sitting area, which included a stone fireplace and a tan chaise with purple throw pillows. Not that Jayla had made much use out of it. Or anything else, for that matter.

She had tried calling Derrick several times, to no avail. Once Joi had picked up his phone with her usual seduction and had claimed she could make Jayla feel better. Jayla had instantly grown nauseated and had hung up.

The vacuum stopped, and slightly comforted by the quiet, Jayla leaned back on the upholstered headboard and ran her fingers through her disheveled hair. The gesture had light catching the engagement ring she still wore. Jayla sighed, held her outstretched hand out in front of her, and allowed the memories to swallow her once more.

It was ridiculous to wear it still, she knew, but she couldn't bring herself to take it off. Part of her, though a small part, still clung to some shred of hope. But as the days had progressed to weeks, and her phone had gone cold from inactivity, it seemed that her sanity had slowly diminished. She'd been able to catch only snatches of sleep since everything happened, and this had allowed her plenty of time to reflect and regret.

Jayla glanced at the digital clock on the nightstand. She saw that she needed to drag her ass out of bed and get to her appointment.

The in-suite bath was just as elaborate as the bedroom, with a Jacuzzi tub, and slate and marble floors that carried up the walls of the glassed-in shower. Jayla washed up in one of the dual sinks, not bothering to so much as glance at her reflection in the framed mirror. Between the lack of food and sleep, she could only guess how hideous she looked. Even more so with the slight discoloration of her jaw, which had only recently healed.

Though this was her third week at Patricia's, Jayla hadn't even bothered to unpack, so now she fished through a few suitcases before settling on some jeans and a T-shirt. She tossed her hair into a ponytail, slipped on some canvas sneakers, and headed downstairs.

Patricia was settled at the marble island in the kitchen, thumbing through a magazine. She hadn't changed from her pajamas; she'd just tossed on a robe, but it was open, revealing a burgundy pajama set with a tank top and patterned bottoms that flirted with her calves. She didn't bother glancing up when Jayla entered the kitchen, merely poured some apple juice in a carafe into a glass and slid the glass over to the empty space opposite her. Jayla eased onto the seat and took a sip from the glass.

"You need to eat," Patricia said. "There is some cereal in the pantry."

Deciding it was better to oblige than to risk arguing with her, Jayla got up and began preparing her breakfast. She felt Patricia's eyes on her as she shuffled about the kitchen.

"You headed somewhere?" Patricia asked.

"Yeah, I have somewhere to be."

Patricia nodded. "I'm surprised. You usually stay up in that room all day and night." She paused for a response, then continued when she didn't get one. "How are you feeling?"

Jayla thought about the previous night's contemplation, the razor blade she'd held in her hand for three hours before deciding to put it away.

"One day at a time," she said.

For a while, it was quiet. The only sounds that could be heard were the sporadic rustling of glossy pages as Patricia flipped through the magazine and the crackling of cereal as Jayla poured milk into the ceramic bowl. Jayla sat down at the island once more, and Patricia looked up.

"You need sleep," she observed.

"Can't sleep."

"Listen, I know this is easier said than done, but you got to get your life together. What are you going to do with yourself?"

Jayla used her spoon to toy with the cereal, her eyes lingering on her ring. "I don't know," she admitted.

"Have you considered what we spoke about the other day?"

Jayla frowned as she thought about the suggestion again. She could see where Patricia was coming from, but she didn't think moving to another city was quite the answer. Besides, what if Derrick . . . ? She sighed, ignored the tug of doubt about the idea.

"I have a friend in Chicago," Patricia went on. "She owes me a favor."

"An old client?" Jayla mumbled, not really sure why it was relevant. Patricia didn't seem to care about the off-wall question.

"Something like that. Either way, she works for a marketing company out there. I could make a call. Get an interview set up for you."

Jayla thought of the thousands of dollars she had saved up in the bank. That was one good thing about the Heartbreaker business. Sure, it had gotten her in trouble, but it had set her up lovely. "I don't see why. I don't need a job."

"I'm not saying you should do it for the money," Patricia said. "I'm saying do it for the distraction. And because that's what normal people do. I don't know how much you got saved up, but no need to touch it right now. Especially if you're not going back into business anytime soon."

"Or ever."

"Or ever," Patricia repeated. Jayla couldn't tell if her nod was approving or doubtful. "But still. I really want you to think about it. Seriously. It's time to pick up the pieces."

Jayla didn't bother responding as she ate a spoonful of the now-soggy cereal, just for compliancy's sake. She didn't taste a thing, only felt the disintegrating bits of flakes in her cheeks before she forced them down her throat. After standing, she carried the bowl to the sink to flush the contents down the garbage disposal. She flicked the switch, listened to the grind and whir of the gears for a moment before switching off the disposal.

"Patricia." Jayla didn't bother turning around. "Thank you."

"For?"

"For not saying, 'I told you so.' For not turning your back on me. I know I sounded like an ungrateful bitch the last time we spoke. I know you told Gloria because Derrick needed to know me." The thought still had her bitter, but not so much about Patricia anymore. More so about herself. "I've always cherished our relationship and appreciated everything you've done for me."

Silence, but she could've sworn she felt Patricia smile.

"Well, I feel I need to thank you as well," Patricia finally said.

Jayla turned. "For what?" she said.

"For telling me what was on your mind that night. And for having some elements of truth in it." She lifted her glass in a mock toast.

Jayla felt herself smile for the first time in a while. It felt good to still have someone in her corner. Someone who hadn't banished her to the depths of hell. Maybe there was some hope left. She caught the clock out of the corner of her eye.

"I'll be back a little later," Jayla said, heading for the front door, grateful Patricia didn't bother stopping her.

Jayla took the elevator to the third floor and stepped into the familiar waiting room. She headed to the reception desk to sign in.

When Melanie called her back, Jayla went in and made herself comfortable on the couch, as comfortable as she could in a psychiatrist's office. Never would she have dreamed of going to a shrink, but after she had gone back to the doctor and they had confirmed her HIV, she'd known there was no other way to keep her sanity. She'd been lost. How would she tell everyone that she had possibly infected them? Derrick, Kevin, Tara, and so many others? She'd had to find a way to make amends.

"How have you been holding up, Jayla?" Melanie asked.

Jayla nodded. "It's difficult as hell, but I'm trying. Every day is a struggle."

Melanie nodded. "In our last session, you touched on your HIV, attempted suicide, your relationship with your family and ex-fiancé, but you never told me the why behind how everything spiraled out of control."

To Jayla's surprise, embarrassment was the first emotion she recognized. But better to get it out and over with. "Well, I was a Heartbreaker."

"And what is that exactly?"

"I was paid to evaluate men and women to judge if they were faithful to their partners. Evaluating their value, much like an appraisal on a house."

"Oh, I see." Melanie nodded as she began to jot notes.

Jayla let the words hang between them, waiting for the judgment, for the disgust, the disapproving words. She relaxed when only compassion registered on Melanie's face as she continued to write.

"You said *was*," she said. "You don't do that anymore?"

"No. No, I don't."

"And why is that?"

Jayla's eyes fell on the ring. It still glittered on her finger, a constant reminder. "I got into some trouble," she said. "I was being stalked. And I hurt a lot of people, mentally and physically. My best friend, my daughter, my sisters, my fiancé . . . everyone who ever meant anything to me."

"And why do you think you did that?"

She didn't have an answer. Jayla stood, crossed to the window to study the downtown traffic. Pedestrians dotted the sidewalks below. A woman rushed toward the train station in heels and a skirt that was extremely tight. A teenager covered in tattoos, and earphones on his ears, nearly broke his neck to turn and look at her. A man in a business suit with a cell phone fastened to his ear didn't even break stride when he bumped into the brunette with the pregnant belly bulging from a floral dress that kissed her ankles. Life. Life went on.

"Okay, tell me about the stalker," Melanie said, shifting gears when Jayla remained silent. "Is that whole thing over with?"

"I guess." She really didn't know. She hadn't been home to find out. Hopefully, the psycho had gotten tired and left her alone.

Jayla turned from the window; the lingering remnants of fear had her crossing her arms over her chest. "I started getting death threats at my house. I didn't pay attention to it at first. Little notes, then packages. Phone calls. I made a lot of enemies with my job, so I just knew it was one of my clients. One in particular came to mind, for some reason. I was concerned with the fact that she was showing up at my house. I never brought any clients to my house, so I wasn't sure how she found out where I stayed. Then whoever it was broke in to my house." Her voice cracked at the memory. "When I went out of town one weekend, whoever it was broke into my house. My sister was there. She was pregnant. Fell down the stairs trying to get away . . ." She trailed off, and Melanie waited patiently before speaking again.

"Do you feel responsible for that?"

"Yeah."

"Do you feel your sister holds you responsible?"

Jayla's eyes fell. "Held," she said softly. "She's gone."

Melanie remained quiet.

All that could be heard were Jayla's jagged breaths as she struggled to remain calm. "Joce hated me for what happened," she went on. "She found out about the stalker and the threats. She was scared. Wanted me to go to the police. I told her no." Jayla bit off each word with disgust.

"I wouldn't go, because my selfish ass didn't want cops all up in my business. So I told her not to worry. And then she . . ." In her mind's eye, Jayla saw Jocelyn's body swinging from the banister, the overturned chair beneath her feet.

"Jayla."

Jayla didn't turn, but she heard Melanie's voice lift as she rose from the chair.

"You shouldn't blame yourself," she said. "You know you would never do anything intentionally to hurt your sister."

"No, it's never intentional to hurt someone," Jayla admitted. "It's always selfish."

"Jayla, you act like you're the only one who can be selfish," Melanie said. "We all can be selfish. Stop trying to make yourself out to be some evil, conniving bitch with no heart. You obviously care. Look at you now."

"Yeah, it's easy to care when no one else cares about you."

"No, it's easy to care when you've cared all along. Now it's just more prevalent since you've lost everything, so there is nothing for you to be selfish with. There's no attention on you."

Jayla took a seat. Her sigh revealed her accumulated exhaustion. "I don't know what to do now," she admitted, resting her head on the back of the couch. "I don't know where to go from here."

"How about up?" Melanie's suggestion was light but hopeful. "They say it's good to hit rock bottom, because you have no choice but to go up. Start living again."

Jayla thought again about how she'd pondered suicide the night before. "I don't know if I can."

"Let me ask you something. Do you play games?"

Jayla frowned and looked at Melanie for what seemed like the first time since the session started. "Excuse me?"

"Games. *Scrabble*, *Taboo*, Charades . . ."

"Um, no, not really."

"Well, I'll use this analogy, anyway. They're all pretty similar when it comes to setbacks. If you play *Sorry!* another player can knock you back to the beginning. If you play *Chutes and Ladders*, luck can have you land on a ladder to take you to the next level, or a chute to knock you lower. Hell, if you play *Monopoly*, the lucky roll of the dice or taking a chance can be the difference between passing Go and collecting two hundred dollars or going to jail."

Jayla frowned and watched Melanie laugh.

"I mean that in life," she continued, "you're going to have setbacks. You're going to have times when decisions or other people or just luck will knock you on your ass. It may seem like you're starting over, but the advantage this time is you're starting over as a new person. You've learned from your mistakes, and you've been through hell and back, it seems. But that has made you a better player. Now, do you want to keep wasting time by regretting the life you had? Or do you want to finally start living the life you want?"

Jayla finished up her session, and when she stepped outside an hour later, the blinding sun had her squinting at the downtown traffic. *One day at a time*, she murmured.

She caught sight of a familiar face and watched as Heather tossed her blond hair behind her shoulder and disappeared into a store. She cursed herself for how she had treated her. Hell, how she had treated everyone. She hadn't been able to relate fully, but after losing everybody, even Derrick, Jayla could see how Heather had lapsed into desperate pleading and groveling in the street. If karma was really a bitch, Jayla had been raped by that shit ten times over.

CHAPTER TWENTY-THREE

"Are you sure you're ready?"

Jayla placed her toiletries in one of the smaller tote bags as Patricia leaned against the bathroom counter, looking on.

"You can stay as long as you want," she continued. "You know that, right?"

"Yes, I know," Jayla answered. "But I've been here nearly a month. Plus, your friend in Chicago wants me to fly out next week for the interview. So I need to get home and start getting myself together." Not only was she tired of living out of suitcases, but she was also tired of her having her life on pause. She crossed into the bedroom and placed the tote bag next to the two matching suitcases in the set.

"At least stay for dinner," Patricia suggested, absently brushing at invisible lint on the comforter.

"Aw, is that Patricia-ese for you don't want me to go?"

Patricia laughed. "I enjoyed having you around," she said. "I must admit, it does get lonely sometimes. And when you get the job in Chicago, then I will really have nobody." She attempted to make the confession out to be a joke, but Jayla knew better.

"Hey. You know I will still come visit and we'll keep in touch." Jayla grabbed Patricia's hand, placed it to her cheek with a smile. "You know I've just got to do what's best for me. Isn't that what you've been saying?"

Patricia nodded and feigned a smile as she tossed one of Jayla's bags on her shoulder.

Jayla felt better. Much better than she had in what seemed like forever. Of course, she still battled the pain, the loneliness, and the guilt, but only time could reel in her numerous emotions—well, time and meds, but she preferred not to bother with the latter. So she took each day one at a time.

They headed outside with Jayla's luggage and stowed in the trunk of her truck.

"You'll call me to let me know you made it home?" Patricia said as Jayla slid into her truck.

"Please, don't worry about me, Patricia," she said. "I'm fine."

Patricia sighed and patted Jayla's leg. "I know you are. You're right. I'm sorry."

"I'll call you," Jayla said with a smile. "And thank you. For everything." Patricia's kiss on her cheek was reassuring. She shut the door, waved once more, and headed down the driveway.

Just as she was getting home, the storm started. The rainfall was a steady stream that dampened her clothes and hair, so she hurriedly slipped her tote on her shoulder with her purse and pulled out her rolling suitcases. She wheeled everything to the front door and, after fumbling with the keys for a moment, managed to get it open and stumbled into the living room. After knocking the door closed behind her with her foot, she locked it and peeled the slick shirt from her body. Soaked. She'd worry about her suitcases tomorrow. For now, she needed a bath and maybe some hot chocolate or something.

After tossing her wet clothes in the laundry room as she passed by it, Jayla crossed to the bathroom to take a quick shower. She found some shorts and a T-shirt and attempted to towel dry her hair as best she could. By the time she was done, the rain was coming down in sheets. Slightly unnerved by the silence, she flicked on the TV and allowed the noise to fill the room.

She headed to the kitchen and pulled the hot chocolate from the pantry. Boxes still were scattered about the house. Whether it was hope or a lack of care, she hadn't bothered to unpack them. Now, with the strong possibility of relocation in her future, she was glad she hadn't.

The doorbell rang and had Jayla spilling a little of the water in the pot as she carried it to the stove. Uncertainty creased her brow as she dried her hands on the dish towel. She crossed back into the living room, where the televised laughter echoed off the walls. Her hand reached for the switch to the porch light as she angled her face to peer through the peephole. Surprised recognition had her leaning back, a deep-set frown on her face. What was she doing here? Then anger had her unlocking the door and pulling it open, observing the figure illuminated by the shadowy glow of the porch light.

"You've got some fucking nerve, showing up to my house after—" Jayla froze when the woman lifted the gun. A split second later, the barrel stared her right in the face.

CHAPTER TWENTY-FOUR

"Get back inside, bitch." Lauren's menacing voice was ripe with hatred.

Jayla felt the fear suck the color from her cheeks. Tracy's sister. The woman who had accompanied Tracy during several evaluations. The woman who was with her sister when Jayla had handed over the tape. Never would she have expected the woman to resort to something like this.

Jayla lifted her hands and stepped back, nearly tripping over the suitcases she had left there just a half hour earlier. Lauren kept the gun in place as she walked in and threw her wet umbrella near the TV. She didn't shift her eyes or the gun as she reached behind her and shut the door.

Jayla heard the lock echo as it clicked into place, and her heart stopped. She could hear her breath roaring so loud, it was a wonder Lauren didn't hear it. She swallowed and concentrated on steadying herself.

"Lauren, what are you doing?"

"Your bedroom," she barked, her voice rising, as she motioned with the gun. "Don't fucking talk to me. Don't open your fucking mouth, you nasty-ass bitch. Get your ass into your bedroom before I kill you right here."

Fear had Jayla inching backward. She couldn't take her eyes from the gun, as if she would see the bullet in the chamber when it was released. She backed into her bedroom, as instructed. With one hand, her eyes still on

Jayla, Lauren shimmied out of the bookbag that was on her back. She tossed it on the bed.

"Open it," she said, her voice deadly calm.

Jayla moved in slow motion as she fumbled for the zipper to unzip the bag.

"Handcuffs," Lauren demanded.

Jayla swallowed. Her heart pounded so quickly, it didn't feel like it was beating at all. She hated having to take her eyes off Lauren, but the way the woman stared, her finger unwavering on the trigger, Jayla knew she had better oblige. So she snatched her eyes from the gun and ignored the panic as she felt around inside the bag for handcuffs.

Her fingers brushed rope, the blade of a knife nicked her knuckle, and she felt the slick surface of a vibrator. The contents of the bookbag unnerved her, and her horror must have been evident on her face, because to her surprise, Lauren laughed.

"I wasn't sure what to do with you," she said, as if the explanation would help. "So I just came prepared."

Jayla shut her eyes, pushed aside some small tubs of some kind of cream, felt the metal of the cuffs, and pulled them out.

"Put them on your ankles," Lauren barked.

With each order, Jayla felt like she was spiraling even further down in this madness, and she wasn't sure if she would make it out alive. Panic had her mind racing. She needed to find a way out. She eased down onto the bed and leaned over to do as she was told.

The butt of the gun rammed into her shoulder, and Jayla toppled over onto the floor, a stinging pain shooting up her neck and down the length of her arm. Jayla shut her eyes against the throbbing pain in her shoulder, grimaced when she heard the subsequent laughter.

"Whew. I feel a lot better," Lauren sighed. "I've been wanting to do that since you gave my sister that tape of you fucking Marcus."

More shooting pain, so raw that Jayla couldn't help the tears that stung her eyes. "She asked me to," she managed to say between gritted teeth. She heard Lauren smack her lips. Jayla was confused.

"Yeah, but you're the nasty bitch who did it," she shot back. "What the hell does that say about you? Going around fucking people's men for money? You like that disgusting shit, don't you? You get off on that kind of shit?"

Lauren leaned over to push the gun against Jayla's temple. "Answer me, bitch." Her voice was ragged. The alcohol on her breath was strong as she hunched an inch away from Jayla's ear. "Do you get off on that kind of shit?"

"I don't do it anymore," Jayla answered, nearly whispering, as she sat there. Time seemed to stand still.

"Oh, I guess that's supposed to make me feel better." Lauren used the force of the gun to push Jayla's head against the floor. It felt like she was trying to push the barrel through her skull. "Oh, so I guess I'm just supposed to forget the nasty-ass shit that went down. 'Baby, don't you want to sample it first?'" she said, throwing Jayla's own words in her face. "'Yes, yes, Marcus. Eat your pussy, baby.'" She lifted the barrel and punched Jayla in the temple with the butt of the gun. Jayla gasped at the impact, the pain like a dagger through one side of her head to the other.

She heard Lauren move away, heard her rummaging through the bookbag. Then silence. Then the click and whir of a tape recorder. Jayla squeezed her eyes as her own moans filled the air.

Yes, please fuck me, Marcus. Her own voice sounded unfamiliar to her.

Oh yeah, baby, I'm gone fuck the shit outa you. Marcus's jagged breathing followed. Then the squeaking of the seats and muffled movement.

Baby, don't you want to sample it first? Yes, yes. Eat that shit, Marcus. Eat your pussy, baby.

Lauren clicked off the recorder, and a mix of disgust and anger had her heaving it at the wall.

Jayla jumped when she heard it crash against the plaster right above her head before the pieces fell on the floor beside her.

"You don't know how deep that shit hurt to hear that," Lauren said. "Do you know how many times she made me listen to that shit? How many times I wanted to kill you after playing it? I know the fucking words by heart."

Lauren was on a drunken rant, and the way she paced back and forth, it looked like something else was in her system too. Drugs maybe? "Marcus is mine." She whispered the words, as if confirming this with herself. "Do you hear me? Mine." And there it was. Jayla caught the quick scratch and jolt of her fingers as she tried to restrain herself. Drugs, through and through. The bitch was on some other type of shit.

"Get on the bed." Lauren motioned with the gun.

Jayla ignored the pain and managed to open her eyes. She struggled to rise. Her legs were weak, so she pulled herself up with her arms and crawled across the mattress, tears flooding her eyes.

Lauren was pacing, nearly stomping her feet with each stride, the barrel of the gun pressed against her open palm. "I can almost see exactly what happens," she went on. "He eats your pussy. You ride his dick. Oh." Lauren turned, amused by her next thought, and pointed the gun in Jayla's direction again. "And I can tell you faked it.

You're a terrible actress." The laugh was psychotic. "But I understand. I've had to do that too. As much as I love that man, he can't fuck for shit." Lauren waited, as if she really expected a response. She just wanted it to be clear to Jayla that she was his number one mistress.

Shit. Jayla shut her eyes as the realization hit. "You're having an affair with Marcus," she whispered.

Lauren half shrugged, like it was no big deal she was fucking her sister's man.

"Tracy doesn't know what to do with him," she said. "Doesn't know how to please him like I do. He loves me, but the bastard insists on staying with her, like she's some damn body. So yeah, I fucked him. Good. Often. Hell, I'd sleep over and sneak a quick fuck while she was in the shower or cooking dinner." Lauren laughed again and had Jayla cringing. She was obviously enjoying this confession. Jayla struggled to sit up against the headboard. Her movements were slow, but she had to get away from this bitch. Lauren was crazy and was having no problem proving it.

"Then she got suspicious," Lauren continued. "Confided in me that she thought he was sleeping around. I tried to reason with her. 'He's a good man. He would never do that to you . . .' Shit like that. But she wasn't hearing it. So she found you. The Heartbreaker. You would be the one to prove once and for all what kind of man Marcus was. You got a taste of my man, and that shit will never happen again. For your information, he *is* mine, and I just share him with Tracy."

Lauren sighed and collapsed on the bed, holding the gun between both hands. Jayla saw the tears streaming down her cheeks and started to panic once more. It was obvious this girl had some sort of mental issue, which made her even more unstable. And dangerous.

"It hurt m-me." Lauren's voice hitched with the flood of emotions. "The longer she stayed with him, the more it hurt. It hurt me that asshole chose her over me. I threatened to tell her everything, so he said he would leave her. He promised he would. But lo and behold, she gets pregnant."

Lauren's eyes were downcast, so Jayla glanced around the room. Looked for a weapon, a phone. Something.

"But after you, he wasn't the same. Started cheating on me. Can you believe it? He started cheating on me and Tracy. Out sleeping with some nasty bitch." She paused, and her eyes were accusatory as she looked at Jayla.

"Lauren." Jayla held up her hands again, so this crazy girl would believe her. She couldn't believe she was tangled in this bullshit because of some sordid threesome between two sisters and the man they shared. "I've never had anything else to do with Marcus after that. I swear."

"That's not the fucking point!" Lauren yelled. "The point is, you were Pandora. You opened the damn box." Her rising temper had her getting to her feet, waving the gun for emphasis. "You were the bitch that brought that shit to him, and after that, he couldn't leave it alone." She turned, pointed the gun at Jayla once more. "Tracy came to you. She came to you weak and scared, knowing that asshole was a cheater, and what did you do? You took advantage. You put a price on her insecurity, her doubts, her fears, and you threw yourself at him to prove you really weren't taking advantage of her."

The whirlwind had Jayla's pain escalating. Now the crazy girl was concerned about her sister again? Even though she was sleeping with the woman's man?

"We joked about killing you." Lauren's sneer had Jayla shuddering. She spoke too casually, as if they were old friends catching up over coffee. She started to pace again, twirling the gun idly as she spoke. "We did. We joked, but I knew my sister would never try something so serious. She was always the weaker one between us. So, I said I would do it for her. Yeah, you fucked her over, but I felt just as betrayed. So I started looking for you. Started watching you. When he started cheating, I didn't necessarily think it was you, but I wanted you for all the nasty-ass skanks he was out there cheating with. Started sending you the little notes and presents, because it was just fun to freak you out, honestly." She shrugged.

As if suddenly remembering something, Lauren rummaged through the bookbag. Her smile was joyful as she removed a sandwich bag filled with white powder. Jayla narrowed her eyes at the cocaine. She had never seen it before up close, but now it was all too clear what was wrong with this girl. She seemed to start drooling as she opened the bag.

Lauren stuck her nose in the opening of the bag and took a huge whiff. She let out a satisfied sigh. After dipping her thumb inside the bag, she raked it across the drug and wiped her thumb across her gumline. The gesture left a powdery residue on each nostril and her upper lip. She licked the remaining powder off her thumb before she continued. "Anyway, when I finally worked up enough nerve to just come over and kill you, you weren't there. But your sister was."

Jayla's vision blurred. Her shoulder and her head were pulsing with agonizing pain, but she tried her best to focus.

"So after we talked—"

"Wait." Jayla blinked, replaying the words. "You talked to my sister?"

Lauren stopped in her tracks. "Yeah. I told her all about you and your little profession. Let her listen to the tape and everything."

"But . . ." Jayla squinted past the haze that silhouetted the woman's frame. She wasn't making sense. "She said you broke in. She said she was trying to run from you and fell down the stairs."

Lauren frowned. "No. She answered the door. I asked where you were, and she said you weren't there. I told her who I was and that I was looking for you to talk more about our business arrangement. When she said she didn't know what I was talking about, I told her everything. We talked for a long while, and I told her about all the stuff you did. Your sister said you probably had an office upstairs, so we were headed up there, and that's when she tripped and fell down. I panicked because, hell, I had a damn gun in my bag. So I left."

Jayla sighed as the pieces clicked together one by one. That was why there was no sign of a forced entry. That was why nothing had been ransacked. That was why Jocelyn couldn't give many details about the incident.

A knock on the door had Jayla's head whipping around. Her heart lifted. She opened her mouth to yell for help, but Lauren pointed the gun in her direction, and Jayla snapped her mouth shut real quick.

"Don't play with me, bitch," Lauren growled as she backed up toward the door, keeping her eyes and the gun fixed on Jayla.

Damn. Having a studio with everything out in the open couldn't buy her any time, Jayla realized. She held her breath as she watched Lauren cross the room and take a quick glance in the peephole, praying that whoever it was didn't leave. She heard Lauren's flirty giggle as she swung open the door.

Jayla's heart sank when Marcus stepped in and leaned down to kiss her wildly.

Lauren snatched her lips from his and looked at Jayla with a devilish grin as he licked her face and groped her titties. "You see," Lauren gloated. "He's mine. I told you he was mine, didn't I?"

Jayla watched in disgust as Lauren kept the gun aimed at her while Marcus removed her titties from her shirt and began licking her nipples. She stared boldly at Jayla, a satisfied smirk on her lips, as she was clearly enjoying how the entire scene was playing out. At one point, Marcus even bit her nipple, and Jayla winced as Lauren moaned from the sensation. Then he yanked down her jeans, lifted one of her slender legs onto his shoulder, and began loudly slurping and sucking her hairy pussy.

"Yes, Marcus!" Lauren quivered as Marcus pulled on a pussy lip with his teeth. He then massaged the sore area with his tongue. "Let me cum all over your tongue, baby."

Marcus sat down, and Lauren squatted over his face, giving Jayla a full view of her kitty as it spread when she widened her legs. She squatted over his face like a frog, and Jayla shut her eyes against the image. Marcus had stiffened his tongue, and Lauren proceeded to bounce on it like it was a dick, gasping at the rising orgasm.

"Watch," Lauren barked, and fear had Jayla lifting her lids. She still managed to keep that gun aimed perfectly, her finger hovering over the trigger. Marcus could have cared less where he was or who was watching.

Marcus moved on to her ass, leaving her pussy wet and swollen. She ground so his tongue was deep in the crack of her ass, and she proceeded to bounce once again when he darted it in her hole.

The entire scene had Jayla's stomach turning all the way over.

Lauren released a moist fart, and Marcus proceeded to sniff it. *Fucking nutcase.* He even opened his mouth over her hole, as if he were eating the rank odor, and then he resumed polishing her asshole. She released another, and he moaned his approval and kept cleaning her asshole with his tongue. Then he was back to her pussy.

With one scream, Lauren released a squirt of cum directly into Marcus's open mouth. He gargled, swallowed, and resumed licking her pussy until the shit was glistening. Lauren laughed hysterically as she lost her balance and fell to her knees, completely weakened from the bust.

"Shit, boy," she said, giggling. She was still giggling when she struggled to stand up.

Jayla was fearful the bitch would accidently pull the trigger.

Lauren angled the gun at her again and smirked. "Damn. Did yours feel like that?"

Jayla wasn't sure if she really expected her to answer, so she stayed quiet.

"You wanna taste my girl?"

Marcus's question had Jayla shrinking back, even as he made his way over to the bed.

"No, please," she whimpered.

He grabbed her by her throat and squeezed, startling her mouth open at the pinching pain. Sure enough, he shoved his tongue in her mouth. Jayla gagged as she tasted the bitter flavor of Lauren's nasty pussy, but he kept assaulting her with his tongue and holding her throat, so she had no choice but to take it all. She choked, struggled not to swallow, but she silently cried as she felt the liquid sliding down her throat.

When he was sure Jayla's lips and tongue were completely saturated, he gave her face a slap. "Better?" he asked.

Jayla coughed, gagged, and spit out as much of the aftertaste as she could.

"That was fun," Lauren said. "Now let's get this over with. It took me a minute to think about how I wanted to do this, and I think it's best if we stage the whole robbery thing. Like, maybe we came in while you were sleeping and shot you. So lay down." She said it so calmly, in such a calculated manner.

Jayla tensed once more. It was all coming to an end. Maybe if she stalled. . . .

"My sister lost her baby," Jayla murmured. "She committed suicide."

Lauren didn't appear fazed. "I'm glad it looked that way. Lay down," she repeated, using the gun to motion to the bed once more.

Jayla opened her mouth to ask what she meant but closed it again as she felt the sadness beginning to choke her. "Did you kill my sister?" she whispered.

Lauren sneered. "You said yourself it looked like she committed suicide," she said. "That's all that fucking matters. But, damn, we did have a time getting her up there. She was a fighter. Huh, Marcus?"

"Hell yeah," he agreed. "Especially when I was fucking her brains out."

Jayla gasped for air as her cries erupted. Not her baby sister. Her nephew was bad enough. But to rape and kill Jocelyn? The pain was excruciating. "Why?" she mumbled between sobs.

Lauren actually frowned at the question, as if the answer was obvious. "The bitch was going to tell you everything," she said. "At first, she was cool with us coming after you, once I told her all about your little business with Marcus. Said to 'do what we gotta do.' Said she was going to stay out of the way, because that's what you deserved."

"Of course, we didn't tell her we were going to kill you," Marcus chimed in, chuckling. "Just have a little fun. Hell, she even fed us a little information about some of the places you were supposed to be, so we could watch you."

Jayla listened to each word, the bitter truth like multiple stab wounds being inflicted. *Betrayal. Damn.*

Patricia once said, you can't trust anybody in this business. She's right.

"But then she started getting all sensitive and shit. 'Don't hurt my sister. I love her,' yada yada. That day y'all went wedding-dress shopping, we followed you to her place and tried to talk some damn sense into her. She kept saying she was going to tell you who we were and go to the police. So like she said, we did what we had to do. But it doesn't matter." Lauren pointed to the bed. "You'll be wherever she is shortly, so you two can hash that shit out then. Lie the fuck back. Now."

Jayla obeyed, scooting back and watching Lauren's brow wrinkle as she appeared to consider something.

"Marcus, help her get under the covers," she said next. "Make it look like she was really sleeping when she was shot."

Marcus stooped to snatch the covers over her body, and Jayla lashed out, connecting a fist with the man's jaw. He doubled back, grabbing his face. He glared at Jayla, and his fist connected to her eye so fast, she saw stars. Seething pain had Jayla moaning as her vision wavered, then darkened from the trauma of the impact. She squinted through the tinted haze, trying her best to focus on the deranged woman still positioned at the foot of her bed.

"You fucking bitch!" Lauren yelled, extending her arm to point the gun at Jayla's head. "Stop fighting, or I'll shoot you right now!"

"Lauren, please," Jayla pleaded, not bothering to hide the tears. "Don't do this. I swear I don't do it anymore, because . . ."

The move was swift. Lauren lowered her arm to Jayla's leg and pulled the trigger, sending the bullet to pierce her flesh. Jayla's scream erupted as a sharp pain reverberated through her thigh. Blood seeped from the wound, dribbled like warm honey down her leg, and pooled on the sheets. Jayla sucked in a greedy breath. She clenched her teeth, struggling to numb the fiery sensation. Lauren immediately began licking the blood off Jayla's leg, while Jayla began passing out from the gunshot wound.

"Now lay back." Lauren was calm again.

Gritting her teeth, Jayla leaned back on the headboard. She felt the dead weight of her leg. She could count each ridge in the headboard as it grated her back. The rich smell of blood was suffocating, and she could almost taste it. Jayla's vision wavered once more, but through the haze of tears and the blur, she saw Lauren's brooding smirk and bloodstained lips. As she watched Lauren's finger stroke the trigger, she let her heavy lids drift close. Jayla knew someone must have heard the gun firing and would come to aid her. These were all just dreams.

Jayla saw herself with Derrick. She was on his back, her arms clasped around his neck, her legs wrapped around his waist, as he ran across the sandy Bahamas beach. He murmured something inaudible before spinning her around. Her laugh. When was the last time she had laughed? Her laugh echoed in harmony with the crashing of waves at their back, and she kissed him. Love. She clung to the sensation with everything in her power.

When Jayla opened her eyes, she saw Lauren's face, but slowly, as if she were watching a movie, the face transposed until it was her own face. Staring back with that malicious grin. And she was pointing the gun. Jayla watched the lips move, *her* lips, even though it was Lauren's voice that came out.

"You know how much I'm going to enjoy killing you?" she said.

Jayla couldn't die. She couldn't give up. Not yet. She wanted to go to Paris. She wanted to get married. She wanted to have a normal life. Not like this. She remembered when she sat in the bathroom at Patricia's, the edge of the razor pressed against her wrist, trying to come up with reasons why she shouldn't end it all right then and there. That was why she had put the razor down, without so much as a nick on her skin. She needed to live.

Jayla didn't bother thinking. Only reacting. With a burst of renewed energy, she grabbed the remote at her side and hurled it at Lauren. Instinct had Lauren dodging the device, and Jayla took that opportunity to grab the bedside lamp and heave it in her direction. It shattered across Lauren's arm, and the impact had her finger slipping on the trigger. A shot rang out, and the bullet penetrated Marcus's chest, sending a burst of blood from the hole. His eyes bulged as he collapsed onto his knees.

Jayla mustered as much energy as she could to lift herself from the bed and dive, shoulder first, at Lauren, sending them both tumbling to the floor. Jayla gasped as she narrowly missed the side of her dresser. The connection with the floor sent shock waves of pain coursing through her body, but she couldn't think about the pain. Only survival. She needed to live.

She watched Lauren climb to her knees, her eyes darting around the floor for the gun.

"I'm going to kill your ass, bitch!" she said.

Jayla watched a calculated move play on her face first before she lunged at Jayla, her hands outstretched toward her neck. Jayla kicked, and her bare foot connected with Lauren's face. Even as blood spewed from her mouth, Lauren lunged again and managed to grab Jayla by the throat. Her fingers were like a vise as they squeezed her throat.

Shit, Lauren was strong. Jayla sputtered as she tried to take a deep breath. Or maybe Jayla was just weak. Her hands came up to grab Lauren's wrists, and Jayla struggled to loosen the forceful grip on her throat. Her head was heavy, and the edges of her vision began to fade. Lauren had somehow managed to maneuver on top of her, and she now stared down at her, murder in her eyes, blood seeping from her clenched teeth to dribble onto Jayla's face.

Jayla's engagement ring flashed on her finger. Her life boat. She collected what little shred of strength she had left, gripped Lauren's black ponytail, which was dangling in her face, and yanked. The force of the pull had Lauren's head veering to one side, and it collided with a sickening thud against the side of the dresser.

"Shit!" Lauren hissed as pain snaked through her head from the impact. Her grip on Jayla's throat loosened just enough for Jayla to take a deep drag of air before she yanked again. This time, the impact left a bloodstain on the oak wood, and Jayla watched Lauren's eyes roll. More blood spilled from the side of her head and trickled down her cheek, like a stream of tainted tears.

Jayla was weak, and she struggled to maintain her grip on Lauren's hair, but the girl was fast. Gravity accelerated the movement as she slammed her forehead into Jayla's still bruised jaw, reigniting the surge of pain. Jayla squeezed her eyes against the ache and felt Lauren shift to reach for something.

The gun. Shit, the gun.

"It's over. It's over," Lauren chanted, like the words were a mantra, her voice almost zombie-like. "It's fucking over, bitch."

Jayla opened her eyes just in time to grab Lauren's wrist as she aimed. The gunshot popped like a firecracker, and the hollow explosion echoed off the empty walls.

CHAPTER TWENTY-FIVE

A dull ache had Jayla moaning, and her heavy lids ignored her brain as it willed them to lift. Her head was tight with wrapped bandages. Every stiff muscle, every bone, every cell in her body felt like it was being squeezed with pliers and immersed in scalding hot water.

Disoriented, she managed to open her eyes into narrow slits. The room was blurry at first, before slowly coming into focus. She saw the stale blue couch, heard the beeping and humming of various machines, saw the needles embedded in her arm as it rested, lifeless, on the starched white sheet. Her encased leg was elevated in a sling suspended from the tile ceiling. Jayla didn't bother trying to move; she just lay there, waiting for what felt like death to take over.

The door opened, and Jayla couldn't even muster the energy to smile when she saw Patricia ease through, an elaborate flower arrangement in her arms.

"I was hoping to get back before you woke up." She spoke in a hushed voice as she walked over to the bedside. "The nurse said you were kind of in and out." Patricia sat the bouquet on the table and rubbed Jayla's arm. "How are you feeling?"

Jayla grunted in response, and Patricia nodded in understanding.

"I'm sure you're weak. Here." She grabbed a Styrofoam cup from the counter and angled the bendy straw to Jayla's lips.

Jayla took an appreciative sip, and the warm water almost stung as it dribbled down her raw throat.

"Better?"

Jayla groaned. The pain was excruciating. Almost numbing.

"I thought you said you were going to call me when you got home, Puma," Patricia teased.

Jayla's lips twitched with the humor, but she didn't even have the strength to smile.

"How . . . ?" The word came out in a raspy gush of forced air, and Jayla could only breathe at the intense energy it had taken just to utter that. The subsequent pain had her closing her eyes. She felt Patricia's reassuring pat.

"From what I was told, your neighbors called the police when they heard the commotion and the sound of gunfire. They found you both on the floor. Both of y'all were passed out cold. Apparently, she woke up in the ambulance, mumbling something about a sex business. But she passed out again. By the time they got you both here, she was dead. Doctors said blunt-force trauma caused brain swelling."

Jayla released a sigh, and her chest tightened from the gesture. *Damn.* Talk about a crazy turn of events.

"What about Marcus?" she whispered.

Patricia frowned. "Who?"

Jayla's throat felt clogged, and she struggled to clear it.

"There was a guy there," she breathed. "Marcus."

Patricia shook her head. "There were only two of you, Puma," she said gently. "Just you and another girl."

Jayla squeezed her eyes shut, the fear bubbling up to sting her chest once more. She swallowed and gasped at the pain. Where the hell was Marcus?

"He must have run off," Jayla said, swallowing another wave of panic. "We need to find him. He could come back."

"Ssshh." Patricia touched Jayla's face, gently lifted her chin to stare her straight in the eye. "I promise, no one is going to hurt my Puma ever again. I know some people who can find him. You have nothing to worry about."

That brought Jayla comfort, and she let herself relax into the pillows.

Patricia stifled tears, but her voice was clipped when she delivered the next sentence. "She shot you in the leg and tried to shoot you in the head, but she missed. Thank God. It just hit you on the outside." Jayla felt Patricia's gentle fingers on the side of her head, above her ear, where the bullet had grazed her. "No brain damage, though you may have headaches and feel yucky for a while. And the other bullet traveled through your leg, and you lost a lot of blood, but they patched you up good. I made sure of that." Her watery smile spread. "When you didn't call me, I called you. Imagine my surprise when the police answered your cell phone and told me to come right over. But I'm just glad you're all right." Patricia leaned down and planted a comforting kiss on Jayla's forehead.

"The hospital told me to make calls to your other family," Patricia went on. "I didn't know how you felt about that, so I said I would wait until you woke up to ask you. Do you want me to call anyone and tell them what happened?"

Jayla sighed once more as everyone flashed through her mind one by one. Jackie, her older sister, who was struggling to come to terms with what she had done before. Tara, her once best friend, who had damn near beat her senseless, and rightfully so, but who probably wished her an agonizing death, anyway. And Derrick. Poor Derrick, whom she'd hurt beyond measure and whom she loved that much more.

Sure she could tell them. They would probably come running too. Cards and flowers, sympathy and regret. It might even be genuine. But it would only be driven by guilt because she was hurt. Not because they were willing to forgive and forget. Jayla didn't want to put them through that.

It was all over for now. She would start fresh, and even though she hadn't done right by them before, she would now. No need to compound the strain and reopen the wounds. Maybe one day, they would find it in their hearts to move on, with or without her.

Jayla's voice came out foreign sounding, raspy from soreness and strangled pain but strengthened with renewed confidence. "No. Don't call."

CHAPTER TWENTY-SIX

Jayla positioned the crutches in front of her, and the tips immediately sank into the dampened soil. She winced as she struggled to hobble on her one good leg, dragging the weak one as best she could. Damn. These things were more of a hindrance than actual assistance. She was better off in a wheelchair. She tightened her grip on the plastic bag she clutched against the crutch handle. At least no one else was in the cemetery to see her pathetic efforts.

She eyed the headstones and sighed in relief when she saw her mother's. JILLIAN MICHELLE MORGAN. LIFE IS NOT A DRESS REHEARSAL. Jayla's lips curved at the quote. "Words to live by," she murmured. She took her time as she shifted to kneel before the granite. She placed the crutches on either side of her and removed one of the fresh bouquets of lilies from the plastic bag. She tenderly placed the gorgeous blossoms against the headstone, the crisp white and purple petals an appreciative contrast to the rigid gray.

"Sometimes, I wish you were still here," Jayla said, resting her hand on the ground. "Other times, I'm glad you're not. Not because I don't want you to be, but because I know you would hate me for what I am, if that makes sense." She sighed. "I'm ashamed of things I've done, Mama. Disgraceful things. Things that embarrass me to even think about, honestly. And I guess it hurts even more because I know you would look at me with disgust. Maybe even ask me why I can't act more like Jackie."

Jayla lifted her head, eyed the rows and rows of markers in succession. "And you're right," she went on. "I was almost right out here with you, Mama. And that scared the shit out of me. I won't detail it to you. You would probably roll over in your grave if you knew everything. But just know that I have changed. I hate that it took me as long as it did, and I hate that it took what it did for my wake-up call. But I'm still here. I have another opportunity, and I'm going to do it right."

The wind picked up, and some of Jayla's hair got free of the neat ponytail at the nape of her neck. She pulled her blazer tighter.

What about you, Jayla?

Jayla smiled. She could almost hear the question, as if her mother had uttered the words out loud. "Well, for starters, I was engaged for a bit, believe it or not. I love him. So, so much. But I hurt him, Mama. Bad. I haven't talked to him in months. You remember, Tara? Well, I haven't talked to her in months, either. I know she is pregnant, and I'm hoping everything is okay with that. But honestly, Mama, she is probably better off without me. They both are. But that's neither here nor there."

She paused. "I actually came today to tell you I am leaving. For good. I'll probably visit from time to time, but I'm going to start living. Finally." Jayla brushed her fingers over the engraved inscription, feeling the letters etched into the stone one by one. "Why, you ask? Because you said it yourself, Mama. Life is not a dress rehearsal, right?"

Jayla looked over at Jocelyn's headstone, situated right beside her mother's. She pulled the other bouquet of lilies from the bag, leaned over, and placed it right underneath the angel wings etched in the fresh stone. She attempted to smile and looked up.

"There is so much I want to tell you, Joce," she murmured, watching a bird sail across the sky. "But let's start with, I'm sorry." A single tear dampened her cheek, and Jayla didn't bother wiping it away. She opened her mouth to speak again and closed it. There were no words.

Jayla touched her fingers to her lips and laid them on the earth once more. Then she picked up her crutches and, using them for support, climbed to her feet. Her movements were slow, but she would get the hang of it.

"Doctor says I don't have too much longer on these things," she said with a chuckle. "I'll be glad when I'm done, so I can get back to exercising. You know I'm feeling lost without my treadmill." She paused, listened to the silence. "I love you both. I think that's what I needed to say."

Jayla turned and headed back to the parking lot. She planned to leave town as soon as possible. But she had one more stop to make.

It was strange being back at his place. Jayla eased her truck up to the curb in front of Derrick's town house and took a breath to steady herself. She wondered if he was home. She wondered if he was thinking of her. Jayla spread her fingers and eyed the ring one last time. The symbol of her love for and life with Derrick. The constant reminder of her quick taste of pure happiness. She rolled down her window and flipped down the little door on his mailbox. On a reluctant sigh, Jayla slid the ring from her finger and placed it inside the mailbox, then flipped the little door shut.

When she gripped the steering wheel once more, Jayla could only smile when she noticed the light imprint the ring had left on her skin. That, at least, would suffice for now.

***

The airport wasn't as crowded as usual, so Jayla was able to make her way through check-in in no time. It was while she was seated at her terminal that she felt her phone vibrating.

"Now boarding all passengers on flight three-twenty-three to Chicago," said a loud voice over the intercom.

Jayla hobbled to her feet, grunting against the crutches. She managed to pull the phone from her purse.

She was shocked, but not entirely surprised, to see Derrick's number flashing on the little screen. He must have found the ring. Her finger hovered over the ACCEPT button. He didn't deserve her. She frowned as the ringing persisted. She loved him enough to let him go. Regretfully, Jayla swiped the screen to reject the call. Starting over meant letting the past go.

Just as quickly, her phone rang again. Jayla frowned at the screen, but this time, she did answer. She definitely needed to hear what Jasmine had to say. "What?" she snapped.

"Auntie." Jasmine's voice was low. "How are you?"

"Jasmine," Jayla sighed, shutting her eyes against the exhaustion. "What do you want? After that whole thing with Jackie, you've got some nerve even dialing my number."

"I know. I'm so sorry, Auntie." Jasmine's breath hitched. She sounded like she was beginning to cry. "I don't know why I did it. I started feeling depressed. Like Auntie Jocelyn. I was angry. I didn't mean for any of this to happen. I've always looked up to you."

Jayla glanced at the line at her gate. *Starting over. Let the past go.* "I forgive you, Jasmine," she said. She may not have felt it completely in her heart, but she would eventually. With time. The smile came as she spoke. "I shouldn't have even gotten you involved in everything. I'm sorry." She wanted to tell Jasmine about the adoption. But not now. Not when they were just getting back on middle ground. "Listen, we need to talk soon. I'll give you a call later."

"Where are you?" Jasmine asked.

"I'm at the airport."

"Airport? Where are you going?"

Jayla sighed. "Chicago. But I'll be back to visit soon. Don't worry about me. But I want you to go to school, you hear me? Get your life together."

"Jayla Morgan?"

Jayla frowned and glanced up when she heard the familiar, yet authoritative voice.

Heather grinned and lifted her hand into view. A police badge glistened like an emblem in her palm and had Jayla's blood running cold.

"Heather—"

"Detective Shaw," she said, correcting Jayla, as she reached to her waist for her handcuffs. "Jayla Morgan, you're under arrest."

"Nah, I don't think so, Auntie," Jasmine said suddenly through the phone. "I got some better shit in store for myself. You, on the other hand, get your life together while you're in jail, bitch."

Jayla's mind fogged over, and she succumbed to a wave of dizziness. "You . . . ?"

"They came to me, wanting you," Jasmine answered coolly. "I delivered. I told you, you would regret crossing me. Checkmate, bitch."

Jasmine's words, sounding so much like Jayla herself, had Jayla screaming, even as Heather was reaching to grab the phone. "You low-down, sneaky-ass bitch! You gone send your own mother to jail?"

Silence.

Then Jasmine's sharp breathing sliced through the phone. "You're not my fucking mother—"

"You think you know everything, but you don't know shit." Jayla pulled away from Heather, fuming at the realization. Jasmine was the ultimate fucking Heartbreaker. "When I see you again, your ass is dead, bitch," she threatened, making the sincere promise of each word clear.

"That is enough, Ms. Morgan." Heather yanked the phone from Jayla's ear and handed it to her partner, who placed it in a plastic bag.

"You don't have anything on me," Jayla said, her voice panic stricken. Shit looked bad, she knew. Especially since Heather had been, apparently, biding her time all along.

"Oh, I have plenty," Heather countered, a satisfied smirk crossing her face. "You forget, we've been watching you for a long time, collecting evidence, getting everything we need to build a solid case. Especially after our informant, Reggie, told us what we needed to know. Solicitation of prostitution, promoting prostitution . . ."

Jayla rolled her eyes. The way she saw it, those misdemeanor threats were hard to prove, *if* they even held up in court.

"Oh, and thanks to Jasmine," Heather continued. "She was just who we needed to put the nail in the coffin on our investigation. So now we're looking at pimping, pandering, racketeering, since you're operating your little prostitution ring . . . Oh dear, we're just getting started."

Jayla was fearful, but more importantly, she was pissed. She had never loathed anyone, but she felt some other kind of hatred for her daughter. It wasn't until Heather grabbed her arm and buckled a steel cuff around her wrist that she figured starting over was going to take a little longer than she'd planned.

THE END OF PART ONE